Praise for Edward St. Aubyn's

Parallel Lines

"Intellectually roving. . . . Real humans—wounded, flawed, and often beautiful—stand behind, and sometimes place themselves in the way of, the ideas the novel confronts."

—*The Washington Post*

"St. Aubyn is worth reading, nearly all the time, because his novels contain brutal and funny intellectual content. He's a briny writer, one who dispatches a stream of salty commentary, sentences that whoosh past like arrows."

—*The New York Times*

"From suicide observation room to cutting-edge art installation, *Parallel Lines* plots quite the journey. . . . In a lesser writer the temptations of sentimentality would get the upper hand, but St. Aubyn is clear-sighted and humane."

—*The Guardian*

"Brimming with wordplay. . . . The novel bristles with ideas. . . . St. Aubyn is at his best in comic set pieces, which recall the brilliance of the Patrick Melrose quintet." —*Financial Times*

"A novel rich in characters and perspectives."

—*The Standard*

"Mordant humour abounds." —*The Telegraph*

"An empathetic excursion into impending apocalypse, and some of St. Aubyn's best work yet."
—*Kirkus Reviews* (starred review)

EDWARD ST. AUBYN

Parallel Lines

Edward St. Aubyn was born in London. His internationally acclaimed Patrick Melrose novels are *Never Mind*, *Bad News*, *Some Hope*, *Mother's Milk* (winner of the Prix Femina étranger and shortlisted for the Man Booker Prize), and *At Last*. The series was made into a BAFTA Award–winning Sky Atlantic TV series starring Benedict Cumberbatch. St. Aubyn is also the author of *A Clue to the Exit*, *On the Edge* (shortlisted for the Guardian Fiction Prize), *Lost for Words* (winner of the Bollinger Everyman Wodehouse Prize), *Dunbar*, and *Double Blind*.

ALSO BY EDWARD ST AUBYN

THE PATRICK MELROSE NOVELS

Never Mind

Bad News

Some Hope

Mother's Milk

At Last

On the Edge

A Clue to the Exit

Lost for Words

Dunbar

Double Blind

Parallel Lines

EDWARD ST. AUBYN

VINTAGE BOOKS
A Division of Penguin Random House LLC
New York

FIRST VINTAGE BOOKS EDITION 2026

Published by Vintage Books, a division of Penguin Random House LLC, 1745 Broadway, New York, NY 10019. Originally published in hardcover in Great Britain by Jonathan Cape and in the United States by Alfred A. Knopf, a division of Penguin Random House LLC, in 2025.

Library of Congress Cataloging-in-Publication Data
Names: St. Aubyn, Edward, 1960– author.
Title: Parallel lines / Edward St. Aubyn.
Description: First edition. | New York: Alfred A. Knopf, 2025.
Identifiers: LCCN 2025053778 (print) | LCCN 2025053779 (ebook)
Subjects: LCGFT: Novels | Fiction
Classification: LCC PR6069.T134 P37 2025 (print) |
LCC PR6069.T134 (ebook)
LC record available at https://lccn.loc.gov/2025053778
LC ebook record available at https://lccn.loc.gov/2025053779

Vintage Books Trade Paperback ISBN: 978-0-593-46874-6
eBook ISBN: 978-0-593-53535-6

penguinrandomhouse.com | vintagebooks.com

Printed in the United States of America
1st Printing

The authorized representative in the EU for product safety and compliance is Penguin Random House Ireland, Morrison Chambers, 32 Nassau Street, Dublin D02 YH68, Ireland, https://eu-contact.penguin.ie.

For M

I

What made the countryside countryside, thought Sebastian, a city boy born and bred, going very fast now, was the enormous gaps between the buildings, the gaping wounds, the wasted space. A rabbit twitching its way through the wet grass, or a desperate squirrel flinging itself from branch to branch, could not explain all that green unpleasant land. Sword in my hand. There must be an invisible city there, a bombed-out city, full of incandescent ghosts; men, women and children, rushing about like human torches, passing on their torment to the innocent woodland creatures, making rabbits hobble and squirrels take flight. Going screwy, chasing their tails around a trunk.

Rapid stabbing motion all over his chest.

He could also see, through the reinforced glass (he wished he was reinforced glass), a herd of cows dotted across a nearby hill, their brown and white hides waiting for the tanners to turn them into shoes. They weren't fleeing or limping because they were tethered by their appetites, wrenching roots from the ground with a twist of their stooped heads and juicing the grass with their slow rotating jaws. Masturbating. Milked for all they were worth. Sometimes, the sound of tearing roots was so loud he had to block his ears and hum to himself. Those shoes in ancient times.

Cows needed three or four stomachs to rip apart the tough fabric of the universe, to break down the cellulites, or cellophane, or cell mates, there was a word for it, the cell phones that bound everything together. A cow could stomach anything, any amount of connectivity. He wished he could stomach anything – anything at all – but he couldn't digest his own thoughts, they came so thick and fast.

Another huge plus about being a cow was that you got to be humanely slaughtered, which explained why there weren't any cows in this hospital, pacing up and down, day and night, working out how to top themselves. They had it all arranged for them. It was a package deal, a luxury holiday, being a grass-fed cow. A cow-fed cow got Mad Cow Disease and who could blame them? It was like crashing in the Andes and having to eat your fellow passengers: enough to drive anyone round the bend.

Dr Carr said the hospital was a temporary measure, but everything was a temporary measure, when you thought about it, with the possible exception of death. Unless you were Tibetan, or whatever, and thought that death only lasted as long as a summer holiday, and then you came back again, wishing you had enough stomachs to stomach the whole thing. It was a package deal, with life on either side, spitting you out one end and devouring you another. Going very fast now. There was a bobsleigh called a 'skeleton' where you went headfirst. That's what he was on, a skeleton, hurtling downhill headfirst, and even if he topped himself, he would soon be hurtling back down again, after a confusing summer holiday in St Bardo, the island of your nightmares, down into a family of absolute cunts, whose only plan was to wire you up to be a suicide bomber. Hurtling down with Very Early Alzheimer's, not remembering a thing about the last time he was squeezed out of his temporary mother's fleshy body, like a sharp little olive stone, left to dry on a saucer before being chucked in the bin. That's where he was now, in the bin, under observation.

Dr Carr said he would visit him again in the Suicide Observation Room. It was a stupid name for this naked little room with nothing in it to help you on your way, not so much as a box of matches or a curtain cord. With a name like that, you would have thought it would be stuffed with pistols and daggers and grenades and cyanide capsules so that people who liked observing suicide had something to look forward to. Modern life being what it was – ever-accelerating – you couldn't expect them to hang about waiting. Or maybe the Observers liked to set a challenge. This room was beyond a challenge, though; it was bloody ridiculous. Even if he ran his skeleton headfirst into the wall, he could only knock himself out trying.

'Go on, knock yourself out trying,' said an Observer.

They were probably lounging at home, watching him on TV, saying in their dead posh voices, 'I wonder if he'll find a way. The last one bit his own tongue off and bled to death and the one before *that* inhaled her own food and managed to choke silently – such discipline! Such gusto! Bravo! Bravissimo!'

'I had to bite my tongue so hard, I practically bit it off,' his Fake Mum used to say every time her sense of outrage was provoked, which was every time she left the house. When she stayed at home, she didn't bite her tongue, she spoke her mind, or pursed her lips.

'This one is simply *dreadful*,' said Dead Posh. 'He's either staring at the cows through a shatter-proof window or being stared at through a shatter-proof door . . .'

'By that fat cow!' Sebastian shouted, swivelling around to see if he could catch her observing him through the strip in the door. He was encircled by cows; he was being cattle-prodded from all sides.

'Oh, God, let's watch *Sharia Law*,' said a Vicious Viewer, 'or *The Euthanasia Channel* – even someone sipping barbs in Zurich, surrounded by adoring relatives, is better than this *dire* episode.'

He was being a dire episode. He wasn't just *having* a dire episode he was being one this time.

'We've upgraded you from a classic *Having* room to one of our superior *Being* rooms,' he lisped, like that Spanish receptionist at the resort hotel where his fake parents had booked a family holiday the August after his first episode. When they were all shown the special room, he could hear his Fake Mum screaming:

If this is an upgrade, what kind of a shithole were you planning to put us in?

But she bit her tongue and instead she said: 'Very nice. Thank you very much.'

Yes, thank you very much for the upgrade. He was now officially Being the worst episode in the history of the universe – the series – the whole thing, whatever. Rapid stabbing motion all over his chest.

He couldn't even star in *Suicide Observation Room*. They would have to kill the series and replace it with *Celebrity Suicide Observation Room* to improve the ratings. They wouldn't let a little nobody like him on a series like that. The only way someone like him could get onto the news was by shooting hundreds of innocent men, women and children, especially children. Bonus points. Even then, there was so much competition for attention he might not make it.

'What?' said the Vicious Viewer. 'That ghastly little bore on *Celebrity SOR*? Don't make me laugh!'

Must slow down, must slow down. Not a bore but a borehole. In the ground. Searching for water. To mend the cracked earth. To dissolve the dust devils into fertile fields of whispering wheat. Sebastian closed his eyes and swayed from side to side. He was being wheat now. He was swaying and he was rustling. It was lovely to feel the warm air, like Gabriella, running its fingers gently through the golden wheat.

He mustn't get so stressed, or so distressed. Although distress sounded like it was the opposite of stress, they were closely related. They weren't identical twins. The identical twin of stress was stress, and the identical twin of distress was distress, but stress and distress were weirdly related, they had a syllable in common, but an uncommon dis.

Shut up. He was being a field of wheat now. He didn't want to be a family of words divided against themselves, he wanted to be a fucking field of wheat.

Why wasn't he allowed a little peace? A little peace with no action.

Why wouldn't they leave him alone? So alone without them.

'Give it a rest, me old son,' he whispered, and went on swaying, until he was startled by the sound of the door being unlocked.

It was Dr Carr, wearing his washable maroon mask. There'd been a Covid case in the hospital and now they were behaving as if it was lockdown all over again.

Ben, the nurse, who was wearing a blue surgical mask, came in carrying two light chairs, which he put about a coffin's length apart from each other.

'Remember, Seb, you don't cross this space, right?' said Ben. 'And put your mask on for Dr Carr.'

Sebastian stayed by the window, immobile until Ben had closed the door behind him. Then he turned abruptly on Dr Carr.

'I don't want to be radicalised,' he shouted.

'I'm sure that none of us want you to be radicalised,' said Dr Carr, sitting down calmly and looking at Sebastian with kindness and concern. 'That's what terrorists do when they want to turn someone into a suicide bomber. Whereas we're all very concerned about your safety, Sebastian, about your bodily safety.'

That was Dr Carr for you. Hole in one. Bastard.

'Fuck you,' he said. 'You're trying to psychoradicalise me.'

He noticed that just by being there, Dr Carr had opened a little breathing space between his thoughts and his reaction to his thoughts, which was slowing things down a bit. Bastard.

If things slowed down too much, he would start feeling the Big Grief, from tip to toe, from Land's End to John O'Groats, from the equator to the pole, from the small blue dot to the ever-accelerating expansion of the universe that might rip the old centres apart. The fabric might be stretched to tearing point. Or it could just be the rolling out of more fabric in every direction at once – because it was literally *making it up as it went along* – making space for itself by expanding.

There was no stopping once he started thinking about it, and if he tried to reverse it, it came rushing in on him until he disappeared, along with everything else, into a tiny black hole in the middle of his body, which then swallowed itself up as well.

He pressed his hands over his ears and scrunched up his eyes. The fuse was lit, there was no turning back, he was thinking about Infinity.

'I'm having a bad word,' he said. 'Begins with an I.' He stretched out his arms as far as he could reach and then brought them back and crushed his palms together. 'The universe,' he hinted.

'Begins with U,' said Dr Carr, not missing a beat. Bastard.

'Your U is my I and my I is your U,' said Sebastian, moving very fast again. 'Mirroring. You were mirroring me, but you know that mirrors are one of my worst things. So, you are *deliberately* trying to push me over the edge, you cold-hearted bastard.'

'Well, that's a very interesting interpretation,' said Dr Carr, 'but I was just trying to point out that the word you find difficult could not be "Universe" because it begins with the wrong letter. We've talked before about some of your bad words . . .'

'No end in sight,' said Sebastian.

'Ah, yes,' said Dr Carr. 'Well, it's certainly true that neither of us can see as far as the end of the universe, but maybe there's something closer to home that you also feel has no end in sight, perhaps that's what you're feeling about your recent setback.'

Dr Carr was trying to be a psycho-nanny-list, trying to turn the big, frightening universe into something more manageable, but the bad words and phrases were stronger than that. They were like the tentacles of the Giant Pacific Octopus in the documentary he had watched the other day in the Telly Room. A bleach-blond American diver, sitting in a folding chair, bobbing up and down on the deck of his boat, had told the story of his life-and-death struggle with one of these monsters of the deep. This bloke was a real man, with more hair bursting out of his short-sleeved pink shirt than an orangutan, and while he held himself spellbound with his yarn, they did a *Reconstruction* of his harrowing adventure: an actor, in full scuba gear, falls backwards off the side of a boat, and down he goes, flapping his flippers, trailing a broken necklace of bubbles, a speargun in his hand, a knife in his belt, and a watch the size of Big Ben on his wrist, hunting for his sunken treasure.

At this point, Diver Boy bangs on about how much one of these – they aren't exactly fish, more like cellophones, or cellulose, there was a word for it, cell pods, whatever – is worth. *Cut to: Dead Posh Restaurants*: tinted harbour lights wobbling across the black waters towards a portside restaurant; cappuccino waves foaming on rocks below a cliffside restaurant. What they all want is octopus. The managers are desperate. Indoors, a besotted man is proposing to Gabriella who, it turns out, has only agreed to have dinner with him to explain, personally and warmly, that she never wants to see him again, although she hopes they will remain friends. Anyway, whatever the special occasion, a waiter always arrives with a tiny morsel of perfectly burnt octopus for which the besotted bloke has taken out a bank loan.

So, imagine Diver Boy's excitement when he reaches the cold dim seabed and sees a fat tentacle draped over a rock next to the mouth of a cave. This was his meal ticket, his mortgage, his alimony, his car payments, a year's worth of diesel and compressed air, all packaged in the bulbous head of the Ocean Martian lurking in his lair. *Reconstruction*: an actor squeezes the trigger, and the spear pierces the darkness of the cave with a confident hiss. To his surprise, there is no cloud of black ink or copper-blue blood; he just watches the fat tentacle slide back, while another one comes out of nowhere and wrenches the weapon from his hand. Then, before he can work out what's going on, a third tentacle curls around his leg and drags him down to the mouth of the cave, where the eight-limbed hunter has now taken up residence, after tricking his half-limbed assailant into expending his useless spear.

At this point, Sebastian was completely on the side of the octopus. He cheered and jumped up and down in his seat, until Ben threatened to take him back to the SOR because he was upsetting the other patients. They were worried about Diver Boy, who was now splayed across a rock, having his mask ripped off by a dish fit for a king; or for a broken-hearted lover, if it came to that.

It was only when he was back in the discomfort of his room that Sebastian had started to recognise the tentacles for what they were: bad words that slithered out of cave mouths and tore the mask from his face, blurring his vision while he ran out of air, his clenched muscles clenched by muscles more muscular than his own. It was happening to him again right now.

'Boom!' said Sebastian, throwing his arms into the air and flinging himself against the wall. The fuse had run out. The bomb had gone off. The infinity bomb, the suicide bomb, the whole thing, shattering the mirrors, shattering the shatter-proof glass. Raining blood and crystal. Sebastian crouched down and sheltered on the far side of the bed, covering his head to protect himself from the lacerating debris.

He could remember a time, while he was working for Mr Morris at Party Solutions, when the bad words had started to lose their grip. After practising a few times in his sessions, he was able to say, without so much as a by-your-leave, 'Don't throw the baby out with the bathwater.' He started to use the phrase so often that his workmates had been able to tease him – in a friendly way. He recognised that they had been teasing him in a friendly way, although it was hard to imagine now. Friendly teasing was a contradiction again but, to do it justice, in his current frame of mind even 2=2 seemed like a contradiction: the second 2 must be different from the first one as it was no longer in the same place. What was it up to? What was its game? Teleportation? Bilocation? Was it having a secret intercontinental equation with its opposite number in Washington, flitting back and forth across the equals sign, fast enough that nobody noticed the empty desks while they were both in transit?

Back then, his workmates had started to use his bad words and phrases, not to torment him, but to make the words that threatened to torment him seem more ordinary. There was only Steve, one of the cooks, who took advantage of Sebastian's openness and deliberately tried to push him over the edge.

'Oi, Seb,' he would shout out, when he was pressing a steak into the frying pan with his spatula, to make it smoke and sizzle, 'do you like *the smell of burning flesh*?'

And then Steve would let out a hoot of triumphant laughter as Sebastian hurried away.

The first time it happened, Sebastian had gone to hide in the pantry where they kept the catering glasses. He sat on the floor, with his forehead pressed to his clutched knees.

'I'm wrestling with my demons,' he muttered to himself, trying to cut at least one of the tentacles that was wrapped around him, but 'the smell of burning flesh' was still dragging him back towards the frying pan and the fire.

Gabriella came in and sat down next to him. At first, she

didn't say a word but just pressed her shoulder against his as a sign of solidarity.

'Don't worry about Steve,' she said eventually. 'Some people are just like that.'

'He's a nasty piece of work,' mumbled Sebastian, looking at her sideways.

He must have looked very distressed because she swept aside the hair that had fallen across his stooped face and turned his head gently towards her, gazing into his eyes.

'Don't let him get to you, Seb; we're all on your side. He's the one with a problem as far as we're concerned.'

He felt as if he was about six, which was quite a lot older than he had felt before, so that was a move in the right direction (or not).

'Okay,' he said.

She ran her fingers through his hair and rested them briefly against the side of his head and it was the loveliest thing he'd ever felt, and he wanted to be with her for ever and ever, world without end, Amen.

The memory of this ravishing moment drove Sebastian out from behind his hospital bed. He paused on all fours, at the corner of the metal frame, glancing sideways; his gaze level with Dr Carr's shoes.

'Can you hear the sound of falling glass?' he asked in a hoarse whisper.

Dr Carr said nothing, giving him the silent treatment.

'We've all been badly cut,' Sebastian went on, speaking rapidly and only just audibly. 'All the woodland creatures have been cut and burnt in this terrible tragedy. It was a suicide bomber. The prime minister said it was "a horrendous and cowardly act" and that the victims were "ordinary men, women and woodland creatures trying to do the right thing" and that his "thoughts and prayers were with the hearts and minds of the families and friends who have lost loved ones". The bomber was captured on CCTV thirty-four times before he arrived at the hospital. He was carrying a black rucksack bristling with copper wires and "Danger! Explosives!" written on the back. With all the CCTVs, there just aren't enough people to look at the footage, but at least you can make a film about it afterwards.'

Sebastian burst abruptly into song: 'That's entertainment!' he roared, before resuming his rapid whisper.

'The explosion blew up all the windows and the mirrors. Some of the cows have been badly hurt. In fact,' he went on, excited by the breaking news, 'the cow who stares at me through the glass door is actually dead and – and Ben is in the emergency room, having pieces of glass pulled out from all over his body. So, he won't be coming back in a hurry.'

'And yet you and I are still here,' said Dr Carr.

'Yeah,' said Sebastian, 'we're survivors. We're bound to be interviewed, so we can tell our side of the story.'

'It's interesting that you say "side" in the singular,' said Dr Carr. 'That suggests that you feel we are on the same side, that we have a shared point of view. Perhaps there is a mirror that was not destroyed in the explosion, a mirror that we have made together, which enables you to see yourself more clearly.'

'Bastard,' said Sebastian. 'That's why you brought me here, because it's the only place in the entire country where there are enough people to be on camera *and* to watch the footage at the same time. It's a fully staffed facility. You're trying to pin it on me! You're trying to frame me!'

'Or perhaps we're trying to frame the mirror, so we know where it ends: what is a true reflection of you and what is something else. I know that mirrors played a very central role in your first episode in the Portobello Road. You felt that they were supervising you in a persecutory way. The whole sky turned out to be made of that kind of mirror and when you shattered it with the blue beam, you felt that you had won a great victory and that you had saved humanity. It was one of the best feelings of your life – at the time. Since then, though, a second kind of mirror, a benign mirror, has come into your life, one that is not overlooking you against your wishes, but which helps you to see yourself more clearly when you step into its frame.'

'If you're so fucking clever,' said Sebastian, 'how come you abandoned me? You and Simon: when the going gets tough, the tough fuck off.'

'As we've discussed, there was a national lockdown and I was unable to see you in person during that time . . .'

'It's your fucking loony bin, you can do what you like. You could have me put down like a rabid dog.'

'I am not the owner of this hospital,' said Dr Carr, 'I am a Visiting Consultant, which is why I was able to get you in here immediately after you found yourself unable to cope. You seemed to like it more than some of the other hospitals you've been in.'

'That was before you abandoned me.'

'I was not legally allowed to visit you for several weeks, but we stayed in touch by phone at all our usual times.'

'But now they've taken away my cellphalopod, my cell mate, my soul mate, there's a word for it, cell phone.'

Dr Carr said nothing.

They both knew that his phone had been confiscated because Sebastian had texted or called Gabriella two or three hundred times a day and that John, who had become the manager of Party Solutions (and Gabriella's boyfriend), had contacted the hospital to complain.

'You could just have me put down,' said Sebastian.

'I think you feel you've been put down all your life—' said Dr Carr.

'Mainly by you,' Sebastian interrupted him angrily, 'because you gave me hope. You said I could have "ordinary unhappiness", but you knew all along that I was never going to be allowed that.'

'Well, that's a very important subject that we can continue to discuss tomorrow,' said Dr Carr.

Sebastian crawled backwards behind the bed again, so as not to watch him leave. He heard Ben unlock the door but did not respond to Dr Carr's farewell. He was trying to replicate the position he was in when Gabriella had sat next to him in the glass pantry. Perhaps if he got it exactly right, he would feel that friendly pressure on his shoulder. He closed his eyes and waited.

2

'Mama!' said Noah reproachfully. 'You're not looking at me! I'm climbing the really high branch now. I've never been this high before. Last time, we said I would climb to this branch *next time* and now it *is* next time.'

'Well done, darling,' said Olivia, watching Noah clamber onto a slightly higher branch, straddle it, and clasp the burr in front of him, like the pommel of a saddle. She was trying to be vigilant without being anxious; ready to catch Noah if he slipped, without assuming that he would. She folded her arms firmly only to become aware of how ready she was for them to spring open into a safety net.

'Giddy up,' said Noah. 'I'm riding on a diplodocus!'

He seemed to have picked up the idea of being in a saddle. There was a free trade of thoughts and impressions between people who loved each other, matched by the passion for secure borders and misunderstandings among those who didn't. She had to give him full credit for putting the saddle on a dinosaur, which she had failed to imagine, although it would have been easy enough if she weren't so preoccupied.

'This time *is* the next time,' said Noah, struck afresh by the insanity of time or of language, or by the acuity of his own mind. It hardly mattered, such was the joy of watching a remembered anticipation collapse into an actual event.

'Yes, time gallops on,' said Olivia.

Francis was already half an hour late and she longed for him to come back. He was much more tolerant of Noah's dinosaur obsession than she was, having passed through a similar phase, in an era of less aggressive merchandising. She had no time for dinosaurs, although a great deal was asked of her. The truth was, she loathed them. They seemed to suffer from drastic design flaws that made their hundred-and-twenty-eight-million-year rulership of the planet unfathomable: the pinhead of a brachiosaurus writhing remotely on its tentacular neck while its tree-felling torso crashed through the undergrowth, and the repulsive flying dinosaurs, instead of folding their wings against their bodies, tucking them into a pair of bony elbows on which they clattered across the ground. Apart from her longing to escape this realm of weird monsters, she sometimes simply longed to let her mind wander freely.

She saw the world as roughly divided between people who felt they were stepping out of solitude into relationships and those who felt they were stepping out of relationships into solitude, with many degrees of each basic view. Even as someone close to the centre of this divide, who was deeply involved with her family and her friends, she still had an underlying assumption that solitude was the natural state from which she emerged to engage in relationships. She couldn't help feeling this must be fundamentally true for everyone, if only they recognised it, but she had met plenty of people from the other tribe, who were surprised and often disconcerted to find themselves alone and who filled their solitude almost exclusively with plans to bring it to an end as soon as possible. They were inclined to say things like, 'We're basically social animals', especially if they had recently found themselves spending several minutes without a device, an alarm, a notification, or contact with their contacts.

It sometimes seemed strange to Olivia that she was on the solitary side of the divide, given that she had started her life sharing her mother's womb with another human being. What could incline a person more strongly to feel that life was all about being close to other people? Maybe the abrupt interruption of both those bonds had made Olivia feel that intimacy was an illusion, or a contingency, or a hoax. Her first companion had become a perfect stranger and her mother had immediately given her up for adoption. Her twin brother was put up for adoption a year and a half later and spent six months in an institution before a family finally took him on. Olivia knew that she had been given a much better start than him, adopted at birth by her wonderful parents, but she would not have had the good fortune to be brought up by the Carrs if her own mother had not rejected her in the first place. Perhaps this experience had formed a layer of ice deeper than the subsequent warmth, but if there was any truth to the great temperamental divide she was envisaging, it couldn't be explained by anything as specific as her personal history. Francis, with a quite different early history, was also in the solitary tribe. Although solitary types might be expected to disavow inter-connectedness, he was obsessed with it in a way often lacking among the people who were most excited by overlapping address books. If the point of life was to discover 'what a small world it is', the idea of a network of all living things, and possibly of all matter (if we understood the true nature of matter), must strike the social tribe as vague and extravagant, and dementedly inclusive. What was the point of turning their attention from a family tree to a global forest that might well belong to someone they didn't know; let alone to the biosphere, which hadn't been fully privatised yet?

Noah had spent a term at nursery school to prepare him for the primary school he was going to this September. After tasting the possibility of successive hours without having to look after him, the return to the old pattern of constant supervision during the summer holidays felt more oppressive to Francis and Olivia than before, kicking off an arms race in the virtuous evasion of childcare. Gone were the days when Francis walked around with a notebook and pencil, cataloguing the progress of the rewilding project going on around them in Howorth. He was now working for Hope Schwartz's NGO, *Not on Our Watch*, and was helping to save Amazonian rainforest, so the unemployed Olivia had started out with a virtue deficit, but in the snatched moments when Francis was looking after Noah, she had started pitching the idea of making six radio programmes about the six most likely causes of the next – which would be the sixth – great extinction. The programmes were now commissioned by Silverline, an independent production company. She was due to record her first interview tomorrow afternoon in their studio in Soho.

Artificial intelligence, pandemics, nuclear annihilation, global warming, asteroids and overpopulation were the finalists for the Silverline production. Strong cases had been made for chemical pollution and misguided genetic manipulation, but despite their many strengths and some passionate advocates, they did not make the final cut. The order of the broadcasts would be up to the BBC, but Olivia decided to start the production with asteroids, as it seemed more relaxing to discuss the only extinction candidate that could not be attributed to human folly or the unintended consequences of scientific genius. Good old asteroids, they just came hurtling towards us, without malice or cupidity, without even sound waves, until they roared through the atmosphere in their final moments. The impact was made by them, but the debris was made by the Earth; the asteroids themselves were vaporised. Meteorites, if they didn't turn into shooting stars or bounce back into space, made an impact not powerful enough to annihilate them, and so they formed genuine alien litter, a topic she would be discussing tomorrow with her guests but which she needed to mug up on right now. She and Francis had watched *Fireball* last night, Werner Herzog's documentary about asteroids and meteorites. Francis, predictably, wanted her to discuss panspermia, the idea that there was life throughout the universe, as evidenced by the fact that some meteorites carried the amino acids needed for proteins, the lipids needed for building cell walls and, most surprisingly, sugars from outer space. Anything beginning with 'pan' – panpsychism, panspermia, and indeed the intoxicating Pan himself – was a big pull for Francis, but there was still an enormous creative gap between the arrival of organic compounds and the formation of life. The theory that those compounds had come to a lifeless Earth, rather than the living Earth being an exception in a lifeless universe, was a reversal of perspectives she wanted to explore with her guests. The much more familiar idea that the universe was filled with stellar factories forging the elements in their furnaces and then dispersing them explosively through space, and that we are 'ultimately' made of stardust, provoked Herzog to step indignantly from behind the camera to say that Bavaria had been a bigger influence on him than stardust.

Since Olivia's commission from Silverline, a touch of apocalyptic rivalry had crept in to Willow Cottage. Noah had only been six months old when Francis accepted Hope's offer to work for *Not on Our Watch*, and so Francis had a head start. It was already four years since he made his grim journey to Ecuador, setting off for the *Oriente*, the Wild East of the country, to have a look for himself at 'The Amazonian Chernobyl'. He was supposed to go every other year, but due to the pandemic had only been once. George and Emma, the owners of Howorth, were friends of Hope's and supporters of *Not on Our Watch*, and had offered him an office with high-speed internet, several comfortable armchairs and a round window overlooking a cobbled courtyard in the old stables. He was probably there now, tracking ecological crimes on drone cameras halfway across the world.

'Mama!'

Olivia glanced up quickly.

'Fuck,' she said, reaching up to support a toppling Noah as he grabbed at the shoots bristling from the burr. Just one moment of inattention, that's all it took. 'I mean, whoops. I'm not encouraging you to use that other word.'

'Don't worry, Mama, I don't need encouraging,' said Noah. 'I already used it at nursery.'

'Oh, really?' said Olivia, on tiptoe, pushing Noah back onto the diplodocus. 'What did Miss Foster have to say about that?'

'That I shouldn't, and I said my parents said it all the time, and she said I didn't have to copy my parents in everything.'

'Well, it is difficult for you if we use words and then tell you not to use them,' she admitted.

'That's right,' said Noah, deliberately tipping from the branch now that he was sure Olivia would catch him. 'That would be pomposity,' he said, foundering into laughter as he let go of the branch and subsided into Olivia's arms.

She caught him as he headed down and hugged him, her face buried in his hair. He was getting so heavy.

'Or hypocrisy,' she suggested and then seeing his disappointment at having reached for the wrong meaning from the penumbra of words he had overheard but not fully understood, she said, 'Anyway, a big word with exactly that rhythm: pomposity/hypocrisy/hypocrisy/pomposity.'

As she turned the words into a nonsense song, she circled around, holding Noah close to her, and they laughed together under the climbing tree.

'Mind you,' said Olivia, coming to a halt and not wanting to stunt Noah's adventurous vocabulary, 'it could be pomposity if . . .'

She could tell he was not listening.

'Dada!' he cried out.

Olivia turned around.

'Ah, there you are,' she said.

'Sorry, sorry,' said Francis. 'I couldn't leave. I was talking to Antero, and I just had to hear him out.'

'Don't worry,' said Olivia, putting Noah down on the ground.

She was prepared to forgive anything involving Antero. He was a guide Francis had met in Ecuador, one of the last of the Cofan who could still vaguely recall the old life of his people, living unobtrusively in the forest, hunting tapir and howler monkeys, growing vegetables, getting illnesses that the shaman could sometimes cure and sometimes not. What he could never forget was the day his father had taken him out for his first hunt. They had been moving quietly through the forest looking for prey when they heard the metallic roar of the first helicopter either of them had ever seen, thudding through the sky, and landing on some open ground near by. They ran away to hide deeper in the forest but watched as tall men in clay-coloured clothes poured out of the entrails of the machine. These men, it turned out, were surveyors from the oil company.

The new illnesses that followed their arrival gradually defeated the Cofan shaman, who ended his career by drinking himself into a stupor in the bars and brothels that sprang up around the new oil camps. Antero's second son died at six months old, having remained as tiny and fragile as a newborn all his life. His older son lasted until he was three. He swallowed some contaminated water, and after vomiting and bleeding for twenty-four hours he died as well. Antero's wife contracted uterine cancer, had a hysterectomy, and spent the rest of her short life in severe pain. Antero was a man, Francis had told her, who seemed to be aloof, but in fact contained a mountain of grief that he had no idea how to approach, let alone invite anyone else to climb with him. All that he dared to want now, and talked to Francis about every month, were tanks to catch the rain before it touched the ground so there would be clean water for other people's children to drink.

'How is he?' she asked.

'He's excited because another thirty big rain barrels arrived and he's going to distribute them around the villages.'

'That's good,' said Olivia, giving Francis a quick kiss. 'Listen, I'm going to pack and do a few hours' work and then catch the eight fifty-five. Are you sure you're happy for me to take the car?'

'Yeah, we've got plenty of food and it's only twenty-four hours.'

'And we've got the ark,' said Noah. 'Dada, can we go and work on it now?'

'Of course,' said Francis, 'we've still got to find a good mast.'

Miss Foster had explained the story of his biblical namesake to Noah's class last term and commandeered the family into a shipbuilding project. Francis had to spend hours a week trying to assemble the ominous vessel from the woods he was committed to leaving undisturbed.

'Is it really going to rain everywhere for forty days and forty nights?' said Noah.

'Probably not,' said Francis, 'but instead of going to the seaside, the seaside will be coming to us, and so it'll be a really good idea to have a boat on our doorstep.'

3

When you thought about it, thought Sebastian, 'thought-provoking' was the stupidest phrase ever invented, because there was nothing, literally nothing, including 'nothing', that didn't provoke a thought. If anyone could find something that didn't provoke a thought, they would make a bloody fortune. Dr Guillotine, being an opponent of capital punishment, who was only trying to make it more humane, was mortified when he was told that severed heads went on thinking for two or three minutes. Even Clozapine, which was tailor-made to turn Sebastian into a moron, provoked the thought that he wished he hadn't taken it. They were reducing his dose incrementally, which was a technical term for far too bloody slowly.

Pill-cutter, pill-cutter, cut me a pill.

'My funny Guillotine . . .' Sebastian sang, holding an imaginary microphone, 'sweet, comic Guillotine.'

Then he threw the mic onto the bed and started pacing the room again.

Sometimes he longed to be back on the bullet train, where the twin magnets pushed each other away, humming along without friction, without opposition, because they were floating on the opposition made by their sameness, above the clatter and the rattle of facts and figures, just gliding through the same-opposite-opposite-same heart of the matter. The trouble was that if the bullet train went too fast it shot a hole in the fabric of the universe, hurtling from one parallel world to another, multiversing through thought-provoking space without rhyme or reason. Then he wished he had wheels and brakes, facts and figures, wished he had the buffers of a destination to terminate the train before the train terminated him.

One good thing about multiversing, though, was that it shook off the track-and-trace merchants. There were no cookies on the bullet train, it was a Faraday cage of secret associations that nobody could supervise.

Earlier this afternoon he had talked to a new bloke in the Common Room, which was unusual because a lot of the patients didn't talk at all, hadn't spoken for years, might as well be dead from a fancy-a-chat point of view. And then there were the ones who never stopped talking. You couldn't chat with them either. Same opposites. Anyway, James, the new bloke, had been in his personal Faraday cage only yesterday. He was lying on a couch at a friend's flat, staring at a Japanese print of a grey heron. And he thought, Japan, Pearl Harbor, pearl, oyster, oyster knife, and he went into the kitchen and found an oyster knife and stabbed himself in the chest, not only to kill himself, but to enter another world. The oyster knife was the key to opening the round red door on the Japanese flag and stepping across the blazing threshold into Tokyo, or Kyoto – they were two faces of the same word, when you thought about it, with good old Kyo, like a master samurai, in the heat of battle, holding his ground, not giving an inch, cool as a cucumber, while his crazy friend To rushed to the front of him, screaming and slashing, or rushed to the back of him, slashing and screaming.

Someone from Health and Safety, or Human Resources, or Frontline Services would have no idea, would not have the slightest clue, that when James was stabbing himself in the chest with an oyster knife, in reality he was unlocking the door to a world of elegance and restraint.

'I was going to become the heron in the print,' said James.

'And fly away,' they had both said at the same time.

To be honest, he had teared-up a bit when that happened, because James, who he didn't know from Adam, was his brother. He kept saying to him, 'I get it, I get it, I totally get it.'

It was all part of a perfect plan once you understood the chain reaction of thought-provoking ideas that led to the heron taking flight. In a way, he was being James's Dr Carr, understanding the chain reaction, but then he did something that Dr Carr would definitely not have done – which showed that Seb wasn't ready to take on the role of a professional psychoanalyst yet, although he had been Dr Carr's apprentice for a long time – he had started wondering if there might be an oyster knife tucked away at the back of a kitchen drawer somewhere in the hospital. They never brought anything onto the ward sharp enough to cut a piece of melting butter, but they might keep an oyster knife hidden away in case the Hospital Administrator suddenly fancied an oyster. Powerful people often had greedy impulses. They just picked up the phone and said, 'Bring me a dozen oysters, Miss Moneypenny, and a bottle of your best methylated spirits.' The feast would arrive on a silver platter, with shattered ice and half-lemons, the whole shebang; but before all of that, Miss Moneypenny would have to find an oyster knife – without suspecting, without having the slightest clue, that it was the key to a portal.

So, if the fat old fart who was running the hospital was having one of his oyster binges, the knife might just be lying around in his private kitchen. They could nick it. He and James could nip in and nick it. And then they could unlock the big red door, and step into a beautiful Japanese landscape, with kimonos and cherry blossoms and ritual suicide: the works, a package deal with Kyo and To fighting back to front and front to back while he and James shot from city to city on the good old bullet train. Magic, absolute magic.

He may have become overexcited and had probably made a

mistake or, in Ben's opinion, had definitely made a mistake, when he started telling James about his plan. Poor old James had been put on some very heavy meds because of his recent episode. The doctors didn't understand what was going on at all and were treating him like some random loony who had stabbed himself in the chest. Still, even in the lead casket of his anti-this and anti-that and anti-everything, of his inhibitors and his blockers and his killers, you could tell that James was getting very agitated at the mention of the oyster knife. He started stammering and shaking and looking around him anxiously. He stared at Seb as if he might be a figment of his imagination tempting him down a path of self-destruction, rather than a true brother who was inviting him on a tour of the Orient. It was only a step away among the origami folds of the implicate order. Things that were thousands of miles away, tens of thousands of miles away in extended space, were bang next door in the origami realm. Telling James about folded space didn't seem to calm him down at all. Soon enough Ben was standing there asking what all the ruckus was about and, after a bit of argy-bargy and to and fro, he marched Sebastian back to his room, locked the door and threw away the key.

So, here he was, back in his room, pacing up and down like there was no tomorrow – not that there was a tomorrow, because by the time it arrived it was today and until it arrived it was just a theory, a sealed window of anticipation among all the rotten floorboards and slamming doors and shattered glass of plans and hopes and fears. It was anticipation's midnight child, hope's shuddering little death, a theory somewhere between twenty-four hours and a second away from being falsified. In the twinkling of an eye tomorrow became today and today got a new tomorrow. It was enough to make your head spin, but it could never spin fast enough to have a face-to-face meeting with tomorrow. You couldn't even do FaceTime instead, like he used to with Gabriella, before she blocked him as a caller.

Stick to the subject, stick to the subject.

If Time was taking tomorrow and tomorrow and tomorrow-sized paces, like Big Bill the Bard said, they would start out by being huge, giant, Fee-fie-fo-fum, twenty-four-hour-sized strides and end up being teeny-weeny, tippy-toe, second-sized steps in the last minute. And even those steps would get smaller and smaller as tomorrow loomed. Frankly, things were confusing enough without good old reliable clock time contracting by 60x60x24 times in the last second of the day compared to the first, just because His Royal Highness, The Mass Murderer of Scotland got a stammer when he was down in the dumps and felt that things were getting a bit monotonous. Murder Duncan, murder Salmon, murder Turbot, murder Sturgeon, murder Donald Duck, murder this, murder that. No wonder he got bored.

'Ch-ch-ch-ch-changes,' Sebastian burst into song, holding an imaginary microphone; lightning bolt across the face; split down the middle; dying for a Ziggy. One brother mad as a hatter, the other a superstar. That's what was really going on.

'Turn and face the strange,' he sang, frowning sincerely, and then threw the mic back on the bed.

Changes were a rolling event, like a wave wrapped around a surfer, they started behind you, before you could notice them, and then they were in front of you, as they came to your attention, but it was all the same surge, made of the same sea. Sebastian crouched down, stretching one arm in front of him and the other behind, and shot through the tube of the wave, keeping his balance with astonishing expertise. Slowly, tentatively, he moved his arms away from the central axis and explored the curling wall of water with his fingertips; feeling with his backward-stretching fingers the upsurge of the wave as it rolled in from the wild open ocean and running his forward-reaching fingers against the tumbling water propelling him towards the shore. It was so beautiful it made him want to scream, and the most beautiful thing about it was that it didn't provoke any thoughts at all.

As soon as he realised that he wasn't having any thoughts, he started to lose his balance. He felt he had overreached, that he should have kept his arms on the straight and narrow, and then the board shot out from under his feet, and he was pounded down by the wave, which was no longer the secret tunnel of Time, just an alien violence that dragged him into its churning undercurrents and expunged all reference points; no up, no down, just around and around.

He lay sprawled on the floor, washed up on the beach, the boom of surf, and the long waves rushing over his ankles.

He'd had billions and billions of thoughts and feelings but only had a handful of memories to show for them. Seashells on a seashore, the shells embedded in miles and miles of golden sand made of broken shells: memories embedded in forgetfulness. Was that the unconscious? Was the unconscious the beach he was lying on? Must ask Dr Carr.

He heaved himself up, blinded by sunlight. The light had taken eight minutes to travel here, from Sunkyo to Kyosun, on the fastest bullet train known to man.

'Wishhhhhh,' said Sebastian, being the bullet train.

The boom of the surf was the little rattler that stopped at every station on the way to his ear.

'The next stop will be Seb's Ear-on-sea,' he announced. 'Thank you for travelling on Sound Wave. Please make sure you take all your concrete music with you.'

Surfing the tubular wave had been a beautiful illusion. By the time he noticed something it had already happened. The light was already pinging the sea before he saw it, telling the sparkling waves they had tested positive for Photon-19. Trillions of new cases a second. He couldn't touch the back of the tubular wave, the beginning of an event, any more than his ears could be where they were, stuck to the side of his head (he quickly checked), and where the boom started in the breaking surf. There was always a gap, a little gap, narrow but infinitely deep. He came to an abrupt halt, as if he had just come to the edge of the gap, to stop himself tumbling in. He held out his hands and stepped back, but the gap was behind him as well: it was everywhere, built into being alive. He wasn't on the edge of it, he was falling inside it all the time.

People complained that there were no live events any more, but there never had been, because of the gap; only more or less dead events.

'Yah,' said Sebastian, straight to camera, dead sophisticated, 'I'm actually in the Very Recently Dead Events industry, and we've been hit especially hard by the lockdown. It's actually been pretty horrendous for everybody who works in the sector and we're going to have to ask the government for an extra injection of Clozapine.'

And the gap wasn't that narrow, when you thought about it, because you couldn't tell when an event began, unless you made a tight little window in clock time, like lunch, or the fourteenth century, or the day they dropped the atomic bomb on Hiroshima, but all the things you saw through the little windows had taken ages to get there. Light from the sun took eight minutes, but light from some of the old stars, the Gloria Swansongs, the Sunset Boulevards of the outer galaxies, had taken millions of years to get here and according to Brian Cox on the telly, they might not exist any more (which was hard to get your head around) although you could still see bullet trains full of luminous refugees escaping from their dying stars. Brian (which was the same word as Brain, if you just put the 'i' and the 'a' in a revolving door and the one that was in the lobby was on the pavement and the one that was on the pavement was in the lobby. Brian's parents probably wanted to call him Brain, but they didn't dare, because he wasn't on the telly yet being super brainy, so they got as close as they dared); anyway, point being that Brian, or Brain, had said that there were more cells in the human body than stars in the sky, or perhaps it was the other way round. Telescopes and microscopes. Looking through the wrong end. Hubble, bubble, snaps and trouble. And when it came to cells, did they belong to Fee-fie-fo-fum or Tom Thumb? Must count for something.

Brian had also said that we were literally made from the elements forged in the furnace of the stars and Sebastian had shouted 'In your dreams, Brian!' because he felt that he was literally made by the atom bomb of his father's *Little Boy* falling on the Hiroshima of his mother's ovary and creating the ruins of his existence. Birthdays were the worst days: regretting being born and hating growing older.

Having a shouting match with the telly usually got him goose-stepped to solitary confinement, but Ben wasn't in charge that day; it was Helio, the dude. Helio said things like, 'What's wrong, Seb, my friend?' and 'Take it easy, man.' He was from Brazil, but he spoke in a very chilled half-American English and laughed a lot and swept his long black hair out of his face, so he didn't spend his whole life walking into lamp posts and falling down stairs.

Falling, he wished he hadn't had that thought.

At least if you fell down stairs you landed on the ground, but when you were falling in the gap, whether it was as big as the Big-Bang-till-Now or as narrow as a human hair, as people liked to say, you were always falling.

He must get out! He must get out right now!

His room was a gap as wide as itself. It was not just hanging over a chasm; it was a chasm.

He ran to the door and started to beat it with the sides of his fists, staring through the slit of reinforced glass.

'Help!' Sebastian pleaded.

'Let me out, you bastards!' he shouted, furiously this time, but as usual nobody could hear his voices.

If he pulled the emergency cord, they would make him eat humble pie, make him beg for a bigger dose of Moronopine.

He didn't want that. Or he did want that. Or he didn't.

Sebastian froze, perfectly divided, or imperfectly divided. Being divided was imperfect and so being perfectly divided was even more imperfect. Same difference.

When his body unlocked, he found himself jumping up and down with pent-up energy, belting out the old lyrics:

Take me to the hospital/ Take me to the show/ I wanna be sedated!

He was already in a bloody hospital. He didn't need to be taken there. He needed to be taken out – not by special ops, or the CIA, or MI6 – but by Gabriella. Bitch. He loved her so much.

He tried to sit on the edge of the mattress, but bounced back upright; sat-bounced, sat-bounced, sat-bounced, trying to relax on a trampoline. He was probably sitting and probably standing at the same time, until you took a snapshot from the Hubble Bubble, the cauldron with a heart of lens.

Getting very slippery now, thoughts all over the place. He'd been locked up in lockdown because he couldn't be trusted to trust himself, but now he wanted to be unlocked and set free in a land flowing with milk and 'honey I'm home' Gabriella.

And then, just as he thought of the word 'unlocked', he heard the door being unlocked. Sometimes it was like that: his mind was a needle piercing through the thick folds of reality and drawing them together with a single thread, and he felt all-powerful, like the first time when the blue beam had shot from his forehead, and he had saved the entire human race from falling under the mind control of the Sky Mirror. Magic, absolute magic. Not that anybody thanked him. You would have thought a quick visit to the palace would have been in order. Arise, Sir Seb; but no, they had sent him to another bloody hospital, like this one but worse.

He didn't stay in these states of – the name he and Dr Carr

had come up with was 'delusional omnipotence' – for long these days, just fluttered past them and singed his wings. Unlike poor Derek, who thought that he was Swami Maharishi Punjaji, or whatever. He even had a long grey beard and wore a pinkish nightshirt and went around the Common Room blessing all and sundry and saying things like, 'Black and white: same thing!' or, 'Hot and cold: no difference!', and woe betide anyone who asked him for an explanation. You'd still be sat there three weeks later with Derek saying that everything was the same, which, since it was the only thing he ever said, was true, as far as he was concerned.

Helio had told him that opinion was divided about Derek.

'That's what opinion is for, man,' he said, getting into Heliospeak. 'It's facts getting divided that's the worrying trend, my friend.'

And Helio had put both his hands on Seb's shoulders and laughed so much, you couldn't see his face any more, because he didn't have a free hand to sweep his hair away, but you could see his nose occasionally bobbing through the curtain of his long black hair. It reminded Seb of the only time he'd been in a school play, and he kept checking to see if the audience was still there. It was.

'You say incredible things, Seb, you should be on TV, on one of those panels,' Helio had said. 'You're a philosopher, like me. You like to think about things and take them to the next level.'

Helio had made a gesture, as if throwing a basketball over the head of a tall opponent. Suddenly, the curtain parted, and you could see his face again.

Anyway, it turned out that opinion was divided about whether to call Derek 'Derek', or whether to call him 'Swami' or 'Precious Guru'. Some of the high-ups thought that it would be 'validating his psychosis' to call him Swami, and others thought that his 'ego structure' was too fragile to take the challenge of being called Derek. Helio told him that he shouldn't really be telling him this stuff, but he knew that Seb had a 'special connection' with Psychology thanks to Dr Carr.

'Derek and Swami: same thing,' said Sebastian, cracking Helio up with his perfect impersonation of Swami Derek.

His own view was that it didn't matter much either way because most people never spoke to Derek. A few people said things like, 'Bless off, you tosser,' but none of it made a blind bit of difference.

And then there was Laura, who had been on the ward for donkey's years. Her white hair had turned yellow, and she had a face like a court summons you'd scrunched up angrily and then fished out of the bin and tried to flatten, but her eyes were as soft and blue as a summer afternoon. She followed Derek around all day saying, 'Bless me, your Holiness', 'Bless me, Swami,' but Derek ignored her, as if he didn't like her being quite so keen.

Sebastian had discussed Derek's case with Dr Carr, and right at the end of the session, Seb said spontaneously, 'If you say "important" fast enough it sounds like "impotent".'

'I think you've got it in one,' said Dr Carr, with a friendly smile.

Seb had half expected him to add, 'And this is the address of your new consulting rooms in Harley Street,' and to hand him a box of engraved cards saying, *Dr Sebastian Tanner, Specialist in enduring psychosis, MD (MA), PHD, THC, CBD, DMT, OBE.*

Anyway, it turned out that when he'd been thinking of the word 'unlocked', it was Helio who had unlocked the door. He came in carrying a little pleated cup with Seb's Clozapine in it.

'Hey, Seb, my friend!' said Helio.

He gave Seb an elbow bump and handed him the cup.

Seb knocked back his meds straight away and took a swig of water from the plastic bottle on his bedside table.

'You swallowed it, right?' said Helio.

'Course I did,' said Sebastian. 'I wanna be a chilled dude like you.'

He approached Helio with his mouth wide open. 'Wanna have a look?'

'No, man, I can see it was real,' said Helio. 'It's just that Ben told me you were being "provocative" earlier.'

'Yeah, well, Ben would find it provocative if the sea turned out to be wet,' said Seb, recoiling from an imaginary wave, clutching his face in alarm.

Helio had to sit on the edge of the bed he was laughing so much.

'You say the craziest things, man.'

'Goes with the territory,' said Seb.

'Shit, I'm not supposed to use words like "crazy",' said Helio. 'It might upset you.'

'I'd be upset if you didn't use the word "crazy",' said Seb, in a fit of gallantry.

Something about the formality of this pronouncement made them both burst out laughing.

It was all getting a bit too much and Seb started to feel uneasy, like he used to when he smoked skunk with Simon back in the day.

Helio took the lead in sounding a more sober tone.

'I got your phone out of the locker,' he said, 'so you can call Dr Carr. But no calls to you-know-who, or any of your old colleagues.'

'Course not,' said Seb, a picture of innocence verging on outrage. 'Why would I do a thing like that?'

'Because you did it six thousand three hundred and twenty-seven times before,' said Helio, 'according to her boyfriend.'

Sebastian froze. He stared out of the window at the gaping wounds and the human torches, and the brown and white shoes dotted across the hillside, and he wanted to die.

'*Porra!*' Helio reproached himself. 'I'm sorry, man, I shouldn't tease you. I break all the rules with you because you're doing so well. You going to be out of this place soon.'

'Not too soon,' said Seb anxiously.

When they had knocked the door of his flat down, he was naked and the gas was on and the room was sealed and he had a box of matches beside him and he had written, THE WORLD'S WORST BOY in the red lipstick he had stolen from Gabriella down the middle of his body, from his heart to his pubic hair, and the word FRIEND on both his thighs. Whichever choice you made he was the worst friend, and when it came down to it, he was the worst boy. It was the first time he'd had a place of his own and he didn't have any blinds yet, so when a neighbour saw him naked, taping the windows, he had reported him to the police for 'suspicious behaviour', which Seb could now see was fair enough. At the time he had thought that if he could burn his body, he would decontaminate himself and then he could be with her as a pure spirit, and she wouldn't be able to stop him.

'No! Not too soon,' said Helio. 'When it's perfect for you, naturally. You're doing so good, Seb.'

Helio put the phone down on the bed remorsefully. 'I see you in a bit, yeah?' he said. 'I come to collect it after your session.'

'Yeah, if I haven't swallowed the battery,' said Seb.

'Don't say things like that!' said Helio. 'Seriously, man! You are making me personally stressed,' he said, putting his hand on his chest, 'when you say shit like that.'

'I was just kid-ding!' said Sebastian, giving Helio another elbow bump, which on a shorter man would have reached his chin.

'Hey,' said Helio, 'now you're doing *capoeira*! Take it easy, man.'

'I'm just kidding,' said Sebastian, taking the phone.

'Okay, Seb,' said Helio with some solemnity, 'I see you in a while.'

He left and locked the door behind him.

4

It was bad enough that the world was slouching towards Bethlehem without having to make six educational and entertaining programmes about it. Starting a new job in August had not been ideal. Noah had enjoyed a long run of being adored at home, and with his birthday in December was one of the older boys in reception, but Olivia still felt guilty about not having spent the last week of the summer holidays with him. Sitting at her desk in Soho, she was fully aware of the irony that having achieved the independence and intellectual stimulation she had been longing for, she was now giving in to a pre-emptive nostalgia for the last days of his early childhood made even more precious by the trouble she had taken to miss out on them.

At least the strain of these maternal complexities was being alleviated by her growing friendship with Sam, the commissioning editor at Silverline. Sam was a woman who seemed completely relaxed in her hedonism, quietly challenging anyone to find a motivation more fundamental or an aim more worthwhile than pleasure, whether it came from gratified appetites or silent virtue, from self-regard or admiration, from struggle or from its absence. However brief or complicated the journey, she seemed confident that it would somehow become suffused with enjoyment, turning frustrations into a down payment on delight, and transforming guilt from an unwelcome gatecrasher into an honoured guest who could always be consulted about what would be wilder, more excessive or strictly forbidden in a world dimmed by obedience and convention. Sam didn't make plans to appease her anxiety about boredom and chaos, nor did she avoid making plans to appease her anxiety about entrapment; she just seemed to take the bewildering view that whatever happened, planned or unplanned, it was eventually going to be fun. Olivia had become fascinated by this faith in the guiding power and the guaranteed advent of pleasure. She had to find out whether the whole thing was an act or not. She had only known her new colleague for a few weeks and, despite her intuition that Sam was authentic, perhaps thrillingly authentic, she couldn't be sure without getting to know her better.

'Yes, I'd love to have a drink,' said Olivia. 'I just have a few emails to send.'

'In an hour?' said Sam.

'Perfect.'

Olivia was feeling browbeaten by the variety of global death threats to which she would have to make some allusion in her series. Extinction felt like a rush-hour train that had finally arrived but was too crowded to fit anyone else on board. The growth in human population seemed to be matched by a surge in the number of Apocalyptic Horsemen. She could imagine David Attenborough saying, with his adorable authority, that it had taken the whole history of the world to produce the Four Horsemen he was told about as a boy, but that over the course of a single lifetime, their number had doubled, and unless something drastic was done, there would be twelve by 2050. Perhaps, in the end, good old Famine, War, Pestilence and Death were always going to cover the case. When it came to extinction events, you couldn't go wrong with Death on your team. Nevertheless, as she surveyed the field, she couldn't help feeling that the paths to universal destruction had been modernised and multiplied in some quite fundamental ways. In the quaint world of the original Horsemen, 'wild beasts' were supposed to be a big threat; the difficulty now was finding a wild beast to be killed by. War, astride its red steed, used to be armed with a sword rather than the twelve thousand nuclear warheads currently at its disposal. Commenting on Yeats's epitaph, 'Cast a cold eye on life, on death, horseman pass by', Auden had said something withering along the lines of, 'It's more likely to be a motorist these days.' She couldn't help feeling the same thing about the Apocalypse. Young motorists with extinction start-ups, hoping to make a killing and retire early without ever having to put on a suit, were clogging the highway to Armageddon. The trouble with the new styles of annihilation, from out-of-control artificial intelligence, or dioxins released into rivers, seas and food chains, or viruses making zoonotic leaps caused by the unprecedented friction between wild and human populations, or butter-fingered bioengineers, grabbing a couple of bats and a racoon dog on the way home for dinner and clumsily dropping the latest gain-of-function smallpox test tube onto some frozen foreign food, was that they made death so complicated. Their juvenile eagerness seemed to conspire against their equestrian role models in confusing ways. Her programme about asteroids, for instance, had made her less rigidly opposed to nuclear weapons. Without nukes there would be no chance of diverting or disintegrating an asteroid that was on a collision course with the Earth; on the other hand, thanks to nukes it might be a matter of total indifference whether an asteroid plunged into the Earth or not. Synthetic carpets, fire retardants and non-stick pans were chock-full of the endocrine-disruptive chemicals that had contributed to a fifty per cent drop, between 1973 and 2011, in the sperm counts of men in Europe, America and New Zealand, as well as damaging female reproductive capacity in less starkly quantifiable ways. With one last plastic-bottled pseudo-oestrogen push, a generous helping of organophosphate pesticides, and enough glycol ethers in our cosmetics, human infertility might yet save the world from ruin.

Knowing that she had *Asteroids* sewn up and could move on with confidence to *Overpopulation* had done something to alleviate her extinction fatigue. Overpopulation was a subject she kept being told was 'taboo' by the innumerable people who wanted to talk about it on her next programme. She was in touch with several GINKS (Green Inclinations, No Kids), the network of ecologically minded people who took seriously the impact of their reproductive choices on the finite resources of the planet. It was thanks to the political implications of this neo-Malthusian angst that the word 'taboo' was so often whispered down the phone. Since the highest birth rates took place in poor countries in Africa and Asia, while many of the strongest proponents of reproductive restraint came from developed countries, any call for lower birth rates could easily be reframed as racist, or as the colonial export of an alien feminism to cultures in which waiting as long as possible to have one child, so as not to interrupt a prolonged education or a promising career, held less appeal. The feminism promoted by the dominant voices at the Cairo conference on population in 1994 emphasised a woman's sovereignty over her own body. So often used to defend abortion, the same argument could be repurposed to defend reproduction. If the choice was based on bodily sovereignty, rather than a utilitarian accountancy of prosperity and suffering, it became incoherent to apply it exclusively to abortion. The justified accusation that the carbon footprint of a child from a rich nation was gigantic compared to that of a child from a poorer nation (except those from elite families) thickening the political smog obscuring the raw ecological toll of adding eighty million a year to the human population. The need for food, clean water and living space was unsustainable, even if most of the people trying to secure them lived in misery.

Olivia's barely acknowledged sense that she might have been better off not having a child at all gave her some sympathy for the

GINKS, but the idea of subtracting her adorable son from the world was of course an unthinkable thought, a quasi-homicidal taboo much more savage than the 'taboo' of revisiting a once prevalent pessimism about the population bomb and the limits of growth. She had been brought up by her psychoanalytic parents to believe that some of our most powerful feelings were hidden in the reservoirs of the unconscious behind a cracked dam that was sometimes swept away by real madness, but in the case of an ordinary neurotic like her just leaked rejected memories and chimerical combinations into her dreams and daydreams, into her decisions and her indecision. Her fleeting, non-lethal fantasies, imagining that her family had never come into existence, rather than imagining its destruction, often took hold of her when she had spent almost the entire day behind the wheel of her car. As a Londoner, a naïve part of her had thought that at least some of life at Howorth would feel like stepping into a Monet, with startling poppies dotting the thick fields, and perhaps some Pissarro poplars shimmering in the distance, and the glowing flanks of a Stubbs horse occasionally trotting into view. Her gallery of expectations was soon replaced by speed cameras and weather apps. She knew now that country life was really all about being on the road, with only a slim chance of fitting in a walk after dealing with the logistics of survival. She drove and drove and drove, to shops and to school and to visit neighbours she didn't especially like (that was also part of the country code) but who lived, after all, within a forty-minute range. She drove everywhere, except to London, where there was no need for a car and therefore nowhere to park. In the country there was no shortage of parking spaces but hardly any opportunity to use them, as everyone was at the wheel, slowing down to pass through yet another village, waiting at a junction for the chance to join an alarmingly busy road, or reversing virtuously up a single-track lane to the nearest passing place.

'Country roads, take me home,' Olivia started to sing in an ecstatic whisper, 'To the place I belong,/ Streets of London, Hampstead hills,/ Take me home, country roads.'

Last weekend, on her way to collect Lucy, Francis had called to say they were a bit low on olive oil, so she made a detour to a petrol station, with a shop attached, where she refuelled and picked up a bottle – wondering, as she always did, why olive oil was alone in having extra virginity.

On the drive home, she told Lucy that Francis would be making his 'famous' paella for them.

'Oh, great,' said Lucy. 'When I tear the head off the shrimp these days, I sometimes can't help wishing someone would tear my head off. Sorry, that was a bit dark.'

'It was pretty dark,' said Olivia, 'but you can be as dark as you like with me.'

'But I don't want to be dark,' said Lucy, 'especially with you. Or perhaps I do; perhaps I just don't want to have a reason to be dark – which is simply childish. Sorry. Sorry to keep saying sorry. Hunter is away on another trip. It's not that I think he's having an affair. It's more like my absence is his mistress. It's a holiday from my darkness that I can't join him on.'

Olivia didn't know what to say, while knowing that she didn't have to say anything. She also knew that it was Hunter, with his surcharge of executive energy, who was finding it hard to live with Lucy's diagnosis. He expected to fix problems, find loopholes, and buy solutions. He did not expect to absorb powerful destructive emotions, without action or judgement, without contagion or despair. He had taken to disappearing for a while, to acquire a company or crush an opponent, to crush, in effect, his own frustration.

Over the weekend, Lucy regained her poise, as she always did, but she was clearly in a more fragile state than usual. Although it had proved useful in the past, Olivia decided to keep away from discussing what she was working on. Forced to pay close attention to her own mortality, Lucy didn't always find it a relief to hear about the more inclusive ways that life on Earth might come to an end. She retreated instead into her role as godmother, helping Noah build his boat in the woods, admiring his dinosaur models, watching *Jurassic Park*, while her godson alternated between frenzied excitement at the next familiar disaster and moments of dread in which he had to plunge his head into Lucy's sweater to hide from the gruesome action. Francis and Olivia had been alarmed when Noah told them he had seen the film at a friend's house, but the big blonde school mother who presided over the viewing said that their qualms belonged 'in the Stone Age'. If the film did have any traumatic impact on Noah, it was passed on efficiently to his parents, who found themselves attacked several times a day from behind a sofa or a door by a tiptoeing Noah, with his arms held close to his chest, emitting weird noises, somewhere between a squeak and a roar, before he headbutted them and pretended to devour their arms and legs.

'What is it about dinosaurs?' Lucy asked, collapsing in an armchair after a tour of Noah's extensive collection. 'When we were young, boys might have a brontosaurus and a T-rex on the shelf and an incomplete set of cards from some cereal packets, but now . . .'

'I know; he has a hundred and twelve,' said Olivia.

'And he's so knowledgeable. He keeps saying things like "late Cretaceous carnivore".'

'I think it's the luxurious terror of knowing they're extinct,' said Olivia. 'Not just extinct, but part of an extinct mass extinction rather than the imminent variety that we're all obsessed with.'

'Well, some of us more than others,' said Lucy, smiling.

'Guilty as charged,' said Olivia. 'But I do think there is

something reassuring about dead civilisations and extinct kingdoms of life: Aztecs, dinosaurs, Ancient Egyptians. They're over and we get to curate their afterlives – in the case of dinosaurs, a paradise of plastic toys ruled over by four-year-old boys.'

'And palaeontologists,' said Lucy. 'Oh, and Steven Spielberg.'

'Yes! He's got dinosaurs *and* Egyptian tombs *and* cuddly aliens. I'm seeing a pattern: luxury terror.'

'Beats the real thing,' said Lucy, 'the unfinished extinctions . . .'

Olivia glanced up from her computer and saw that Sam was still busy. Although she had one more email to send, she would have postponed it if her new friend had been ready to go out. She didn't dwell on this faintly compromising eagerness but moved on rapidly to her final effort, thanking the doctor who had agreed to be interviewed about endocrine-disrupting chemicals. As Olivia wrote a sentence about the tug-of-war between infertility and overpopulation, wondering whether to use a more original phrase than tug-of-war, but leaving it in place, she felt a flush of shame at having imagined not being a mother. Sperm counts were plummeting around the world, at least in countries rich enough to afford the little curlicues of convenience provided by the endocrine disruptors, and there she had been, idly imagining a life without the child she was blessed with. If she had been at Willow Cottage, she would have been giving him something to eat, and then kneeling by the bath as he sat among the crackling bubbles, narrating the improbable circumstances that had led to a pterodactyl making a screeching attack on a diving submarine. She would have read him stories as he lay in his dinosaur pyjamas, in a heap of soft toys and blankets beneath the smiling faces of the solar system glued educationally to the ceiling above his bed. She would have been a little bored, but now she could afford to feel enormously moved, knowing that Francis would be taking care of the whole thing.

As she sent her best wishes and signed off the email, Olivia imagined a future in which humans had become the dinosaurs for a new dominant species – a superorganism of giant-brained cockroaches, for example, whose hard-shelled ancestors had survived one of the mass extinctions anticipated in her forthcoming programmes.

'Look, she's getting into her car to drive to the local supermarket!' a young Roach Sapiens might well be telling his mother sixty-six million years from now as he played with his keratin-based human dolls.

'Really, darling? What kind is she?'

'Late Anthropocene omnivore,' the erudite little monster would explain to his hard-working cockroach mother.

'Are you ready?'

Olivia looked up, shaken out of her daydream, and saw Sam standing at the edge of her desk.

'Yes, yes, I've just finished. Perfect timing.'

Sam smiled as if to warn her that perfect timing was something Olivia would have to get used to if they were going to hang out together.

5

When Sebastian said that he was serious about wanting to meet his Bio Mum, Dr Carr had given him the silent treatment. Silence was an uneven paving stone, deliberately put there to trip him up, to send him windmilling down the street, careening into a bobby on the beat, or tumbling into a passing pram occupied by a pair of tomato-faced little squallers. Silence made him fill in the gaps, the gaping wounds, see the invisible cities in the countryside. That's what it was all about, bringing out secret connections. It was the Ebola of conversation: blood, sweat and tears, together at last after decades of tragic separation. Talk made the world mean one thing, or two things, or several things, but silence could mean anything, anything at all. It could be leaden, or it could be golden, it could be helium, hydrogen or plutonium.

'Someone like Professor Brian Cox,' said Sebastian, gazing dreamily at the ceiling, 'would probably say that silence was ultimately forged in the deafening furnace of the stars.'

'I think you feel that your mother has been calling to you very loudly,' said Dr Carr, 'but that she's been silent for so long, she might as well be inhabiting another galaxy.'

'Oh, piss off,' said Sebastian. 'I was just being *The Sky at Night* or *Secrets of the Universe*, or whatever.'

The silence was definitely plutonium after that. Nausea. Shortness of breath. Pulling out tufts of hair. Fatigue sliding down the walls. Fear of radiation sickness was trending strongly these days. You couldn't get hold of iodine for love or money because all the survivalists, who kept hidden pouches of activated charcoal in their flak jackets and had special sleeping bags with kitchen stoves and recycling centres built into them, were stockpiling iodide tablets to help cope with the nuclear fallout. Iodine was made from kelp, so once he was out of the hospital, he was going to go to Scotland to swim with the seals among the swaying branches of giant brown bubble wrap. Munch his way through a couple of tons of the good stuff. That should do the trick. If he saw a mushroom cloud in the distance, he could set off to help those less fortunate than himself who hadn't had their daily quota. He'd be like a Bio Mum to them, bulging with natural energy from all the iodine in the kelp. He'd be their hero. 'Let me help you with that, madam . . . I wouldn't eat those if I were you, sir, my Geiger-counter is crackling like a fresh bowl of Coco Pops . . . What a lovely baby! I happen to have some hand-dived Scottish kelp in the back of my van if you'd care for a few strands.' That sort of thing. Mr Morris would be proud of him, catering to the needs of the community. He might run into Gabriella with her own tray of kelp canapés, or iodine truffles.

That's what he was going back to: care in the community. It was a step forward and a step backwards. Same difference. Back to the old halfway house where he felt halfway at home. Maybe they could help him track down his Bio Mum. He'd be able to see Dr Carr in his natural habitat, instead of behind bars in the hospital zoo. He'd be an ambulatory schizophrenic, whistling *Carmen*, as he ambulated down the boulevards, a cane in one hand and a tuft of hair in the other. *Torre adore/ la di-da di-da.*

Helio had said that he would come to see him in the halfway house. He also said that Seb should come and visit the studio he shared with his girlfriend, who was another Brazilian artist. When Seb asked him what he painted, Helio had said, 'I work with light.' Seb imagined that he wrote catchy things in neon. During one of his episodes he had been walking down a street full of galleries near Piccadilly and he had seen the word VACANCY – like a hotel sign, hanging in one of the windows – and it had sent him into a spin, and he didn't dare read any of the other messages, because they obviously belonged in the thought-provoking category, which he regarded as the prison he wanted to break out of and not an artistic space he wanted to be ushered into. He had really hated them for doing that: piling on the pressure when he could barely cope, and so, to be positive, he hadn't said anything to Helio, who was a sort of friend. He didn't want to hurt Helio's feelings by saying how terrified he was about going to see his work, although he was already frantically trying to make sure that he wasn't asked to admire what would probably be lots of bad words humming and hissing in coloured neon against a white wall, burning into his brain like a cattle brand.

Helio was an artist, so he could do art therapy – as long as they didn't go to his studio. If he had been an actor, he could have done drama therapy. Or a gardener could do gardening therapy, or a cook could do cooking therapy. There was hardly anything left that wasn't therapy. Even war must be a relief for some people. Imagine if you had been amassing an army on another country's border for months and months, or you'd been working on a special rocket design, you'd be gagging to invade, or to show off your big new rocket. There would be loads of catharsis and getting in touch with your angry side, all very therapeutic, but to the nice old granny who was walking away from the house where she'd lived for fifty years with the man whose corpse was now buried under the rubble, along with their dog and her favourite teacups, it might not feel like therapy at all.

'One man's therapy is another man's trauma,' said Sebastian.

'Perhaps a part of you,' said Dr Carr, 'thinks it would be therapeutic and another part of you thinks that it would be traumatic to reconnect . . .'

'What?' said Sebastian, who had been imagining Kim Jong Un hopping up and down and clapping his hands with delight as his latest missile pierced the white skies above the Korean Peninsula.

'Your Bio Mum.'

'Oh, yeah,' said Sebastian. 'No. Who cares? She must be a horrible person; abandoning her own flesh and blood.'

The silent treatment.

'Or maybe she had a good reason,' said Sebastian. 'Maybe I'm the good reason. She might be lovely. She probably is lovely – or was. Maybe she's dead. Now you're making me anxious. Why did you have to bring her up? I was thinking about missiles. I was perfectly happy thinking about missiles, and you had to bring her up. She didn't bring me up, but you had to bring her up. Typical.'

'What strikes me, Sebastian, over the years we've been working together,' said Dr Carr, 'is how much better you've become, despite some difficult times, at bringing yourself up. As you know, the hospital committee has decided that so long as you stay on your current dose of medication and continue to see me three times a week, you're now ready to return to Heron House.'

'And fly away,' said Sebastian.

'Ah, yes, James's Japanese print,' said Dr Carr, who had been told all about the portal and the oyster knife.

Sebastian was relieved that he wasn't seen as an escape risk, but he was also a little alarmed at being so well understood. Perhaps he *should* escape to a windswept island, somewhere like Heligoland, where he could get away from being interpreted by Dr Carr, or Copenhagen, or Stockholm syndrome, or Mystic Meg. Then he realised he'd lived alone on a windswept island almost all his life and that he'd had enough.

'Spot on, Dr C,' he said. 'You're on fire today!'

'We'll have to pause now,' said Dr Carr, with a friendly smile. 'Our next two sessions will be by telephone, but after that I'm pleased to say that I'll be able to welcome you back to the consulting rooms in Belsize Park.'

'Excellent,' said Sebastian, 'the good old consulting rooms.'

Dr Carr got up to leave Sebastian's new, unlocked room: his halfway house to the halfway house: his quarter-way house.

'I won't throw your books on the floor like I used to – promise,' said Sebastian.

'Thank you, Sebastian,' said Dr Carr, with a warm laugh. 'We'll have to see what happens, but I'm pleased that you've set an intention to leave them on the shelves!'

And then he was gone.

6

'But isn't everything political under the surface?' said Lizzie, who was looking perplexed by the familiarity of the menu, as if fighting against what she always ended up choosing. 'Cutting down a tree; singing the national anthem; putting up a statue or, more likely these days, pulling one down?'

'Everything is also bloody under the surface,' Olivia replied to her mother, 'but that doesn't mean we want to have blood pouring out of our eyes and ears.'

'Thanks for the vivid imagery,' said Lizzie. 'I feel myself leaning towards the minestrone.'

'We've lost the luxury of being bored by democratic politics,' said Olivia. 'We expect North Korea and Russia to punish their citizens for having the wrong thoughts and using the wrong words; it's just perplexing when Harvard and Oxford feel they have to join in.'

'Well, at least they're not trying to control the same thoughts and words,' said Francis. 'We need as much diversity in our dictatorships as possible.'

'To diversity in dictatorship,' said Olivia, raising her glass.

'It would be bad luck,' said Lizzie, pointing to her glass of water.

'If ever a toast needed bad luck . . .'

'Maybe I should order a glass of wine,' said Lizzie, wondering why she was so indecisive this evening.

'Go for it, Mum,' said Olivia, 'you only come here two or three times a week.'

'Luigi's is the still point of a turning world,' said Martin piously. 'It hasn't changed its menu since 1984.'

'The year we were all famously luxuriating in our indifference to politics,' said Lizzie.

'Orwell may have got the date wrong,' said Olivia, 'but the Ministry of Truth is now tightening its grip by the hour.'

'It's very Ministry of Truth for the Tories to call themselves the Conservative and Unionist Party when they behave as if they were running the Cultural Revolution,' said Francis. 'There's nothing they don't want to destroy, no union, international or internal, that they don't want to smash, or put at high risk of breaking apart.'

'So, what is it you want to toast?' said Lizzie, who had poured some of Martin's wine into her spare glass.

'How about something helpful?' said Francis, raising his glass with gallant optimism. 'Rewilding the world and uncovering our true nature?'

'Gosh,' said Martin, '*vaste programme*, as de Gaulle said to the heckler who shouted, "Death to all idiots!"'

They clinked their glasses, despite the extravagance of the toast.

'And to democratic politics becoming boring again,' Olivia added.

'They weren't boring in the 1930s,' said Martin.

'Only because we had an epidemic of dictatorships on our doorstep,' said Olivia.

'I wonder how boring it was for Emily Davison to throw herself under George V's horse at the 1913 Derby,' said Lizzie.

'It must have been terrifying,' said Olivia, 'but we weren't a democracy yet because women didn't have the vote.'

'It is true,' said Francis, 'that most developed nations only have a choice between what Gore Vidal called "two branches of the Property Party . . ."'

'I'm rather fond of my property,' said Martin.

'I'm sure I would be also – if I had any,' said Francis. 'And the vote just slides from one branch to another without anything much changing, except who occupies the White House.'

'Assuming the previous occupant agrees to leave,' said Olivia. 'Assuming the Ministry of Truth agrees that the voting machines weren't rigged . . .'

'All of that may have made democratic politics less "boring",' said Lizzie, 'only—'

'I apologise for interrupting,' said the waiter, 'but have we made any decisions?'

'I must have done in my time,' said Lizzie, 'I just can't remember how. You lot go ahead.'

The others ordered while Lizzie frowned with concentration.

'The way this government is headed,' said Martin, buying his wife some time, 'twenty-four-hour nursing will be redefined as a nurse turning up twenty-four hours before you die from not having had an essential operation.'

'I'll have the minestrone and then the burrata,' said Lizzie, handing back the menu with the relief of someone who has stopped holding everyone up.

'Great,' said the waiter. 'Can I just ask if anyone has any allergies?'

'Boris Johnson and his predecessor,' said Olivia.

'I'll try to make sure the chef doesn't put either of them in the pesto sauce,' said the waiter with a laugh.

'Another part of me wishes he would put both of them in,' said Olivia, as the waiter walked away, 'finely chopped.'

'It's the gourmet in you,' said Francis.

'Interesting that he chose pesto, given that it was Francis who ordered it . . .' said Martin.

'Oh, for God's sake, darling,' said Lizzie, 'he's not one of your patients. It wasn't a hidden allusion to the need for political pest control, or to Camus's masterpiece . . .'

'What?' said Olivia. '*La Peste*, I think that's really far-fetched . . .'

'Or,' said Lizzie, finishing her point calmly, 'whatever free association was going through *your* mind.'

'How can you be so sure?' said Martin.

'Isn't the question how the two of you can be so sure,' said Olivia, 'since your job consists of making wild guesses about what's going through other people's minds?'

Francis took a gulp of red wine, having witnessed quite a lot of Olivia's in-house mockery over the years.

'They're not guesses,' said Martin, 'we're just pointing out what we've already been told. It's a form of literary criticism in which the text is the unconscious.'

Francis had so many things to say about this last statement that he didn't know where to begin.

'You have to stop interpreting at some point,' said Lizzie.

'And do what?' said Martin.

'Have fun, make a joke, relax . . .'

'How would I make a joke without interpreting the absurdity or the incongruity of something? And aren't you trying to make sense of feeling so indecisive this evening?'

'It's because I keep thinking of one of my patients,' said Lizzie. 'I'm the one who can't stop.'

'There you are,' said Martin, 'neither of us can stop; none of us can stop. It's just a question of whether we are seduced into judgement: the interpretation that tries to bring interpretation to an end, to close the matter, to imprison the culprit – but there's always another case, another news item, another stranger on the bus, another feeling we would rather not be having. We might as well stay open-minded and surrender to the endlessness of it. What could be more relaxing than interpreting one's dreams while still having them?'

'Dreamless sleep,' said Francis. 'Real unconsciousness beyond the reach of interpretation, not "The Unconscious" of your business model, which in fact depends on constantly breaking into consciousness to have any meaning at all, not to mention stopping people from asking for their money back. How many copies do you think you'd sell of *The Interpretation of Dreamless Sleep*?'

'Tens of millions,' said Martin. 'It's the final frontier.'

Despite Francis's smile, Olivia felt she should draw the subject away from her parents' profession and back to her own current obsession.

'So, anyway, we're agreed that a society is malfunctioning when politics invades every aspect of life.'

'You're not entirely blameless,' said Lizzie, 'wanting finely chopped prime ministers in your spaghetti sauce.'

'When I was doing my training,' said Martin, 'the attitude was very much "as to changing the world, let our patients do it for us". We were discouraged from expressing strong political views. The ethos was that psychoanalysis or psychiatry stayed in the room or the ward where they took place. Recently, under the pressure of what Olivia is talking about, Dr Bandy Lee felt that the case of Donald Trump was so extreme that she had to draw attention to the danger he presented despite a warning from the head of the medical faculty at Yale that she was breaking the American Psychiatric Association's Goldwater Rule that no professional can comment on the mental health of a public figure without having examined them and getting authorisation for the statement.'

'As in Barry Goldwater?' said Olivia.

'Yes,' said Martin.

'Was he the model for a deluge of commentary on the mental health of a public figure?'

'Well, he successfully sued *Fact Magazine* for publishing an article called "The Unconscious of a Conservative. A Special issue on the mind of Barry Goldwater",' said Martin. 'It claimed that well over a thousand psychiatrists thought he was unfit to be president. The point is that the rule is under pressure in this increasingly politicised atmosphere. Nevertheless, the APA has strengthened its position on the issue and strangely enough received an increase in federal funding soon after.'

'Hunter has a signed photograph of Barry Goldwater,' said Olivia. 'His father, who was an oil man, used to back all the presidential candidates from both sides of the race. Hunter says it was his first lesson in hedging.'

'It seems so quaint,' said Francis, 'that a British MP, if he owns one share of BP stock, must "declare an interest" before taking part in a debate about the fossil fuel industry, whereas an American politician is considered a complete failure if he hasn't received tens of millions of dollars in bribes from all the fossil fuel companies, as well as their opponents.'

'Since everyone else has been analysing Trump relentlessly,' said Olivia, 'wouldn't it be better if the words "narcissist" and "sociopath" entered the general vocabulary with real explanatory power rather than just being grandiose alternatives to "wanker" or "jerk"?'

'Dr Lee's defence was that she had not said that Donald Trump was a paranoid schizophrenic, for instance; she had simply said that he was dangerous, which is not a diagnosis. She also said that as a psychiatrist she had been trained to cure the patient, but in such dangerous times she felt that psychiatrists also had a duty to protect society.'

'Perhaps there should be another sort of Goldwater Rule,' said Lizzie, 'a Goldwater Variation, making it an obligation for aspirant world leaders to have a minimum amount of analysis before they hold high office.'

'Hang on,' said Olivia, 'you want politicians to get a certificate from a priesthood of psychotherapists before they can get a job?'

'Well, we can only dream,' said Lizzie, 'but I think it would be sensible for someone to have a hundred sessions before they're allowed to change the tax code and five hundred before they're given control of nuclear weapons.'

'It may not be enough,' said Martin. 'If we go on with our strange cult of resentment. The politician who knows how to stir it up will always win – making people proud of what they used to be ashamed of is such an intoxicating alchemy. Someone who could bring that off would need more than five hundred sessions if only because manipulators always waste so much time trying to manipulate their therapist.'

'It is hard,' said Olivia, 'to see how someone would be set free by the truth if they don't want to be set free and aren't interested in the truth.'

'Especially when an unexamined life always commands the highest price for an autobiography,' said Francis. 'Lying about lying by a former world leader: nothing is more certain to start a bidding war.'

'Still,' said Lizzie resolutely, 'if George W. Bush had been given his five hundred sessions, perhaps we wouldn't have had the Second Gulf War. Since the pretexts for the war were knowingly fabricated, he might have worked out that his burning desire to invade Iraq was driven by other motives. If he had glanced in the direction of competition with his overshadowing father so many lives and limbs might have been saved.'

'How come?' said Francis.

'Well, his father flew dozens of missions in the Pacific during the Second World War,' said Lizzie. 'He was shot down four times and rescued four times. On the last occasion, he was the sole survivor. Most of his crew were captured, tortured and executed by the Japanese. Of the other two men in his own plane, one was burnt alive and the other wore a parachute that never opened. Bush swam through the water, bleeding from his forehead and being stung by so many jellyfish that he was vomiting uncontrollably by the time he climbed into a lifeboat and was picked up by an American submarine. After that he was demobilised, covered in medals. George W., by contrast, avoided the Vietnam War by joining the Texas Air National Guard.'

'Buzzing around Texan air space,' said Francis, 'must have drastically reduced his chances of being shot down by anti-aircraft fire and bailing out over shark-infested waters. Mind you, with the gun laws in Texas, you never know. You can probably pick up an air defence system at Walmart in El Paso.'

'I wouldn't be surprised,' said Lizzie. 'But my point is that Bush bought his exemption from Vietnam at the price of feeling less potent than his father. When he was magically transformed from draft dodger into Commander-in-Chief he was strongly motivated to show that he was a greater warrior than his father by going "all the way" to Baghdad – to bag dad. His father had stopped short of conquering Baghdad because he was not a fantasy warrior and knew the real cost of war. He also stopped short of Baghdad because the mission of the First Gulf War – getting Iraq out of Kuwait – had been accomplished. When George W. dressed up as an airman, just like his pa, onboard an aircraft carrier – the same type of vessel from which his father had flown into combat – and stood under the orgasmic banner "Mission Accomplished", the mission in question was taking place in his unconscious mind: he had proved that even if he couldn't be a hero in the Second World War, or in the Vietnam War, he could be *the* hero of the Second Gulf War; he could invent the entire thing! Back in the real world, nothing at all had been accomplished for the American people, or in terms of making the world a safer place. On the contrary, a long, illegal, unnecessary, destabilising and unsuccessful war had just been launched.'

'Coo-wee,' said Olivia, 'Freud didn't live in vain.'

'The culmination of the Great Unconscious War,' said Lizzie, 'was that George W. had two terms as president, making him twice as big a man as his relatively brave, well-informed and sober father. My case rests. Ah, and my minestrone has arrived. Thank you.'

'And here's your PM-free spaghetti,' said the waiter, putting the dish down in front of Olivia with mock solemnity.

She shot him a smile.

'I like the Goldwater Variation,' said Martin.

'Surprise, surprise,' said Olivia.

'If a depressed patient came to me,' said Martin, 'and said that she was going to restore her enthusiasm for life by biting on a cyanide capsule, I would ask her to pause and look at her plan more carefully. If only we had been able to talk to the patient who said he was going to restore sovereignty to Parliament by destroying the sovereignty of Parliament and governing by plebiscite.'

'Do you think that patient was depressed as well?' said Francis.

'I'm not sure,' said Martin, 'but he would certainly have schizoid leanings . . .'

'There are a lot of them about,' said Olivia.

'Indeed,' said Martin. 'Yes,' he seemed adrift for a moment, '. . . to accommodate such a root confusion. I think it's significant that both the referendums were about dissolving a union. To someone who is themselves disunited, leaving the European Union and threatening to disintegrate the United Kingdom might feel like the most authentic choices. Johnson is treated as cynical and opportunistic for writing two editorials overnight, one in favour of Brexit and one against it, and only deciding which one to publish at the last minute, but I think there's a genuine split consciousness under all that egotism and cunning and cleverness. There are parts of his mind that are only tenuously acquainted with other parts, and that's why his gift for taking up contradictory positions – let's have a party to celebrate social distancing; let's restore sovereignty to Parliament by dealing it a death blow, etc. – is so disturbing. If only it were mere hypocrisy.'

'Apart from all that,' said Francis, 'isn't this sort of national decline just what happens when we have Etonian prime ministers? Eden and Macmillan gave us the Suez Crisis and the Profumo Affair; Cameron and Johnson have given us Brexit and Partygate. The public demanded a long pause before entrusting the country to Etonians again, but when they did, it turned out that nothing much had changed. The international fuck-ups were based on the same arrogance and exaggeration of Britain's autonomy and the scandals on the same combination of self-indulgence and mendacity.'

'It's not a school that teaches its students to run the world,' said Lizzie, 'it teaches them to feel entitled to run the world. The competence is expected to come from the funny little people who didn't go to the Hogwarts School of Anarchy and Arrogance but were swots in some lesser institution.'

'What I like most is that it's a registered charity,' said Olivia. 'It's the rest of the country that should be registered as a charity for helping people recover from the impact of letting Etonians into Downing Street.'

'I disagree with all of you,' said Martin. 'I think it's the only perfect school in the world. It makes an entirely reliable promise: those who go to Eton will become Etonians; those who leave Eton will become Old Etonians. The mission is the brand. It has a hundred per cent success rate, which schools claiming to want their students to reach their full potential, or be the best possible versions of themselves, or make a positive contribution to society, can't possibly hope to achieve.'

'It sounds very confidence-building and integrative,' said Olivia, 'not at all conducive to schizoid tendencies.'

'Except that in a democracy you have to pretend to believe in something other than yourself,' said Francis, 'and your secondary school.'

'Oh, yeah, I'd forgotten about that,' said Olivia.

'It seems to me,' said Francis, 'that this Goldwater Rule has got things the wrong way round. Isn't it when you *have* examined a patient that you are bound by confidentiality not to make any public statement about their mental health? If you are simply interpreting information that's on the public record, then I don't see why it isn't just part of an open discussion.'

'It's a question of lending professional authority to the discussion,' said Lizzie.

'What's wrong with that?' said Olivia. 'I don't want to listen to a commentary on the World Cup Final from four people who have never seen a game of football before and don't know that the object of the game is to put the ball into the back of the other team's net.'

'I'll give you a concrete example,' said Francis. 'During the Brexit campaign there was an influential cartoon based on the fantasy that Turkey would make a successful application to join the EU. It depicted a turbaned Turk on a magic carpet, flying in to take advantage of our foolishly generous welfare system . . .'

'And our marvellous education system,' said Olivia.

'It wasn't clear that he was heading for Windsor,' said Francis, 'but my point is that Boris Johnson's grandfather, Osman Wilfred Kemal, changed his name during the First World War, when Britain was fighting against Turkey (his motherland against his fatherland), to Wilfred Johnson, adopting his maternal grandmother's name. He was a Turk who had already arrived in Britain, probably by boat rather than magic carpet, but whose grandson went on to lead a campaign that benefited from treating the arrival of Turks in Britain as a menace. Is there some schizoid potential there?'

'Absolutely,' said Martin. 'And Johnson's great-grandfather, Ali Kemal, was a very distinguished politician and journalist who was horribly assassinated during the 1920s, which must also have produced a strong sense of conflict between feeling that high office was both a very natural and a very dangerous thing to aspire to.'

'So,' said Francis, 'we have historical facts on the public record that are suggestive. They involve no indiscretion, no special knowledge of private matters, no examination. They can be treated with sympathy and understanding, but why should you and Lizzie, who are especially well placed to understand the impact of those sorts of intergenerational forces on people's minds, be banned from commenting?'

'I agree,' said Olivia. 'Down with the Goldwater Rule!'

'Well, I won't entirely accept that as a toast,' said Martin, 'but I will drink some wine with you.'

'Hedging your bets, just like Hunter's dad,' said Olivia.

'I'll join Martin in not coming to a final judgement,' said Lizzie, 'but I will drink to the Goldwater Variation and demanding more sanity in public life.'

7

Since Hunter had stretched out on the narrow pallet bed in his whitewashed cell, pressing his arms rigidly to his side so as not to fall off, a slanted rectangle of sunlight had moved across the worn terracotta tiles, past a rustic wicker chair with a frayed white towel folded over its back, until it narrowed into a bright blade underlining the crucifix on the wall. The window was too high to tempt him with the charms of the Perugian landscape but provided enough light for him to take in the crushing simplicity of his surroundings. Did a crucifix count as furniture or interior decoration? Was it an instrument of torture or an instrument for ending torture? Both-And, Hunter, Both-And. That was the paradox he bounced off if he ever tried to penetrate it. At least there wasn't anyone hanging from this one, just the bare geometry of salvation through torture.

He couldn't help thinking that he might have stayed at home, floating in the hammock at *Plein Soleil,* watching the slim metal branches and the red, white and black leaves of the Calder mobile reconfiguring themselves in the breeze; speed boats unzipping the silky waters of the bay; Lucy, her hair wet from swimming, leaning over to kiss him and tell him that lunch was ready; or walking around the network of trails looping through the garden Francis had rewilded for him; now a refuge for frogs, un-silencing the spring, and floppy-winged butterflies dipping and rising among the tall grasses, and lizards darting among the drystone walls.

'Might have stayed': the emptiest tense of all, not just past but conditional, the breeding ground of yearning and regret and counter-factual speculation. Summer was over, and Lucy's wet hair had remained short since he had shaved it all off four years ago. After a few months of radiotherapy and chemotherapy, she had complained that she was starting to look like Benjamin Franklin. The long, unpredictable wisps dangling from the base of her skull, like tantalising footnotes to a lost manuscript, made the comparison to the Founding Father's hairstyle painfully apt and one evening Hunter had simply offered to shave her head. He did it with the tenderness of a mother who has promised not to let any shampoo sting her child's scrunched-up eyes and has a flannel ready and a shower running at the right temperature to prevent any rogue suds from reaching the tear ducts.

Lucy's head stooped over the basin, lightly supported by one hand, as he ran the razor gently through the foam, making the baldness deliberate.

At least he had a bottle of Unico in his bag, knowing that the little abbot had a nostalgia for that rich Spanish wine. He and Lucy had grown fond of Father Guido over the years. At first, they had used the AGM as an excuse to invite him to *Soleil*, but they had gone on inviting him even after selling *Digitas* and its Happy Helmets, of which *Capo Santo*, partially owned by the Vatican, was a subsidiary. The trans-cranial stimulation game had proven less straightforward than he and Saul had imagined back in the days when they were still talking to each other. Although he had sacked Saul years ago, one of the attractions of parting with Happy Helmets was that it felt like sacking him again. He also didn't mind distancing himself from the facile equation between technological convenience and happiness, not to mention the physicalist assumption that lay behind the Happy Helmets, that the brain and the mind were identical. His one regret was that the sale had lost Olivia her job. *Digitas* was now owed by *Cogito,* a Silicon Valley amortality company, which exploited the fear of death by offering to download its customers' consciousness onto a 'non-biological substrate'. Its name was supposed to imply that if a person's *cogito* could be downloaded their *sum* would come along for the ride. Hunter thought that the famous Cartesian motto was the wrong way round: that the *sum* obviously came before the *cogito*, that being must precede thinking. The *ergo* in the middle was the culprit responsible for inverting the natural order, making it look as if the challenge of being was to prove its incontestable existence, whereas the challenge was to find some way of putting up with it. If we weren't being we certainly wouldn't be thinking, let alone thinking how to prove we were being. Anaesthetists would have a lot more lawsuits on their hands if every time we stopped thinking we stopped being. And so on and so forth. Then Hunter imagined arguing the other way around. The problem was the narrowness of *cogito*. Thinking was just a subset of consciousness, and all knowledge was an appearance in consciousness. We only know the world by inference from the one thing we know directly. Being was inherent to consciousness – we couldn't have consciousness except by being conscious. And so on and so forth. Anyway, he had been delighted to sell *Cogito* the expertise accumulated by *Digitas* over the years. Attempting to translate brain scans of people in allegedly desirable states of mind into trans-cranial stimulations that would generate similar states of mind in other people came with the disclaimer that one person's equanimity was another person's seizure.

Oh, God, he wanted some Unico, not more *cogito*. He could feel his blood sugar plummeting. He could argue anything and its opposite because he was so hungry. If he had eaten something, he probably would have settled for the absurdity of proving Being through one of its derivatives, like thinking, or for that matter belching or screaming.

In any case, even without the *Capo* pretext, it turned out that he and Lucy liked having the sweet and cheerful Guido to stay once a year. What were the odds of two agnostics making friends with an abbot? What were the odds, if it came to that, of Hunter Sterling ending up in a fucking monastery? And where was the sweet and cheerful Guido? Was this some sort of spiritual trial? What had he signed up for? He was supposed to be here for three days. Perhaps there was a great hotel near by he could move into and just pop over to see Guido for a couple of visits. In fact, maybe he should cut loose and go back to *Soleil,* but then he'd be with Lucy again.

'Get me out of here!' said Hunter, lifting himself off the bed.

It turned out that his cry of protest had been drowning a timid knocking on the heavy wooden door. He lunged over and opened it.

'Guido! What a surprise!'

'But I live here,' said Father Guido, blinking behind the slightly thicker lenses of his new prescription.

'No kidding,' said Hunter.

'And you just happened to be passing by . . .' said Father Guido, getting into his stride.

'A poor and weary traveller,' said Hunter, 'looking for shelter from the storm.'

'Yes, please, *caro* Hunter, you are so welcome. Come, we will go to my rooms and have something to eat. You must be hungry after your journey. It is such a pleasure, such a pleasure to see you and to have you here as a guest of the monastery.'

The piercing sincerity of Guido's welcome cut through the high-handed irritation that had been building up in Hunter. He saw that his banter had in fact been a confession: he really was looking for shelter from the storm and he wasn't going to find it by retreating to the life he needed shelter from. Perhaps it was his turn to experience gratitude, an emotion he was in the habit of eliciting or extorting from other people. Gratitude felt like a threat, like the passive form of the generosity he was usually in charge of; and yet, as he followed Guido silently through the cloister, with his head bowed and his vision a little blurred, he realised how much he longed to have something to be grateful for, something bigger than his big personality and his legendary willpower and his huge income; or perhaps 'bigger' was precisely the wrong word, or at least from the wrong category of words, because what he needed was a rest from measuring and comparing, winning and losing; from beating the market, beating cancer, beating the system, or beating himself up for not beating them.

Guido continued to say nothing as they moved into a smaller cloister. The wisteria branches twisting around the columns of the arches would have been almost indistinguishable from the natural imagery that crowded much of the stonework, the sculpted branches and trees and grapes and flowers, if not for the colourful death of the yellow, brown and russet leaves that still clung to them. The chorus of Dylan's famous song had worked its way into Hunter's mind: *Come in, she said, I'll give ya shelter from the storm*. The words seemed to go around and around in a cloister of their own. Although the health app on his phone would have recorded very few steps, this walk seemed to be going on for ever. He patted his pockets and realised that he had forgotten his phone on the rough grey blanket of his bed. His cell was in his cell, where arguably it belonged, and if he didn't go back to retrieve it and sat through a standard-length dinner, he would be separated from it for the longest time in years. His sense of alarm was muffled by the pensive cloister. Was it Guido's small steps that were taking so long? Was it the silence between them that made the sound of each step more emphatic? Or was it the feeling that instead of ordering for everyone, as he so often did, he was now the prisoner of an altogether different hospitality?

The light was fading by the time Guido turned the heavy iron ring and opened the arched door to his private quarters.

'Come in,' said Guido, 'take shelter from the storm – that's what you say, yes?'

'That's the one,' said Hunter.

He took a handkerchief from his breast pocket and hastily wiped both his eyes. He knew that Guido had seen the gesture and that it didn't surprise or perturb him. Perhaps this happened to everyone. *Aperitivo lacrimoso*, thought Hunter, trying to keep his distance. His distance from what? Guido had invited him because he already knew that Hunter was burnt out. And why struggle to keep his distance? On the inexplicably drawn-out trek from his cell to these rooms, the ideas of defeat and victory seemed to have become less distinct, as they might for a soldier who suddenly longs to surrender rather than die, who has changed his mind about securing a posthumous medal by trying to take the machine-gun post single-handedly and simply wants to live a little longer. If he didn't admit that he needed refuge, he wouldn't get the refuge he needed. He had to come out with his hands raised, even if one of them was still carrying a bottle of wine.

The vaulted ceiling and the faded fresco of a haloed friar surrounded by songbirds and other enchanted creatures, with a walled city and its monastery in the valley far behind him, was just what Hunter would have expected, but nothing had prepared him for the turmoil that followed his request for a corkscrew.

'We will find one, do not worry, *caro* Hunter,' said Guido, standing perplexed by an open drawer. '*Manfredi, dov' è il cavatappi?* Do not worry, Hunter, Manfredi will find it. It is a mystery – not a great mystery, *certo*, but a little one – because we always keep it in the same drawer. It is always here but it is not here!'

'If it looks like a mystery and sounds like a mystery . . .' said Hunter.

'It is a duck!' said Guido. 'Yes, you told me this English expression, I remember. Excuse me, I haven't drunk wine for many months, and now you bring me this beautiful bottle . . .'

'Don't worry,' said Hunter, 'I'm relaxed about it. I can always pull the cork out with my teeth.'

'No, please, I don't think this is a good idea,' said Guido. 'Manfredi will find something. And Giuseppe, who works in the garden, has a penknife he has shown me many times which has a corkscrew, so finally we have a solution . . .'

Manfredi soon brought in a corkscrew and then some rabbit stew, a bowl of wild rice, some cheeses, and an orange polenta cake. Although he only drank one glass of the wine, Guido seemed a little flushed and light-headed and refused the offer of more. Hunter, by contrast, who had rapidly finished the rest of the bottle, grew uneasy at the thought that there might be nothing more to drink. He felt less vulnerable than he had on arrival and was enjoying his reprieve. Still, after devouring most of his own present, he also felt inhibited about demanding more alcohol. Instead, he rested his hand possessively on the stem of his empty glass and turned it slowly on the tablecloth.

'I have some local wine,' said Guido, answering Hunter's prayers. 'Very simple, nothing like this magnificent wine, but perhaps with your cheese you would like another glass.'

'Simple is great,' said Hunter decisively.

The second bottle undermined the calming effects of the first and soon Hunter found himself even more defenceless than he had felt before starting dinner.

'Nowhere to run and nowhere to hide,' he said, with a sudden melancholy.

'This is the place you have run to,' said Guido, 'and where you are hiding, so perhaps it is not necessary to run from it and hide from it. Eventually we must rest.'

'I'll need lessons,' said Hunter.

'So do I,' said Guido.

'You mean you get compassion burnout as well?'

'Maybe what gets burnt out is not compassion,' said Guido. 'It is the parts of us that have not understood compassion completely. It is our personalities, our nerves, our bodies, our vanity. Compassion is just love in the face of suffering and love does not run out with use – it grows stronger.'

'I'll take your word for it,' said Hunter.

'Believe me, I am taking other people's word for it also,' said Guido.

'My problem, Guido, is a lot uglier than that. The compassion doesn't just run out: it turns into resentment and sometimes into hatred, as well as speculation about the life I might have had rather than the one I do.'

'"Might have" does not exist,' said Guido.

'Exactly!' said Hunter. 'I was thinking the very same thing earlier this evening, but for a non-existent dimension it sure in hell generates a lot of negative emotion.'

'I think this is the wrong way round; it is the negative emotion that creates this dimension: when I am unhappy, I imagine things might have been different. When I am happy, I have another fantasy: that things might continue to be the same . . .'

'You guys are the experts on generating extra dimensions out of negative emotion!' said Hunter. 'You've made heaven and hell out of the fear of death.'

'If this is true,' said Guido, leaning forward and putting a hand on Hunter's arm, 'then perhaps paradise is just the absence of hatred and fear – we don't have to wait; in fact, we cannot afford to wait. This story of heaven and hell is really a continuation of what is happening before we die: it is where we are left whether we continue to know it or not.'

'Are you sure that's not heretical?'

'I am sure that it is!' said Guido. 'But also, it is not: it is just logical. Whoever makes the judgement, it is made when we die. This is our chance. If we are going to find out about love, this is our chance.'

'That's what I'm afraid of: I am wasting my chance by feeling anger and resentment.'

'But a feeling is just a feeling,' said Guido. 'It is like the shadow of a cloud; we don't have to pay so much attention to it.'

'So, what's the cloud in this little allegory of yours?'

'I don't know!' said Guido. 'I am not a poet! Maybe it is the principle of love, a little more substantial than the shadow – the shadow cannot bring rain, for example.'

'If it's not the feeling and not the principle, what's the real thing?'

'It is the light,' said Guido, 'not just the things we see, but the thing that makes it possible to see.'

'That reminds me I should call Jade about an installation,' said Hunter. 'Sorry, what you said made me think of Turrell. But the love you're talking about is too big for me. I just get the cloud and its shadow.'

'This is true for almost everyone, I think,' said Guido. 'Most of the time I am also lost, although I have many more things to help me remember than most people. I try to remember, but there are many, many distractions. This distresses me so much that I am going to go on a retreat to the hermitage where the Blessed Fra Domenico used to live.'

'Ah, the model for the *Capo Santo*.'

'Yes, I think he was someone who understood that when you get to the source, compassion does not burn out – it . . . it burns; it just burns – with no "out".'

'Pity he took a vow of silence,' said Hunter, 'he could have told us how that works.'

'Show not tell was his philosophy, I think,' said Guido. 'The rest of us have day and night, cloud, no cloud, *chiaroscuro*, but if our minds were like the sun, there would be no "out", only – I have not the words.' Guido expanded his arms and rounded his eyes and puffed out his cheeks. 'Always the beginning, again and again.'

Hunter had a fleeting sense of that explosive radiance, of that enduring energy, of that self-renewing love, and then he thought that he was just tripping out on a metaphor, and that the sun would run out of fuel one day and have its own burnout, and that in his current state of exhaustion if he were asked to do a kindness for someone he would just – in fact he *was* just, no conditional needed, pouring himself another drink.

'I'm a poor student,' he said.

'No, no,' said Guido. 'You are tired because you have been looking after Lucy and worrying too much.'

Hunter stared blearily at the solar radiance of the halo in the fading fresco, smiling faintly at Guido's generous but misguided interpretation. He wanted to get away, not from someone who was dying, that would be asking too much; but from someone who was so preoccupied with dying. Lucy had responded well to all her therapies. She was not in pain or impaired. Her prognosis was uncertain, she might easily live for many years, and even had a chance of living for decades, but she was enchanted by a perfectly understandable terror of her diagnosis and felt obliged to allude to it directly or indirectly half a dozen times a day. He sometimes imagined that he would one day be lying on his deathbed still listening to her talk about her white cell count while he slipped away and was finally allowed to release his grip on her fearful hand. He wondered whether they would ever be able to drop into the life they were having or, if he stayed with her, he would have to remain in a jet stream of anxiety as she hurtled towards her fascinating plot in the common cemetery.

'The old hermitage . . .' said Hunter, wanting to change the subject. He was thinking about what he had come here to stop thinking about, or at least had come to think about more magnanimously, or freshly.

'It is very beautiful in the hermitage. One can feel the atmosphere of Domenico,' said Guido. 'I have not tried the *Capo Santo*, but in the hermitage, it is very clear.'

'Maybe the effect was not locked in his skull, let alone magnetically transferred to someone else's.'

'This is a great mystery, not a small one like finding the *cavatappi*,' said Guido.

'I expect Manfredi to come through with the solution any minute now,' said Hunter. 'It's been hiding in the refectory: the brain is a transceiver in the extended field of the mind.'

'A universal field, perhaps,' said Guido modestly.

'Maybe,' said Hunter, 'with smaller fields of species, traditions and families nested within it; Sheldrake fields structured by habits which constitute a kind of memory and explain the "atmosphere" of the hermitage that your transceiver brain can pick up as well as contribute to.'

'Manfredi will bring us the answer, no doubt,' said Guido with a smile. 'But tell me, Hunter, what is this new company that now owns the *Capo Santo*? I think they do not have the same respect for the gift that Fra Domenico made when he allowed himself to be scanned in his deep mystical condition. The Cardinal – Lagerfeld – was many times complaining about the diminishing sales, problems with supplies, and so on, many, many complaints.'

'It's an amortality company . . .'

'What is this?'

'Staying ahead of death: lots of theories of rejuvenation, freezing people until there's a cure for what's killing them, downloading minds into machines . . .'

'Ah,' said Guido, '*vedo*, but why search for amortality when we have immortality?'

'Because immortality depends on dying first,' said Hunter. 'And a lot of people don't believe in it anyway.'

'It may be true, it may not be true,' said Guido, 'but amortality is certainly not true, so it is just silly to believe in "staying ahead of death", no?'

'Sure. I sold *Digitas* to *Cogito*, I didn't buy *Cogito* for *Digitas*.'

'The only way to stay ahead of death,' said Guido, 'is to contemplate it with – I don't know the word exactly – enthusiasm? Not for death, that would be morbid, but for reality, for how it is. When you are kind enough to ask me to *Soleil,* you say, "Please prepare a bed for Guido," you do not say, "Lock the gates! Double the security! Alert the Interpol." We must make room for death because whatever it is, it is coming to visit.'

'It's not a real invitation without a date,' said Hunter.

'That is why the room must always be ready. Then we can stop worrying about when it will arrive, we can . . .' Guido slowly expanded his arms as he had done earlier. 'Always the beginning again and again.'

'Yes,' said Hunter, sinking back into his chair and looking at the small, stout, bespectacled Guido, who seemed to be holding a burning sphere in the air between them.

8

Karen's front door was freshly painted in the same alarming red Olivia had almost walked away from on her first visit twenty years ago. Pausing before ringing the bell, she suddenly yawned uncontrollably, as if she were trying to expel the anticipated boredom of the next hour or two. She put her hand to her mouth and took in the deep breath her body was forcing on her. She could hear the muffled sounds of Karen moving about the house, probably carrying a depressing plate of biscuits from the kitchen to the sitting room, where it would lie on the table between them untouched. Karen would say, 'Help yourself,' and Olivia would reproach herself for thinking, I certainly didn't get any help from you, and then smile and say, 'No thanks.'

She had almost cancelled today's visit, but Karen had been strikingly anxious about reconfirming the date, and besides, now that their meetings were reduced to an annual tea, cancellation would have brought their relationship close to extinction. Their conversation, if not entirely extinct, sometimes felt like trying to persuade despondent pandas to mate in captivity. Or perhaps it was worse, thought Olivia, remembering the photograph Francis had shown her of the last passenger pigeon, alone in its cage in the Cincinnati Zoo in 1914: perhaps she was visiting Karen to emphasise her isolation. She had no desire to integrate Karen into her family life or to be the lost daughter Karen could show off to her small circle of friends. Each year they made polite enquiries about people they had never met and would never meet, but who had acquired the fake familiarity of having been mentioned so often. It was a psychologically awkward situation sustained by Olivia's moral stubbornness. She felt that since she had taken the initiative of contacting Karen, she had a duty to stay in touch with her until the end. Their first meeting had been charged with a presumption of intimacy, but over time their lack of a shared past and Olivia's reluctance to create a shared present consolidated Karen's original rejection. Olivia sometimes wondered if she was taking her revenge by not including Karen in her life, but it felt more complex than that, as if she were embarrassed by having so obviously benefited from being adopted. The hope Karen clung to was that she would one day meet Noah, a redemptive object just outside the blast radius of her decision to give Olivia away.

'I'd so like to see him,' Karen had said last year. 'You don't even have to introduce us. I could, I don't know, watch him play football, or something. It would mean the world to me.'

For Olivia the question was whether Noah, who stood innocently at the edge of the adoption crater, would suddenly tumble into it if he were introduced to Karen, or even knew of her existence. She had discussed with Francis how disconcerting it might be for Noah to meet his mother's mother after thinking he had known her all his life. They had decided that he shouldn't be told the truth until he had some chance of understanding it. Even then, it might not entail a meeting with Karen, just be an explanation about a part of his mother's past.

'It gives him the enriching possibility of a third grandmother,' Martin had said. 'If he didn't love Lizzie, it might be a relief, but as it is, it can only be a bonus of one sort or another: additional love from Karen, or additional gratitude for Lizzie.'

'In any case, it's the truth,' Lizzie had said serenely, 'which is always the best starting point.' She seemed to have expended whatever rivalry she felt on the period of Olivia's first contact with Karen.

'I don't think Noah should meet her unless he asks to,' said Francis. 'The whole thing is just a footnote to his family history unless we build it up. If he wants to meet her, we can make it as easy as possible.'

And that was where they had left it, with some years to go before they even had to address the question seriously.

Now she really must press the doorbell before she was swallowed by another yawning fit or gave in to her strong impulse to run away.

'Hello! Hi! Great to see you!' said Olivia, giving Karen a hug almost before she had crossed the threshold. 'How are you? It's so nice to be back. I like your new hair.'

'You seem very cheerful,' said Karen.

'Don't worry, it won't last,' said Olivia, jokingly. 'But I am, I am feeling cheerful! It must be seeing you again. How have you been? You look well. You're very dressed up.'

'Now you're making me feel like I should change,' said Karen.

'No, no, not if you're going to a job interview.'

'Maybe it is a sort of job interview . . .'

'Well, that's mysterious. Should I be here?'

'Oh, yes . . .' said Karen. 'Perhaps I feel it's always a bit of a job interview seeing you, and that I haven't been given the job yet.'

Isn't it more of a case of having resigned? thought Olivia. Although she had made every effort to keep things superficial, there seemed to be something more combative about today's encounter.

'Really? Well, at least it's not a surprise,' said Olivia. 'I hate surprises. Maybe it's because the biggest surprise in my life was finding out about you, and so I suppose I associate them with – well, you know, emotional effort, confusion, identity crisis – that kind of thing, and now, of course, with peace and understanding, but we only got to that bit when we were past the surprises.

It's not my father, is it? You haven't finally found out which maximum security prison he's been doing his weight training in all these years?'

'God, no,' said Karen. 'I would never spring something like that on you, and I never want to see him again for the rest of my life. Some things are impossible to forgive.'

'I suppose, unless that's your central project,' said Olivia.

'Yes, if you think it's the only way to be free or good, but it's a funny kind of freedom if you're obliged to pretend you love someone you hate in order to get it.'

'I'm not an expert,' said Olivia, 'but I think you're obliged not to pretend.'

'I think you're right,' said Karen, 'which is why it's never going to happen.'

Maybe she hadn't forgiven Karen, thought Olivia, not in the extreme way they had just been touching on, but in a listless sort of way in which she couldn't really be bothered, precisely because she didn't think her freedom, or her goodness, depended on it. Martin was fond of mentioning Donald Winnicott's idea of the 'good enough' mother, neither overprotective nor neglectful, aware of her children's needs, as well as her own, and so on. Maybe she was a 'good enough' daughter in relation to Karen, not rancorous or reproachful or demanding but, while persevering with the basic fact of their relationship, refusing to pretend that a great love had sprung up between them.

'How's Charlie?' asked Karen.

'Oh,' said Olivia, 'I'm going to see him this evening, strangely enough, but I hardly see him these days as he has an American girlfriend who he seems very in love with, and he spends most of his time in the States – in fact, he's returning tomorrow. What else?' Olivia soldiered on. 'I have a new best friend at work, called Sam, who I have a sort of crush on. She's mischievous and good at the same time, but despite the huge cultural pressure to discover my lesbian side, this relationship isn't heading for the bedroom but perhaps towards the kind of closeness where news isn't quite complete until you've shared it with the other person. We'll see.'

'Oh, yes, that's what I have with Anne,' said Karen.

'How is Anne?' said Olivia. 'Did you go to Windermere this summer?'

'I sent you a postcard.'

'Of course!' said Olivia, conjuring a false memory of the latest card that might distinguish itself from the colour-saturated tributes to bunting and boating that arrived every summer, accompanied by stoically cheerful notes about rainy days, over-crowded hillsides and the cranky charms of Anne's cottage, with its 'relic from the 1950s kitchen' and its wood-fired boiler.

'How are things at work?' said Karen.

'Well, I'm a bit stressed because I have to do an interview tomorrow,' said Olivia. 'Not a job interview like you,' she smiled, 'but one for the programme I'm working on.'

'Oh, yes, the six things most likely to destroy life on Earth,' said Karen. 'You told me about it in one of your emails when we were rearranging the date.'

'That's the one,' said Olivia.

'No wonder you seemed so jolly when you arrived,' said Karen. 'Sometimes real catastrophes are reassuring because you can stop inventing them – or remembering them. I was on a plane once that suddenly dropped several thousand feet, and I thought, Ah, thank goodness, this is the real thing.'

'I don't think that's how I would have reacted,' said Olivia, 'but I can imagine what you mean.'

'I think it's partly to do with being right,' said Karen, 'a kind of pride at not being neurotic for once. Of course, I *was* being neurotic . . .'

'Neurotically calm,' said Olivia.

'Yes, the calm during the storm,' said Karen. 'I wouldn't be here if I'd been right. The oxygen masks didn't even fall out of the ceiling.'

'Oh, no, poor you,' said Olivia, 'you didn't get the chance to "put your own oxygen mask on before helping others". Isn't that what they always urge you to do?'

'Yes, I think so. It's been such a long time since I've been on a plane,' said Karen. 'So, what is your interview going to be about?'

'Overpopulation.'

'Well, I've made my own modest contribution to that,' said Karen.

'No, no, that was population; it's the other mothers who have been overpopulating the planet, apart from me of course.'

'How is Noah?' Karen asked wistfully.

'Well, they keep discovering new species of dinosaurs, so every time Francis and I think he might move on to something else, he gets dragged back by a new extinct predator. We've tried to explain that birds are dinosaur descendants, hoping to turn him into a bird lover, but it's been a complete failure so far. Although we live in a nightingale hotspot, there aren't any nightingales in *Jurassic Park*.'

'There's always Hitchcock, if he needs a horror film to turn him into an ornithologist,' said Karen. 'I'd love to meet him sometime. I keep up with all the latest dinosaur news in case you want a free babysitter one day.'

'Well, that really is keen,' said Olivia, imagining a Trojan tetradactyl at the gates of Willow Cottage, with Karen hidden uncomfortably inside.

The doorbell rang, startling Karen.

'Oh, I don't know whether I . . .' she said, leaving what she didn't know unsaid.

Perhaps there was a visitor after all, thought Olivia. She might be about to meet Anne after all those introductory postcards. Or perhaps it was just a package for a neighbour, the scourge of the age of delivery, or someone canvassing for the next election. No, Karen was asking the person to come in, so it must be someone she knew. She could hear the mumbled thanks of a male voice. It was a strange feeling. In all these years she had never met Karen with a third person present. It felt as if an unacknowledged rule was being broken.

When she came back into the room Karen was accompanied by a nervous-looking man in his early forties. Olivia had a vague sense of having met him before but had no idea where it might have been.

'I don't think that's fair,' said the man. 'You didn't say there would be someone else. This is the first time we've met in living memory, and you invite a complete stranger without so much as a by-your-leave.'

He turned abruptly and disappeared from the doorway for a moment.

'I'm sorry,' said Karen, 'I've probably done the wrong thing as usual. Please don't go.'

'Hang on, hang on,' he said, putting his head back around the edge of the door and staring at Olivia. 'You're the nice lady from the party when I used to work for Mr Morris. You were at that party in the big house and you asked me to sit down and take the weight off, and I was very grateful because it was my first time as a waiter and I had just made it across a complicated carpet with all the vines wrapping themselves around my ankles and dragging me back into the black lagoon – no, no, hang on, it was Aladdin's garden – A lad insane. That's what I was expecting, to be swallowed by the carpet. And you were expecting too! A baby – or two. That's why you had all the canapés, which saved me dropping them on the floor, and you defended me against that wanker John, who stole the love of my life.'

'Yes!' cried Olivia, partly marvelling at the coincidence and partly desperate to stop him talking. He seemed a little deranged, but also had an atmosphere of vulnerability that aroused her maternal protectiveness. 'The Happy Helmets party.'

'Happy Helmets – so likely – have you got one, by the way? If only it was that easy – I could really do with one now.'

'This is Keith,' said Karen, a hostess under strain.

'Sebastian,' said Sebastian.

'Oh,' said Karen, 'sorry, I always forget.'

'What do you mean "always"?' asked Sebastian. 'We've never met before.'

'Well, strictly speaking . . .'

'It's a bit late to be strict,' said Sebastian.

'Keith,' said Olivia. '*The* Keith?'

'Yes,' said Karen.

'I told you, I'm called Sebastian,' Sebastian shouted. 'I don't have two identities. I've got a lot more than that,' he added, suddenly letting loose a wild high-pitched laugh.

Olivia wavered for a moment but decided she would deal with her own feelings later. 'Yes, "Seb", that's what that . . . what your colleague called you.'

'How do you know that Mr Morris used to call us colleagues?'

'I didn't,' said Olivia. 'How could I know?'

'That's what I asked you,' said Sebastian angrily. 'Don't mirror me!'

'I'm sorry,' said Olivia. 'I just meant to say that I didn't know.'

'Were you spying on us?' said Sebastian. 'Only Mr Morris said "colleagues".'

'No, I wasn't,' said Olivia, thinking of Karen's phrase "the calm during the storm", but in her case knowing that it was the product of pretence and compassion, rather than deeply fulfilled pessimism. 'I wasn't very mobile, being heavily pregnant with Noah.'

'That's your nephew,' said Karen helpfully.

'My what?' said Sebastian. 'Hello, Uncle Seb, pleased to make your acquaintance,' he lisped, with an imaginary handshake. 'Hello, nephew Noah,' he said in a deep voice, 'the pleasure's all mine, I assure you. My fucking what?' he shouted in his own voice. 'My nephew! But that means . . . I'm sorry, I know you're a nice lady and everything, but I came here for a private chat with my Bio Mum, who I've never met before, and it was supposed to be a Special Moment, and now I've got a nephew and you're here.'

He clutched his head to prevent it from exploding.

'To be honest, I don't think I can handle it all at once.'

Olivia got up and walked over to him and held out her hand.

'Well, I'm your Bio Sis, Olivia, and I didn't know this was happening either, but it's a pleasure to meet you – to meet you again, that is, knowing who you are this time.'

Sebastian frowned for a moment and then looked disconnected. Olivia realised that she really was mirroring him now and almost dropped her hand, but Sebastian reached out and took it.

'The pleasure's all mine, I assure you,' he said mechanically. 'How old are you?'

'The same age as you,' said Olivia.

'But that means . . .'

'Yes,' said Olivia, 'we're twins. I shouldn't be the first to tell you, but Bio Mum has laid on a lot of surprises for us this afternoon.'

'I hate surprises,' said Sebastian.

'So do I.'

'It must be genetic,' said Sebastian.

'Or maybe most of our surprises haven't been enjoyable,' said Olivia.

'Yeah, yeah, that's probably it,' Sebastian agreed immediately.

'Well, here we are,' said Karen, with lonely nostalgia, 'together again at last.'

Sebastian ignored her, pacing up and down, still clutching his head.

'Twins!' he said. 'But that means we were together in the same . . . place. I'm sorry, I have these bad words. Usually, I can handle them much better but if I'm stressed, I get stuck, and now I can't say it.'

'We all know what that place was,' said Olivia. 'So you don't have to say it to be understood.'

'Overload,' said Sebastian, twirling both his index fingers around his temples, as if he were secretly communicating to Olivia that someone in the room was off their rocker. 'I mean, "colleagues" – I hadn't heard the word for donkey's years and then Kapow! You've got to admit it's strange, right?'

'It is,' said Olivia. 'If you had only heard the word from Mr Morris and then it comes up again when you meet someone you first met when you were working for Mr Morris . . .'

'Right! You see, *she* gets it,' he said to Karen sharply. 'I need a glass of water.'

'Of course,' said Karen.

Olivia heard the crinkle of pharmaceutical foil in Sebastian's pocket. He took out a strip and popped two pills into his palm, knocking them back the moment Karen returned with the water.

'Overload,' Sebastian said again. 'I must go. I can't actually handle this. Don't take it personally, I know you're a very nice lady, but I can't get my head around being a twin, being half of a double act. All my life I've felt like I was . . . inadequate, not complete, not whole, and now this feels like – like scientific proof.'

'Let me give you my number at least,' said Olivia, but Sebastian didn't seem to hear. He rounded on Karen, changing his tone abruptly.

'You, on the other hand, you *can* take it personally,' he said to Karen. 'I'm leaving your house. I can walk now. I'm not a baby. I'm not a human ashtray. I can walk now and I'm walking out. You can't just do this without so much as a by-your-leave, you can't just say I'm a twin and I used to share the same place in your body with this other person. You can't just *do* that to someone. I'm leaving now and if I'd had a scalpel back in the day, with a mother like you, I would have performed my own bloody Caesarean, cut the old umbilical cord, and given myself away at birth to this nice lady's family so we could have stayed together.'

Sebastian strode down the hallway, shouted 'un-fucking-believable', and slammed the front door behind him.

'Tmesis,' said Olivia.

'What?' asked Karen.

'Splitting up a word with another word: unbelievable becomes un-fucking-believable,' said Olivia. 'In my first conscious act of solidarity with my twin, I have to agree with him that it was the perfect choice of word. What you've done this afternoon is un-fucking-believable. I'm leaving as well.'

'Can't we at least talk about it?' asked Karen in a voice that seemed to know the answer that Olivia didn't bother to give.

She took her coat from the hook in the hall and stepped into Mafeking Street. She looked in both directions but couldn't see Sebastian and so she started her walk back to the Underground, wondering how she could get hold of him without having to ask Karen, who she intended to punish with silence. It was lucky that Francis and Noah were in the country, as she really wanted to talk this incident through with her real parents, and her known brother. At home, she would have had to contain herself through a bubble bath and a bedtime story before she could try to make sense of the storm that was building up inside her.

9

He hated his Bio Mum. He hated her washed-out eyes, like a watercolour left in the rain. He hated her disappointed mouth, like an old leek at the bottom of a crate. Despite their dire reputations, hatred and anger were better than fear. That's probably why people got into them, they felt more powerful, more vigorous. Fear was a porcupine rolled up in your throat. He had chosen hatred and anger, but now he could sense that ache in his forehead, as if the blue beam was going to shoot out and do battle with the Sky Mirror, like it used to in the good old bad old days. He had shattered himself by shattering the mirror. That was the trouble with hatred and anger power, you couldn't use it without blowing yourself up. It reminded him of that programme about the Cold War: back in the sixties, the Defence boss, Robert Somebody, had called American nuclear policy 'assured destruction' and then a witty critic had added the word 'mutual' so the acronym would be MAD. He had taken his meds back at his Bio Mum's so that he wouldn't go mad, so that he could have this dull ache in his third eye instead of the blue beam burning into the sky and mutually incinerating them.

In his imagination his Bio Mum had been young and blonde with rosy cheeks, like an old-fashioned poster for the joys and benefits of milk. He had thought she would open the door in an apron, and the whole house would smell like *The Great British Bake Off*, with something delicious in the oven, something she was making especially for him, not that little plate of hard biscuits he had seen on the table when he was pacing up and down the back of her front room. He realised he had pictured her being younger than him, which, if it had been true, would have made the Virgin Birth look like a push-over. He would have had to be born before his mother existed – eat your heart out, Jesus Christ. You'd need a wormhole between different universes to bring that off. They didn't have that sort of technology yet, let alone back in the day, unless it was a secret government programme, or it had happened when he was surfing the multiverse.

Thank goodness he was seeing Dr Carr tomorrow, because psychologically, in psycho logic, he had probably been imagining she was still the same age she had been when *he* was a bun in the oven. He had longed for her to be young and pretty and incredibly cheerful, so they could make a fresh start and turn him into Aladdin instead of a lad insane. He had arrested her development to free himself from his own arrested development. He was going to tell Dr Carr his interpretation and, without getting his hopes up, he thought it was just the sort of thing Dr Carr would think was bang on target. An ICBI, an intercontinental ballistic interpretation.

The biggest thing they would have to sort out was the shock of discovering that there had been *two* buns in the oven. He felt divided about being a twin. On the one hand, he was outraged that he hadn't had his Bio Mum to himself even before he was born. He had been forced to live in an overpopulated womb – he could say 'womb' now that he had wolfed down his meds and escaped from the siege of Mafeking Street. Not to mention being in the front seat on the top floor of a double-decker bus, which was one of his absolute favourite things. On the other hand, he really loved his Bio Sis and wished they had never been separated. They were twins after all, peas in a pod, piled on top of each other in a double-decker womb. He must have been on the top deck back in the day, that's probably where he'd developed a taste for it – you couldn't look back far enough for the origin of things. Imagine if there had been three or four or five or six of them, that would have been like construction workers living in a converted ship container in Qatar, air-conditioning a desert for fans of the beautiful game. It must have been strange to be separated at birth. He felt now that he had been missing Olivia all his life. It made him want to cry. He had been cut in half, deprived of his best friend, the only person who really understood him, the only person he had ever been close to. It was the tragedy of birth, or the birth of tragedy, depending on how you looked at it.

Mind you, twins did staggering things sometimes, like Romulus and Remus, who founded Rome. Did one of them kill the other? He couldn't remember the whole story, but he'd had a Ladybird book about it when he was little, which his Fake Mum used to read to him. Yes, yes, one brother had killed the other, he could remember now, because his Fake Mum used to say it showed that greatness was easier to achieve if you were an only child. She probably knew he was a twin and had been trying to put him off in case he ever found out. Bitch. It must have been Romulus who killed Remus otherwise the city would be called Reme, not Rome. 'There was once a dream that was called Reme . . . The decline and fall of the Remen Empire . . . Give way! I'm a citizen of Reme.' It didn't have quite the right ring to it, when you tested it out, so if somebody had to get killed, it was probably just as well it was Remus. Mind you, both Romulus and Remus had been brought up by a wolf, which was a difficult start by any standards. It put his own dodgy upbringing into perspective. Like his Fake Mum used to say, 'There's always somebody worse off than you,' which really used to upset him because he felt so dreadful in the first place, he didn't want to think about the people who were suffering even more. With a start like that, if Romulus had been arrested for giving his brother the chop, he could easily have pleaded diminished responsibility.

'Senator Krupke, we're misunderstood! Deep down inside us there's a wolf/ There's a wolf, there's a wolf/ There's a female wolf/ There's a multi-breasted wolf!' Sebastian sang at the top of his voice.

'Oi, pipe down,' said another passenger.

Whoops. He had started behaving as if he was the star of a musical set on a bus, which was always a mistake (unless you were the star of a musical set on a bus).

'Sorry, I got carried away,' Sebastian called out, without daring to look behind him.

He loved *West Side Story*. He'd seen it at least a hundred times, and that was his favourite song. Now he had the tune in his head, he continued playing around with it quietly under his breath.

'My daddy beats my mummy/ My mummy was a wolf/my grandpa was a tyrant/ My grandma was aloof/ My sister is so lovely/ Her brother is insane/ Goodness, gracious, no wonder I'm a pain/ I'm a pain, I'm a pain, I'm a total pain . . .'

'Oi, I've warned you and I'm not warning you again,' said the angry man.

Whoops, he must have turned the volume up without meaning to, but he just couldn't stop himself now. This time he really made sure he was saying the words in his head. 'Senator Krupke, I'm down on my knees/ Because nobody wants a fellow with a mental disease.'

He was almost sure he hadn't sung it out loud, but he glanced around nervously at his heckler, a grim, unshaven man a few seats behind who looked like he wanted Sebastian to get carried away, not by *West Side Story* but by a police van. You could tell just by looking at him that he was a nasty piece of work.

Talking of Nazis, they used to do experiments on twins. Although 'experiments' wasn't quite the right word, because in an experiment you were trying to find out something that you weren't sure of yet, whereas Dr Mengele preferred experiments where the outcome was already known, namely, a definite and horrible death: assured destruction without so much as a 'mutual'. For instance, if you put someone in a chamber and created a vacuum, they just splattered all over it, time after time.

'Let's verify that result again,' Dr Mengele whispered, hoarse with pleasure.

'*Ya vol, Herr Doktor.*'

'Either you get off the bloody bus or I'll throw you off,' said the nasty man, gripping the rail behind Sebastian's seat and leaning down threateningly.

'I'm sorry, I'm sorry,' said Sebastian. 'It's just that I've got all these ideas going through my head.'

'Well, we don't want to bloody hear them, do we? So, get off the bus.'

'I've met my real mum today for the first time,' said Sebastian, 'and it's brought up lots of emotion. I'm adopted, you see.'

'Yeah, well,' said the man, who seemed a bit thrown by Sebastian's candour, 'you need to get a grip, mate.'

'I do,' said Sebastian. 'I do need to get a grip. I'm going to see my doctor tomorrow.'

'You'd better ask him for some shut-up pills,' said the man, trying to restore his reputation for hostility.

'I will,' said Sebastian. 'Some shut-up pills, some pipe-down pills and some keep-your-thoughts-to-yourself pills.'

'Are you taking the piss?'

'No, no, I really mean it,' said Sebastian with desperate sincerity.

'Right, well, this is my stop,' said the man, 'thanks for ruining my journey. Fucking looney,' he muttered as he turned his back.

Perhaps that was his Bio Dad, thought Sebastian. Perhaps the Fates or the Furies, one of the Terrible Triads, or one of the Special Ks, Kismet or Karma, had arranged for him to meet his Bio Mum and his Bio Dad on the same day, as well as his lovely, long-lost sister, Olivia. After the birth of tragedy, or the tragedy of birth, there was no stopping the train until it arrived at Gravesend or Death Valley.

'He was a nasty man,' said a voice behind him.

Sebastian turned around and saw a nice-looking black lady holding a bag on her lap.

'You must have been reading my mind,' said Sebastian.

'I'm no mind-reader, darling,' said the nice lady, 'but I know a bully when I see one. You were just singing to yourself. Nothing wrong with that – I do it all the time! I don't know why everyone is so angry these days, but you mustn't let it upset you.'

'I won't,' said Sebastian. 'I won't, thanks to you. You're a very nice lady.'

'Oh, don't flatter me,' she said. 'I just say what I see.'

'That's what I do!' said Sebastian. 'But it hasn't always been to everybody's liking.'

'Never you mind, just sing your heart out, darling,' she said.

'I will,' said Sebastian. 'Thanks.'

He waved at her as he started down the stairs.

This was the stop for the halfway house. Perhaps now he'd met his twin his halfway house and her halfway house could join forces to make a whole house. Perhaps they were the missing bits in each other's jigsaw puzzles, and all the pieces were going to fit together at last, and it was all going to be all right. Perhaps.

10

Martin stood up politely while Carmen, his last patient of the day, left his consulting room, closing the door behind her. Between the click of the first door and the clunk of the street door, there was an interval, like a pianist who pauses above the keys at the end of a performance, to let the music resonate in silence, an interval in which he could take in the whole atmosphere of the session. In a single recollection he revisited the cave system of associations his patient had just been wandering through, the unhappy collision with a low-hanging stalactite, the glimpse of galloping bison on the wall, the passages as narrow as a birth canal and the vast chambers with an opening to the sky, the frustrations, and the breakthroughs.

Carmen was not fruitful in breakthroughs, if only because she had moved to London from California burdened with what turned out to be a Lacanian analysis. Jacques Lacan's psychoanalytic school had eventually had its membership of the International Psychoanalytical Association revoked and so, strictly speaking, Carmen had not been analysed at all, but that didn't mean she hadn't been harmed, if only by imagining that she had already been analysed. The authoritarian obscurity of Lacan's writing combined with the brutality of his clinical methods formed a compound that any Borgia would have been thrilled to keep in the hollow of their ruby ring and tip into the goblet of an enemy who was not yet entirely convinced that suicide was the best way forward. His prose appeared to have been written by an alarmed squid, escaping in a cloud of ink from the terror of not being able to live up to his craving for intellectual greatness. He had no time to waste on the difficulties of his patients when he was so busy creating insurmountable difficulties for his readers. His *courtes sessions* could last as little as two minutes, before the tormented analysand was thrown back into a waiting room crowded with acquaintances, and the next victim was summoned to the Procrustean couch. To Martin, who felt that the regularities and rhythms of analysis provided a cradle in which the analysand could safely reconnect with the most primitive parts of their mind, this method was obviously inept and often dangerous. A Lacanian analysis, as Carmen exemplified, was the natural refuge of someone determined to avoid getting better but hoping to look as if she were trying, if only to sometimes preface her self-centredness with the phrase 'my therapist says', rather than the naked first-person singular which would otherwise appear at the beginning or, at the very latest, after a derogatory comparison, in the middle of every sentence she uttered. If not quite equivalent to choosing Charles Manson as a spiritual guide, the choice of a Lacanian analyst was a match for any list of charlatan gurus whose sexual predations, fundraising frenzies and abundance of 'crazy wisdom' turned out to be no substitute for enlightenment, generosity and sanity. When he had to take on a patient who had survived a Lacanian episode, Martin not only had to interpret the pattern on the vase, which was always the case, but also reassemble the vase from the bag of shards handed to him by his predecessor.

Quite apart from the double workload created by Carmen's therapeutic history, it turned out that she had connections with Martin's world which would have prevented him from taking her on if he had known about them at inception. These things sometimes happened. One analysand might turn out to have a friend in common with another, and Martin would have to make sure he didn't import the role they played in one psyche to the role they played in the other. One patient's wife might become another patient's mistress, which didn't mean that he could vigorously oppose the husband's view that his jealousy was a paranoid fantasy that was driving his poor wife mad. Of course, he would have preferred to have known that Carmen was a friend of Hope Schwartz's before taking her on. Although Olivia, Noah and Francis had not had to be rescued from under the rubble of Willow Cottage, Hope had registered on the Richter scale in some way that Martin had been too tactful to enquire about but knew had shaken the last days of his daughter's pregnancy.

On top of these complications, Carmen was one of those adamantine narcissists for whom insights were indistinguishable from insults, since the only insights worth having were bound to throw into question the perfection whose image she expected to see reflected in every object around her. The idea that any of these objects were subjects in their own right was a heresy that had to be annihilated, making it very difficult for the analyst to interpose himself between the gaze and the mirror. She was at the opposite end of the spectrum from the zealous neurotic who lines up all the bright pebbles of insight she has gathered between sessions and brings them to be admired, along with the new notebook she had just bought as the vessel for the eighth volume of her dream diaries. Carmen and Sebastian were, in their very different ways, his most difficult patients. Sebastian because of the depth of his disturbance and Carmen because of the depth of her resistance. Of course, there would be no analysis without resistance since everyone would be walking around in a perfect state of self-knowledge, but ordinary resistance often took the form of clinging to a cherished self-image while longing to get rid of its unpleasant side effects. It became more ferocious when it was protecting an archaic defence linked to survival, sometimes to the point of root confusion, like a convict who never makes a prison break without first handing the warden the schedule of his attempted escape and showing him the laundry chutes and storm drains which he plans to use, only to be thrown into despair by the injustice of getting caught yet again.

Carmen's prospects of freedom were even more remote since she mistook her prison for a palace. Her cherished self-image had no unpleasant side effects since it was an image of perfection. Unpleasant side effects could only come from giving it up. She went into analysis not to set herself free, but because it was her ideal habitat: instead of having to bring the subject back to herself, as she must be forced to in the outside world, in the analytic setting it would have been a categorical error to take any interest in the only other person in the room. What heaven! No more tugging at the leash as the naughty puppy of conversation strained to find another topic. It was all about her, with the puppy anaesthetised on her lap. Sebastian's case was extreme in the opposite sense: he had no cherished self-image, only cherished images of being someone else. The unpleasant side effects, in his case, came from being alive, while the siren song of non-existence played like muzak in a broken lift. His great advantage over Carmen was that he desperately wanted to change and that thanks to his analysis he had been changing, showing great resilience after the setback of his two months in hospital this summer. Martin was seeing Sebastian tomorrow morning and however volatile it might be, the session would make a bracing change of dynamic from the opulent rigidity of Carmen's self-regard.

Martin switched off the lights of his consulting room and climbed the basement stairs to the kitchen. He was going to have dinner with Lizzie and his two children. It had been a long time since they had been alone together. Martin would have to lay the table and open some wine and put some nuts in a bowl, the light duties that made up a little for his incompetence as a cook, but he was looking forward to the particular intimacy of the basic family, without in-laws and grandchildren.

'Hi, darling,' said Lizzie, who he found preparing a chicken in a large black pan on the central island of the kitchen.

'Hi,' said Martin. 'I was just thinking how much Lacan has to answer for . . .'

'Well, it's not an answer we could make head or tail of,' said Lizzie, 'so it's just as well he can't give it. Why has he come up?'

'Discretion forbids me to go into it,' said Martin.

'So, you have a Lacanian survivor to look after,' said Lizzie.

'Hmm,' said Martin, revealing nothing.

'I had one once,' said Lizzie, 'and it was a horrible victory for Lacan in that I wanted to throw him out three minutes into the session. After a few weeks, though, we'd learnt to make a profitable use of all fifty minutes.'

'Not as profitable as seeing ten patients in the same fifty minutes,' said Martin.

'Yes, but then I would have been less sane than my patients,' said Lizzie. 'It's no use asking people to internalise the analyst if she's madder than they are. By the way, Charlie is just outside. He's putting a visitor's permit in his car.'

'Oh, good,' said Martin, just as the doorbell rang. 'Ah . . .'

'Hi, Dad.'

'Charlie!' said Martin, giving his son a hug.

'Is Olivia back yet?' said Charlie.

'No, she went to see Karen,' said Martin, as they walked into the kitchen together.

'On the annual visit?'

'Exactly.'

'They seem to have the special quality of being portentous and pointless at the same time,' said Charlie.

'Oh, I think the pointlessness got the upper hand a long time ago,' said Martin, 'but you know Olivia, she'll go on doing the right thing.'

'Why is it the right thing to go on doing something pointless?' said Charlie.

'The inane conversation still takes place in her mother's house. It's like a ruined church on consecrated ground.'

'It can always be deconsecrated,' said Charlie. 'Half the people I know seem to live in a converted chapel.'

The front door opened, and Olivia walked into the hall briskly, unlooping her scarf and throwing it on a nearby chair.

'Were you talking about me?' she said as she joined them in the kitchen.

'What on earth makes you think that?' said Charlie, kissing her hello.

'Well, Watson, since it's almost impossible to get any of you to stop talking, if you all three fall silent when I come into the room, I assume that's the reason.'

'Busted,' said Charlie.

'I don't think Watson would say "Busted",' said Olivia, 'unless he's moving to America.'

'By Jove, Sherlock,' Charlie corrected himself, 'your powers of observation never cease to amaze me!'

'That's more like it,' said Olivia.

'I was arguing that you should be able to do what you like about Karen, with no sense of duty entering into it.'

'It's more baked-in than entering in,' said Olivia. 'In any case, I might not see her again after what she did this afternoon. It was "un-fucking-believable", to quote my other brother's assessment.'

'Your other brother?' said Charlie. 'You mean you've met Keith?'

'Sebastian,' said Olivia. 'He was renamed by his adoptive parents.'

'Wow, that's huge,' said Charlie. 'Thank goodness I'm leaving the country. I'm feeling what Mum must have felt twenty years ago, or whenever it was you first went to see Karen – possessive, jealous, anxious. But how are *you* feeling? What was he like?'

Lizzie, who had been overlaying the edges of thinly sliced potato across the bottom of a pan, paused. Martin, by contrast, found himself opening a drawer and clasping a handful of knives and forks.

'I'm listening,' he said, conscious that this was not the perfect description of trying to avoid hearing Olivia's account of her meeting with Sebastian.

'Do you have to lay the table at this exact moment?' asked Olivia, more puzzled than annoyed, but annoyed enough.

'I'm sorry,' he said, hoping his reputation for equanimity would survive his strange behaviour. 'I don't know why I felt the call of duty at that exact moment. Maybe I needed Charlie to talk me out of it.'

'Don't lay the table, Dad,' said Charlie.

'Fine,' said Martin, laying the knives quietly on some napkins, trapped.

'So, tell us about Sebastian,' said Lizzie. 'Does he look like you?'

'No, we couldn't be less identical,' said Olivia. 'He's quite stocky and prematurely aged, while seeming to be incredibly young. He's rather touching, but very vulnerable. When Karen unveiled her big surprise, he had to swallow some pills in a hurry, like someone who is trying to head off a seizure or an episode or a stroke. I felt very sorry for him. As well as being quite edgy, he didn't even know he had a twin, *and* he was meeting Karen for the first time. It was so unfair on both of us, but especially on him. How dare she do that without warning us? I mean, I'll get over it, but he seemed extremely disturbed.'

‘Poor both of you,’ said Lizzie. ‘It was terribly irresponsible, but I can imagine that she might have got lost in a fantasy world where it was a beautiful, redemptive act – the reconciliation at the end of a Shakespeare comedy – or at least a sentimental scene from Dickens.’

‘Well, back here on planet Earth,’ said Olivia, ‘she just confirmed what a completely hopeless mother she is, in case we hadn’t taken that in. She said, “Together again at last”, not bothering to notice that two out of three of the participants in this beautiful reunion had no memory of ever having been together in the first place, and one of them didn’t know there was a third party involved. It was utterly selfish.’

Martin felt the impossibility of the mental acrobatics required of him: to attend to his daughter’s account of her deeply significant meeting with her twin, and to forget the entire story so that he could listen to it freshly the following morning from Sebastian’s point of view. Only half an hour ago he had consoled himself with the thought that ‘These things happen’ when considering the overlap between Carmen’s history and his own world, but the sort of overlap that existed between his world and Sebastian’s history belonged to another category with the label ‘These things do *not* happen, *cannot* happen and *must* not happen’. And yet, in a sense he was lucky that it had taken so long for his daughter and his most traumatised patient to know each other for who they were. He had watched them sitting next to each other at Hunter’s party four years ago and, from that perspective, the discovery of their relationship had been a long time coming.

‘The amazing thing is that we’ve met before,’ said Olivia.

The remark shadowed Martin’s thoughts so closely that he almost said, ‘I know’, but managed to say, ‘Oh, no.’ Not so much a Freudian slip as a Freudian swerve. ‘Really?’

‘Yes,’ said Olivia, ‘at that Happy Helmets party we all went to just before Noah was born. Sebastian was a waiter, and I remember noticing that he was in bad shape and making an excuse to chat with him for a moment. It's so strange that I felt protective towards him without knowing we were connected in any way.'

'Not that strange, given your nature,' said Charlie.

'Maybe, but the feeling was much stronger than any general sense of concern or goodwill. There were parts of him that didn't seem to fit together. He was paranoid but very responsive to friendliness – a strange combination of trust and mistrust. Something good must have happened to him as well as all the awful things.'

'Maybe he's had some help,' said Lizzie. 'People who are very disturbed often get lost in the psychiatric system and don't get the psychotherapy they need. They just get the pills.'

'Unless they meet heroes like you and Dad,' said Charlie in a tone that was only slightly flippant, 'who are prepared to take on the most extreme cases.'

'Whether he's had help or not, he certainly needs more,' said Olivia. 'Perhaps we should try to connect him with somebody – obviously not you. Or perhaps he is already getting help, which is why he's not entirely paranoid. I'll find out when I see him again. I just don't want to ask Karen for the moment.'

'Yes, perhaps you should wait a few days until you're less angry,' said Lizzie.

Yes, a few days, thought Martin, or ideally, a few months. Not tomorrow morning, at any rate. Could he ask Olivia what time she was doing her interview, or would that seem strange? There was so much work left to do with Sebastian. He wasn't going home, after this explosive revelation, to a family of three psychotherapists, but to a halfway house, with a code on the door, a curfew, and a nurse on night duty. The discovery that he had a twin would lead to fusion and confusion, to a sense of identification with Olivia but also of further alienation from Karen. There were now no brakes on his split mentality, which didn't start with his first episode or his adoption, or his emergence into a world containing his vile father, but had started at conception in his mother's divided womb. It was enormous enough that he had met his 'Bio Mum' for the first time, but the circumstances couldn't have been more disruptive. Martin stared at the kitchen floor, in a kind of proleptic paralysis, feeling that his silence was inherently suspicious, but that anything he said would turn out to seem duplicitous once his relationship with Sebastian became known.

'Any thoughts?' Olivia asked him.

'No,' said Martin, searching for perfect banality. 'Yes, I mean, of course he should be helped as much as possible.'

'I could take him on,' said Charlie, 'brother to brother, *hermano a hermano*, preparing him for the incredible challenges of having Olivia as a sister.'

'I take this quite seriously,' said Olivia.

'I know,' said Charlie. 'I'm being a bit silly because I think we're all rather stunned.'

'Right,' said Lizzie, closing the oven door and rinsing her hands under the tap. 'Shall we all go and sit down and have a drink?'

'Wonderful,' said Martin, not because sitting down warranted such high praise, but because he was being released from the immediate pressure to comment on Olivia's predicament.

II

There might be a shepherd in the Himalayas or a surfing instructor in Tahiti who had a more delightful journey to work than Francis, but he felt that his walk back and forth from Willow Cottage to his office in Howorth Park would merit inclusion in *The World's Hundred Greatest Commutes*, the sort of feature designed to make its readers envy and, if possible, destroy the fragile beauty and sublime remoteness of the places featured on its list. Herds of bellowing yaks would cascade over the nearest cliff as much larger herds of amateur photographers and part-time contemplatives were lured to the mountains by the disastrous popularity of the article. He imagined the despairing Tahitian surfer paddling further and further out into the fatal swell to escape the beach party whose monstrous sound system was drowning the boom and hiss of the surf breaking on the sands of his once secret cove. Francis sidestepped a fallen branch, as if the noise of it snapping underfoot might provoke the stampede of tourists he had been imagining. Perhaps one day he would have to book months in advance to go on a tour of these woods, like buying a ticket to see Botticelli's *Primavera* in the Uffizi. He could join a safari led by a local guide, listening to her praise the mushrooms springing from the ground and the berries ripening in the bush, while she selected bursts of seasonal birdsong from the playlist on her smartphone, synced to camouflaged speakers distributed among the trees, but just for now, he could listen to unrecorded birds and, as he stepped out of the woods into an open field, enjoy the dusky pink light catching isolated clouds and chalky vapour trails that seemed to be underlining invisible sentences in the deepening sky. What was it they wanted to emphasise so much? Emptiness? Space? Wanderlust? Kerosene?

Despite these grounding daily walks, the virtual nature of his work sometimes superimposed lingering images of Ecuadorian forests on the Howorth landscape he knew so well. Today, such was the vividness of the photographs he had been admiring on the screen of his desktop computer before heading home, he half expected to see the blood-red eyes and the scarlet, black and yellow scales of a newly discovered species of canopy snake hanging from the branches of the first oak tree he walked past in the park. At least that species of arboreal, snail-hunting snake would not suffer the ignominy of becoming extinct before it had been given a Latin name: *Sibon marleyae*. How could its ancestors have known that they were evolving in forests impertinently rooted among some of the richest gold and copper deposits in the world? Its habitat must be cleared and although the snake was non-venomous, the mining industry could make up for that oversight with sulphurs and heavy metals. The showrunner in charge of the wrestling match between Gaia and Mammon needed to be re-educated in the basics of entertainment. It was no fun watching poor Gaia being spun, strangled and slammed to the canvas time after time by a flaxen-haired, steroid-soused giant with *Human Greed* written in gold letters on his red polyester leotard. A little variety was needed, an unexpected come-back, a reversal of fortunes, otherwise the ratings would plummet, and nobody would bother to watch any more, except for Mammon's base, lounging in their *Corporate Evil* easy-chairs, in basements cluttered with *Blood and Treasure* sweatshirts and muscular wrestling figurines, needlessly cheering as their oily hero, after headbutting the referee, brought himself crashing down yet again on his supine opponent.

Not on Our Watch might more accurately be called *On Our Watch* since it entailed viewing hours of footage taken by drones hovering over illegal gold-mining and logging operations, as well as spending further hours in video conferences with local activists, or New York attorneys, or with the patrons who bankrolled the organisation. Francis had only been on one visit to Ecuador, accompanying Hope to the *Oriente* before the pandemic. That was where he had met Antero and been taken on his first 'Toxic Tour' by Hank, a yarn-spinning former alcoholic – or, in his own volcanic mind, a dormant alcoholic, sober for twelve years but ready to erupt at any moment if he found himself stranded downwind of a crêpe Suzette. Hank was also a former employee of General Power but was in no danger of relapsing into their employment, regardless of his proximity to a barrel of crude, since his new job consisted of bearing witness to his old company's crimes and misdemeanours. He was determined to keep confessing, whether he could be heard or not, over the whine of the outboard engine, as he steered Hope and Francis in his fibreglass canoe through river waters rich with polycyclic aromatic hydrocarbons towards the Cofan village where Antero lived. 'It was wrong what we did,' Hank shouted, scanning the river beyond the prow as he told the barely audible story of how he and his colleagues used to encourage the indigenous people to rub crude oil over their bodies by claiming that it was good for their skin, for aches and pains, and was also a cure for baldness. When he finally cut the engine and tilted it expertly out of the shallow water, letting the canoe drift towards a beach where friendly villagers were waiting to help haul it onshore, he was still shaking his head in repentant disbelief at the memory of that cruel and facetious deception.

Ecuador was the first country to enshrine the Rights of Nature in its constitution. In the Galapagos, its most westerly territory, marine iguanas still clambered tenaciously onto rocky, foaming shores, and finches still managed to take flight despite the theoretical weight of adaptive radiation they carried in their thirteen varieties of independently evolved island beaks. It was on the Amazonian edge of the country where the rights of nature were being less successfully defended. Pipelines, powerlines and dirt roads radiated through the forests like fissures on a hammered windscreen, slow jungle streams glinted with the iridescent sheen of oil, and sticks thrust into fields of bright crops emerged dripping with the drilling waste which had been poured into unlined pits and covered with a thin layer of soil. The *Oriente* accommodated almost every impulse of eco-tourism, from awe to rage, from biodiversity to bio catastrophe, with plenty of ethnopharmacology and shamanic practices to help visitors from Ibiza and San Francisco feel at home. Francis had struck a balance between the sort of toxic tours led by Hank and the pro-business toxic tours, more urban but no less engrossing, emphasising untreated sewage, overcrowded housing and poverty as the likely sources of the explosion of disease among the indigenous peoples and agricultural settlers. No doubt they had contributed. It seemed like yet another needless dichotomy, especially since the overcrowded housing wouldn't have been there without the industries that created it.

After a fortnight in Ecuador, Francis and Hope had flown to California for a few days. Francis wanted to check up on the rewilding project he had been organising for Hope, Hunter and their neighbour Jim Burroughs. They hesitated to accept Jim's invitation to dinner on their first evening back, but finally agreed when they heard that Bob Glazer, the CEO of General Power, and Sheryl Forbes-Gonzales, its COO, were guests at Titan Ranch and were leaving the next day. Francis could still remember the evening vividly. The contrast between the Ecuadorian refineries belching black and orange flames, like dragons guarding the buried treasure of a devastated land, and the hospitable flames dancing in the hearth of Jim's virile but sumptuous drawing room was so incongruous that it heightened all his impressions of that evening.

For Francis, who was strongly inclined to discount a person's appearance in favour of their character, Bob Glazer nevertheless looked like a turkey arrested halfway through its hubristic metamorphosis into human form; its wattle not yet fully absorbed into a chin; its scrawny neck thrust forward to disguise the stubbornly avian ratio between a restless little head and a majestically swelling torso. Anybody who doubted that the intestinal microbiome formed an additional organ, with its own visceral intelligence, only had to glance at Bob Glazer to accept that he must indeed have a second brain tucked away in his belly, since the one in his head could not possibly be large enough to run a company with four times the income of Ecuador and a far more combative sense of its own sovereignty. His sinisterly pale face, which looked as if his thoroughly white parents had dipped him in a river of bleach, as an extra precaution against lynching mobs, might have disappeared altogether behind his enormous glasses, if he hadn't removed them so often to wipe the lenses, a nervous habit which seemed to Francis like an unconscious confession that however salient it was, he could not see what was in front of him.

'We can't allow little countries like Ecuador to screw around with big companies like General Power,' he announced, settling down in the armchair he had occupied before dinner.

'Hope tells me the affected area is the size of Rhode Island,' said James Burroughs, lobbing some kiln-dried logs onto the already exuberant fire.

'Seriously, Jim, this whole environmental craze is out of control: it's like being asked to go for a run in the woods without stepping on an ant. It's highly sensitive, and all, but I don't think anyone in this room wants to drive into a gas station and find there isn't any gas for sale, because we had to pay out a billion dollars to every lying son of a bitch who claims to have eaten a contaminated carrot. We adhere to the highest standards required by the countries we invest in.'

'Do you ever invest in persuading them to keep those standards as low as possible?' said Hope.

'Well, we have a fiduciary responsibility to our shareholders. With all due respect, we're not running a family foundation or a non-profit, we're running General Power,' said Bob, 'and the "plaintiffs" in this case are just a bunch of anti-gringo farmers and indigenous peoples who got suckered into a class action suit by a crooked New York attorney.'

'I'm sensing some hostility,' said Hope.

'I'm going to destroy him,' said Bob, almost vaguely, as he stared at the writhing flames reflected in his glass of whisky, like a burning forest on the shores of a tannic lake.

'It must be a tough time to be running General Power,' said Jim.

'It's a hell of a tough time,' said Bob, animated by a sudden rush of compassion. 'We've got "ethical funds" disinvesting from the extraction industry. It's so damned fashionable, even the Rockefellers are suing Exxon with money that they only have because their great-granddaddy created the parent company. We should slap a RICO suit on them.'

'Isn't that for organised crime?' asked Francis.

'Well, shaking down the greatest corporations in the country is an organised crime.'

'Oh, for God's sake,' said Hope. 'You can't use the law to get immunity from the law.'

'Well,' said Bob, knocking back his drink, 'actually, we can.'

'Exxon's own scientists warned them they were wrecking the planet back in the seventies,' said Hope. 'The organised crime is the cover-up.'

'Nobody is wrecking the planet,' said Bob, exasperated by

the need to clear up that fallacy yet again. 'Carbon is food for plants. It's a natural fertiliser. If you look at the facts scientifically, we've had a carbon deficit for thousands of years and now we're just beginning to close that gap. We've got some hungry trees out there. From their point of view, this is Thanksgiving.'

'You think they have a point of view?' said Hope. 'I didn't know there was a shaman hidden inside the oilman. Break out the ayahuasca and we can have a truth and reconciliation ceremony.'

'Bobby has always loved trees,' said Sheryl Forbes-Gonzales, feeling it was high time to deploy her legendary diplomatic skills. 'He drove his parents crazy pretending to be Tarzan when he was a kid. We have neighbouring plantations in South Carolina – Jim's been there, duck shooting, so he knows that we both love trees personally.'

Bob Glazer let loose a feeble impersonation of Tarzan's signature cry as he set off on his liana swing through the zoological hullabaloo of a Hollywood studio.

Sheryl's white suit shook with mirth; she would never be able to get enough of Bobby's sense of humour until she replaced him as CEO.

'Jim has shown us some of the work you've been doing here with the three ranches,' she said to Francis, awestruck. 'It would be an honour if you came to Plum Grove and helped turn it into a biodiversity hotspot. We could team up on that, couldn't we, Bobby?'

'The more game the better,' said Glazer, stubbornly unsentimental.

'He loves animals,' Sheryl whispered, blowing Glazer's tough cover. 'We could probably get Bo to join in – she's another neighbour.'

'If Bo had her way, we'd have herds of elephants charging down the Charleston freeway,' said Glazer.

'The three properties form a pretty sizeable block of land,' said Sheryl, 'but everyone knows that Bobby's place, White Plains, is the finest plantation in South Carolina.'

'Well, that's what the realtors like to say,' Glazer admitted, as if boasting were something he couldn't manage all on his own.

'Golly, Jim,' said Hope, yawning theatrically and resting her hand on his forearm. 'We had dinner last night in Quito with the local guys from *Not on Our Watch* and I think we'd better head home while I can still drive. We came straight from the airport, and I have a guest back at the house I haven't even said hello to yet. Are you coming, Francis?'

'Oh. Sure. Yup,' said Francis, rubbing his eyes, blowing out his cheeks and hoisting himself out of his chair. 'Sorry, Jim, I didn't get any sleep on the plane. Let's stay in touch about the wilding,' he said to Sheryl, as she gave his jet-lagged back a sympathetic but carefully calibrated rub. It was Bob Glazer, after all, not her, who would soon be deposed on a charge of sexual harassment.

'Greenwashing sons of bitches,' said Hope.

'Sure,' said Francis, 'but it's still a chunk of land and we might as well use it.'

Sheryl's proposal would turn out to be the first of many wilding propositions that came Francis's way through his frequent contacts with the rich patrons and, in some cases, the corporate opponents of *Not on Our Watch*. He continued to take a pragmatic view of these opportunities, while Hope continued to enjoy the moral luxury of pouring scorn on offers that came from the enemy camp without preventing him from accepting and dealing with the consequences of its problematic invitations.

The pandemic had stopped Francis from returning to Ecuador, but even after four years and all the drone footage, he could remember how strange it had felt to be visiting an ecological trauma in a region he had previously associated with two of his scientific heroes, Alexander von Humboldt and

Charles Darwin. In 1802 Humboldt had climbed Chimborazo, the volcano only a hundred miles south of Quito which Francis had seen from the plane. At the time of Humboldt's ascent, it was thought to be the highest mountain on Earth and although it had lost that distinction to Mount Everest, its position on the bulge of the equator meant that it remained the world's highest point relative to the Earth's centre, if not to sea level. Humboldt reached over nineteen thousand feet, higher than any European had yet climbed, but found himself separated from the summit by an uncrossable crevasse. Nevertheless, it was on those icy slopes, abandoned by his porters at the snowline and breathing perilously thin air, that he realised 'in a single glance' that 'Nature is a living whole and not a dead aggregate'. Collecting samples for curiosity and classification was replaced in his mind by a preoccupation with the idea that individual phenomena were only 'important in their relation to the whole'. He saw the resemblance of vegetation at the same altitudes across continents; he understood keystone species before they had been given that name; he even made the connection between colonialism and environmental degradation when he recorded the effects of deforestation and cash crops, and the overexploitation of the bark of the chinchona tree, harvested for its anti-malarial quinine. Simon Bolivar, after his great war of independence from the Spanish, planted a million trees in honour of his friend Humboldt, 'For the protection and wise use of the National Forests of Columbia.' Humboldt's emphasis on the 'relation to the whole' made him an ecologist, rather than just an explorer, geographer, biologist, geologist or political historian, although he was all those things as well. Francis was drawn to his drive towards a unity of knowledge, which included poetry and philosophy and imagination in the pursuit of science, not just specimens and measurements. Although much celebrated in his day, Humboldt had been largely forgotten in the English-speaking world, as science became more and more specialised, but he now seemed urgently contemporary, especially in the *Oriente*, where the science of dead aggregates had joined forces with the oil and mining industries to reduce the world to numbers, commodities and diseases. As Paul J. Getty had pointed out, 'The meek shall inherit the earth, but not its mineral rights.'

Charles Darwin, during the voyage of the *Beagle*, was constantly reading Humboldt's *Personal Narrative of Travels to the Equinoctial Regions of the New Continent* and had been deeply inspired by his predecessor's descriptions of South America and his holistic approach to science. He stopped in the Galapagos in 1835, three years after they had been annexed by the new Republic of Ecuador. There, he collected the samples, including the distinct species of finches from the various islands, which would later form a key part of his theory of evolution. Overwhelmed by seasickness and homesickness on his five-year voyage, he didn't realise the full significance of his discoveries at the time. Francis liked the idea of this gradual revelation; cases of evidence from around the world, strapped in the hold, waiting for a theory to bring out their deeper meaning. It was not only a slow-motion epiphany, but an expanding one: if evolution was taken seriously, it was itself evolving. Just as the wilding to which he was devoting his life could not, by definition, be tamed by a fixed outcome, evolution would lose its meaning if it could not move into new fields and adapt to new intellectual pressures.

When Hope and Francis arrived at Yab-Yum from Jim's dinner party, Carmen Van Dyke was already there to greet them. She ran into the hall, like a ballerina running onstage, her back arched, her head held high, taking light, rapid, equal steps, her little cries of joy subsiding as she wrapped her arms around Hope and rested her head sideways on her shoulder with a deep sigh.

'You're home!' said Carmen.

'Hi, baby,' said Hope. 'This is Francis.'

'Hi, Francis,' said Carmen, opening her eyes, but not releasing Hope from her embrace. 'She's back.'

'Yes,' said Francis, ambushed by jealousy. After mature consideration, he and Hope had decided in Ecuador that they simply had to set aside whatever attraction they felt for each other, given Francis's loyalty to Olivia and to his newborn son, not to mention the sorrows of intercontinental affairs, in which 'I miss you' replaces 'I love you' as the central term of endearment. They behaved with such discipline, and Hope, to his surprise, had done nothing to wear down his resistance, even when they had been put in the same room in the Cofan village. They hadn't wanted to seem ungrateful when they were shown into a small wooden building with a mosquito net suspended over a mattress covered with a brightly embroidered bedspread. Their hosts clearly assumed that they would be spending the night together, and they did, clothed, with their backs to each other. They had such a long history of thinking it was a bad idea to get together, but that didn't prevent Francis from lying awake feeling mugged by the damp heat of the equatorial night; searching for tears in the mosquito net that might allow yellow fever, dengue, malaria or Zika to invade their bloodstreams; listening to the hum of life in the forest and trying to make out individual notes; hearing the occasional cough or murmur from another building and wondering what a racket he and Hope would have made if they hadn't followed their wise, wise policy of restraint. Hope would, of course, have been wonderful in bed, so wonderful that Francis couldn't help feeling that he might have been superfluous. Better to let her be wonderful all on her own. Along with that night of heroic chastity, the pollution, the piranhas, the caiman and the danger of attracting unwanted excitement discouraged Hope from peeling all her clothes off and swimming naked in the rivers, but she was back home now, with Carmen tugging her towards the pool. Francis could see the outline of Carmen's nipples through her white T-shirt and knew that her gold leather miniskirt was only a button away from falling to her ankles, but it was the thought of Hope gliding through the steaming waters of the pool that made him determined to go straight to bed.

'I am so, so tired,' said Hope.

'Oh, come on,' said Carmen, taking both Hope's hands and walking backwards through the drawing room. 'It'll help you relax and sleep better.'

'Are you joining us?' Hope asked him.

'No, no, I'm, um, well, shattered, really shattered,' said Francis.

He threw himself onto the bed in his guest room, a little aggrieved (he was only human) to be missing out on the no doubt virtuoso threesome that Hope and Carmen would have laid on if they had all been together. What he was really missing, though, was Olivia and Noah and home. He felt that sudden but unmistakable sense that he had been away long enough. He was supposed to spend five days at Yab-Yum, but he now felt that his stay would be too long, especially with the balletic Carmen flitting from room to room in search of Hope. He wouldn't need much time to check out the wilding project, which was only four years old, and in any case had some local supervision. He took out his computer and looked for earlier flights, but before booking one felt that he should have a word with Hope. He hesitated to go to the pool but decided to approach cautiously and retreat if there were any danger of entanglement. They might, after all, just be swimming. Anything was possible.

The sliding doors of the drawing room were open, and he was able to slip onto the terrace silently. He could hear conversation. That was a good sign.

'So, what have you been up to while I was away?' he heard Hope asking.

'Oh, the usual,' said Carmen, 'me, myself and I.'

'All three of you? I hope it wasn't too crowded.'

'We get on really well,' said Carmen. 'We did a lot of yoga and thought a lot about all the sweet things we'd do when you got back. How about you? Did you guys connect in Ecuador?'

'No, no. Francis has a newborn kid . . . It's complicated.'

'The One That Got Away!' said Carmen.

'We kinda moved away from each other,' said Hope. 'It was elegant and a little sad, I guess. I still really like him.'

'Ah-ha,' said Carmen. 'Well, it makes a change from having to throw out all the people who get addicted to you.'

There was a long silence after this remark that made Francis step quietly back through the sliding doors, feeling that he had not chosen the ideal moment to present Hope with his revised travel plans. He told her at breakfast the next day and she seemed as relaxed about them as she seemed about everything.

He had wanted to get back to Noah and Olivia, as he wanted to get back to them now, and somehow the memory of that first big return enhanced his desire to return home this evening after his short familiar walk. He could see the lights in Willow Cottage at the end of the darkening path and he moved towards them with the eagerness of someone who has been too far away for too long.

12

Good old Helio, true to his word, had asked Sebastian over to dinner at his flat, which was also his studio. Helio wasn't only a psycho nurse; he was a light artist. Sebastian had never been in a flat like that before. It used to be a warehouse back in the day. The room was very deep, with a big window at the far end so you could look out on the canal. There were ducks quacking and paddling about, as happy as ducks in a canal, and people jogging along the footpath, as happy as people jogging along a footpath, improving their cardiovascular health. The whole room was undivided, except for the walls around the bathroom. There was a mattress on the floor in the corner, at the canal end, opposite the bathroom, and then, towards the middle, a kitchen and a dining table Helio had picked up in a Brick Lane market for twenty quid, and three old armchairs arranged around a computer. The rest of the room, more than half the space, was a studio, with a converted stove for bending glass, and several gas cylinders, and multi-socket plugs, and different types of glass, coated with chemicals. The electrified gases produced colours of their own, but you could add to the variety by modifying the inside of the tubes. It turned out that making art was a very scientific process, especially light art, which was not only scientific, but often linguistic as well. Seb hadn't thought about art that much, but when he did, he thought about saints full of arrows, or vases full of flowers, or rooms full of people, or whatever. It was all about the objects you were looking at – various kinds of portraits really, even if it was a portrait of crows in a field, but this art was different because instead of making art representing light with paint, you were making art representing ideas with light. Instead of squishing oily colours out of metal tubes, you were radiating airy colours out of glass tubes. It was a lighter light. One of Helio's pieces was called *NOBLE* – the word NOBLE in white letters – because apparently there had been a very famous piece called *NEON* in white letters, back in the day when light art was finding its feet, but Helio said that *NEON* didn't actually use neon gas, so although it appeared to be self-referential, it wasn't, scientifically speaking, because electrified neon naturally glowed red. He had written NOBLE because all the gases used in light art belonged to the family of noble gases, but also because it was practically impossible to find a person who behaved in a noble way, so it was really a lot to ask of a gas. Or perhaps the only truly noble thing in the world was this family of gases. It was a sort of joke, but not the sort that made you laugh out loud.

'It's crazy, man,' said Helio, 'we project a class system onto the Periodic Table. It's an accident of birth to be a noble gas, an undeserved privilege. It's like the Lou Reed song, right? "Men of good fortune, very often can't do a thing": noble gases don't bond with the lesser elements, the atoms don't even bond with each other, but then, like Lou goes on to say, those men can destroy whole countries – so we can use the noble gases to make protests, right?'

Helio switched on a piece which had DERAEPPASID written in huge red letters.

'Now that, my friend, *is* neon,' he said.

'It's "disappeared" written backwards,' said Seb, who was good at spotting patterns.

'That's right!' said Helio, and then added to his girlfriend, Isabella, 'The man got it in one.'

DERAEPPASID, it turned out, was written in the same script as a famous sign for Cinzano from the olden days when neon was used for advertising rather than art. The point was that in Helio's country, Brazil, there had been a dictatorship which 'disappeared' its enemies, meaning that it killed them, but nobody ever got to see the bodies. Now Helio was making the Disappeared conspicuous, but only in the form of a word. Then it got a bit complicated. Helio said that a word was not the same as the thing it stood for, so he was making the absence of the bodies even stronger. He was advertising the disappearance, which was a topsy-turvy idea, and that's why he'd written it backwards. And then Helio had talked about signifilers and signifinders, or whatever, and to be honest, Sebastian had got a bit lost at that point, but the red glow was so intense that he just stared at it in wonder.

'The light is shining on us as well,' he said.

'That's right,' said Helio, clapping his hands. 'If the light didn't shine on us, we'd disappear!'

'Yeah, right,' said Seb, 'but we'd still have our bodies.'

'The Disappeared still had their bodies, but we couldn't see them,' said Helio. 'He's good, yeah?' said Helio to Isabella, pointing at Sebastian.

And then they'd had dinner. Isabella had made a vegetable feast because she didn't think it was fair to kill animals. Cutting up vegetables was all right, everybody was clear about that, peeling them, frying them, boiling them. Everyone except Sebastian, that is, who started thinking about the plant's point of view. Sometimes he didn't know where to draw the line when it came to ideas like cruelty or having a point of view. He could imagine that even a mountain didn't want to be blown up for its stone, or have its veins gouged out for silver. Isabella was very gentle and friendly, and so Sebastian had fallen in love with her, as he did with everyone who was kind to him.

It turned out that Helio was very political and that he considered himself 'a child of the military dictatorship' because his parents had conceived him in 1985, which was the last year of its twenty-one-year rule. He was also very het up about President Bolsonaro, who was nostalgic about the dictatorship, but didn't think it had gone far enough. 'Their biggest mistake was to torture and not to kill,' he had said, although they had done plenty of killing, and disappearing, but not enough to meet his exorbitant standards. Sebastian already had President B down as a total wanker, with his love of torture and killing and the way he had gutted all the environmental safeguards in the good old Amazon, a big source of oxygen, one of the ignoble gases that did the hard work of keeping life going, but for some reason when he heard that President B had four sons in a row, and then had a daughter in what he called 'a moment of weakness', Seb had become even more upset. He couldn't help thinking about that poor little girl whose father gave interviews saying cruel things like that about his own daughter. How did it feel, having a dad who publicly humiliated you? Of course, Helio was already on to it and had done a piece about it, which he showed Seb on his computer. It was a light-sculpture version of a famous painting called *The Birth of Venus*, which Seb had seen posters of, with a girl standing on a giant shell among the waves, and she was so beautiful and radiant, but then as a sort of joke-not-joke, Helio had renamed it *A Moment of Weakness*, to teach President B a lesson.

After dinner, just when Seb was starting to think that all Helio's work was in the joke-not-joke, play-on-words, art-about-art game, and just when he was beginning to get a feel for that sort of thing, and secretly thinking that at least with a painting of a chair you didn't need an explanation, you just thought, It's a good old chair, Helio had said to Isabella, 'Shall we go for a walk?' and she had smiled and said, '*Con certeza. Vamos.*'

And then Helio picked up a remote control and lowered the blinds on all the windows. The walls and ceiling were already white, and now, with the blinds down, every surface was white. Helio typed something onto his computer and all at once the entire room turned into a lush, towering forest, with the canopy stretching into the ceiling and trunks the size of trucks growing out of the floor, and a red and yellow tropical bird in curving flight vanishing behind a tree with howler monkeys sitting in the branches.

'It's too much,' said Sebastian, laughing nervously.

'Come,' said Isabella, taking his hand and helping him get out of the armchair.

There was a faint path through the forest, hardly different from the rest of the ground, a sinuous line among the trees that had an obscure history of being used by the animals that were walking that way, and as Isabella moved very slowly along it, almost pretending to walk, with Sebastian following her and Helio behind him, the forest shifted and changed, inviting them deeper into itself, with mushrooms bursting out of the leaf litter, and a brilliant, spiny caterpillar undulating along a giant, waxy leaf. Although they continued at a snail's pace, the forest enveloped them, like a parent reaching out to catch and embrace a returning child.

The entangled foliage parted mellifluously until they came to a clearing. Isabella held back her hand and they paused. Above them, through the breached canopy, they could see the inky, roiling sky shuddering with lightning. A jaguar padded to the opposite edge of the clearing with the unhurried ferocity of a feline predator that only pounces at the end of its hunt. It paused and from the black sky a flash of lightning streaked into the middle of the open ground. Rain pelted down, splashing onto the leaves and branches overhead and raining a second time, so loudly that Sebastian had trouble believing he was still dry and involuntarily held up his hand to protect himself from the exploding tropical water drops. After about half a minute, the rain stopped, the forest disappeared, and the lights went back on.

'It's called *The Jaguar Brings Down Fire from Heaven*,' said Helio.

Sebastian was too stunned to speak. The space was not just depleted but wiped out. It wasn't like the end of a favourite track, it was a full bereavement, a loss of something much more convincing than the poor bare room he was back in, as if he had been swimming among many-headed, ever-changing waves and suddenly they had disappeared and left him stranded on an endless beach, a silent desert where the sea used to sing and play.

'The jaguar is the Prometheus of the Amazon,' said Helio. 'It brought us fire from the otherworld and taught the human race to hunt with tools, and the punishment for this master of civilisation . . .'

'Can we go back?' asked Sebastian.

'You see – he loves it,' said Isabella.

And so, they had walked through the forest again and again. The scene never changed but each time it brought Sebastian a bright and bruising confusion, which disturbed him but made him want more. After the third time, Helio said that enough was enough, which you couldn't really argue with – once you knew what enough was.

The trouble for Sebastian was that he hadn't had enough, and even now, as he lay on the narrow bed of his room in Heron House, looking at the faint brown stain around the ceiling light, as he so often had, wondering what a water mark was doing so close to the electric wires, he was longing for the whole room to be disappeared and replaced by *The Jaguar Brings Down Fire from Heaven*.

13

Strangely enough, it was Martin rather than Francis who seemed thrown by Olivia's decision to spend an extra night in London. His response included an almost imperceptible hesitation she only picked up because it was so untypical of him to be anything but spontaneously warm and welcoming. Francis, by contrast, encouraged her to accept Sam's invitation to go to Sadler's Wells that evening. Olivia had last been there with Francis to see a performance of *The Statement*, choreographed by Crystal Pite, who was collaborating on one of the pieces being performed that evening. *The Statement* had remained a reference point for them, partly because it had been one of the last things they had seen before live performance was shut down by the pandemic, but mainly because of the thrilling way in which the voiceover, describing an opaque corporate crisis with the spins and twists of plausible deniability, was turned into the spins and twists of whiplash dance. Euphemisms became menaces and clichés lies as four executives evaded and intimidated each other around and across a boardroom table. Despite its curved edges, designed for reconciliation and fluidity, it came to seem more like a spear for 'Upstairs' to stab 'This Department' in the back and extract the exonerating statement the piece was named after. She knew that Francis had bought a download of the performance and would sometimes watch it when he felt disgusted by the implausible denials of companies like General Power. Although Olivia as a rule wasn't in the market for the idea that things were meant to be, she ended up feeling exactly that way about her return to Sadler's to see the same brilliant choreographer and dance company.

Sam warned her that the main piece might be 'a bit of a busman's holiday' since it was called *Figures in Extinction*, but Olivia found that the opposite was true. Perhaps because some form of extinction was the dominant topic of conversation in the Silverline offices, its transformation into music and dance was even more of a holiday for her than it might have been for someone who had managed to spend a whole day without considering the subject at all. The jerky figure of a besuited climate-change denier took on a similar role to the voiceover in *The Statement*, but his absurd contortions and his libertarian and 'science hoax' rhetoric were not the central theme. He was a satirical counterpoint to the elegiac celebration of hunted animals, melted glaciers, forgotten forget-me-nots, dehydrated inland seas and vanished trees. His extinction was the only one the audience longed for, but it would come too late to save the golden toad and the white rhino and the school of hand fish shimmering in a band of light to the right of the stage. The more ingeniously a species was represented, the more crushed Olivia felt by the fact that it no longer existed. And yet for a moment there was a pure joy in seeing a flock of passenger pigeons brought back to mimetic life, and in watching the immense curving horns of a Pyrenean ibex make a parenthesis for the audience to embrace the afterthought of its regret. A kneeling dancer strained his muscles to hold the horns on his extended arms, his head bowed as if to ask forgiveness for replacing the creature to whom they rightfully belonged.

Olivia cried, exhausted by the sixth extinction, but exhilarated by the beauty being remade in other forms. She thought of King Lear carrying Cordelia in his arms and saying, 'She's dead as earth', and then wavering between despair and delusion until he died imagining he was seeing her lips move. The comparison with earth was sometimes thought to be a miniature of that wavering mentality, pointing to the supposedly inanimate ground out of which graves are dug but evoking at the same time the fertile soil from which life springs. How long would 'earth' continue to offer that ambiguity as less and less life sprang from it – not to mention its shrinking capacity for fresh graves. For a moment she pictured humanity as a mad old king, the unruly ruler of the Earth, staggering onstage with his dead child in his arms, vacillating between a fake 'hoax' and a faint hope. She was pleased to have finished her programme about asteroids before embarking on the human threats to the biosphere. The last mass extinction was caused by an asteroid hurtling into the Yucatán Peninsula, as any young dinosaur expert could tell you several times a day. Luckily, human intelligence was taking control of the minuscule threat of accidental collisions by devising collisions of its own, but even NASA's ability to deflect asteroid Dimorphos by crashing a spacecraft into it, was a symptom of advances much more likely to cause extinction than the asteroids themselves: the faith that technology would produce solutions to everything, including the problems created by technology, the continued pursuit of the dominance of nature, the virile cult of rocket launches that punch holes in the stratosphere and rain down emissions on the ozone layer, the implicit abandonment of the home planet for the moon shot of colonising fantastically hostile extra-terrestrial environments, the extraction and exhaustion of rare Earth elements; the list went on. Even the history of rocket science originated in the Luftwaffe's search for more ingenious ways to terrorise and lay waste to London in the closing years of the Second World War. Although they were designed by the same man, the V1 rockets that devastated London preceded the Apollo rockets that landed a man on the moon, and the first atom bomb preceded the first nuclear power station. The precedence wasn't only in time but in number: there were over twelve thousand nuclear warheads in the world and under five hundred nuclear power stations; there were hundreds of thousands of missiles and only a handful of spacecraft. Like family fortunes that turn overdoses into art galleries and finance peace prizes with dynamite profits, certain branches of science struggled to establish their sunny side, for example, by offering the holiday of a lifetime spent briefly orbiting the Earth for fifty million dollars (or for the budget-conscious, fifteen minutes of suborbital flight for half a million dollars); or by explaining how the energy that had boiled Bikini Atoll, harnessed by the right reactor, was the same energy that boiled the water in your kettle.

'That was a wonderful way to have our hearts broken,' said Sam.

'Or mended,' said Olivia. 'Thanks so much for bringing me.'

They hugged quickly as the standing ovation died down and before the practicalities of getting to dinner eclipsed the immediate impact of the performance.

'I love it when something makes you think of everything,' said Sam, as they walked to Moro through the wet streets. 'Do you know what I mean?'

'Yes,' said Olivia, 'but it can only do that by being about one thing and going into it deeply.'

'Exactly, and then it expands underground, like a root system,' said Sam. 'Here we are!'

Once they were at their table in the teeming restaurant, Sam ordered a bottle of Rioja.

'My treat,' she said.

'But you got the tickets,' said Olivia, wondering vaguely if she was being seduced.

'I know, but it's been such fun working with you, I wanted to thank you. Anyway, we've got to celebrate being halfway through the *Apocalypse* series. It's no small thing to have nukes and asteroids and overpopulation in the bag.'

'If only we could get them into one bag, they would sort of cancel each other out,' said Olivia, looking up from the menu.

'The trouble is we'd be in the bag as well,' said Sam. 'You may have thought it was a strange choice of show . . .'

'No, on the contrary, I loved it. I don't want to escape, I want to, if such a word existed, *inscape*.'

'It does exist!' said Sam. 'It was invented by Gerald Manley Hopkins to mean something like the individual form of something, its unique design, that kind of thing, but I think it should be used more generally in the spirit of going deeper to get free: the-way-down-is-the-way-out.'

'It's the only way out,' said Olivia, 'even if you have a helicopter waiting for you in the prison yard.'

'Always helpful in a jail break,' said Sam.

'Even then,' said Olivia, 'you would have to dig your way into the prison yard.'

'Or lower yourself down on some knotted sheets,' said Sam. 'We're sounding like a couple of hardened convicts.'

'Everyone has been trapped somewhere, but some people more than others,' said Olivia, suddenly thinking of Sebastian and feeling that it was time to break her silence and get his number from Karen. She was quite surprised at herself for having punished Karen for so long. It felt needlessly cruel but at the same time forced her to recognise the reservoir of resentment she felt towards their Bio Mum, as Sebastian called her.

'One of the most depressing things about the current batch of super-rich is that they seem fully committed to escaping, not just in the local sense of wanting to buy New Zealand and turn it into a billionaire's country club,' said Sam, 'but in wanting to leave our troubled planet behind altogether and piss off to Mars or swap Europe for Europa.'

'It's funny you should say that!' said Olivia. 'At the end of the performance I was thinking about rockets and leaving the home planet behind, not especially about the super-rich, admittedly . . .'

'Don't spoil it,' said Sam, 'we're having a One Mind experience.'

'Strange unexplained phenomena,' said Olivia.

'The Jamón Ibérico,' said the waitress, putting down a plate of dark gleaming ham between the two women.

'Her timing made it sound like the Jamon was the explanation we were looking for,' said Sam, 'the fibre-optic cable of telepathy.'

'Well, it's no worse than some of the other theories of consciousness rattling around,' said Olivia. 'The "Metaverse" is made to sound like a dimension we want to escape to on our rocket phones, whereas in fact it's what we're all desperate to escape *from*.'

'To the Verse,' said Sam, 'where your mind is no longer the stale bread being pecked at by a swarm of digital pigeons each time you go online.'

'Those sharp beaks and clockwork heads and filthy feathers. I was going to check up on Noah, but now you've put me right off,' said Olivia, dropping her phone back in her bag. 'So much of my anxiety about Noah is generated by the fact that I *can* check up on him. My parents just had to assume that I was okay a lot of the time; it must have been so relaxing. Now I feel guilty if I don't take my phone into the shower.'

Some Vegetable Mezze joined the Jamón on the table.

'Our concept is sharing,' lisped Sam, 'as a waiter once said to me in a restaurant I never went back to. The food was delicious, but I couldn't get past the "concept". I can just about put up with conceptual art – if I'm caught in a thunderstorm and there's a warm gallery across the street – but conceptual food is out of the question.'

'They should have asked you if you had any word allergies.'

'He would have run out of notepad before he took my order,' said Sam. 'I'll tell you another phrase that was weighing on my mind when I bought the tickets for tonight. "Topical trash": it's a typically haughty label Nabokov liked to use to dismiss a certain kind of fiction.'

'Well, trash can't be good,' said Olivia, 'but topical needn't be trash. Did you think that extinction was a bit too trendy?'

'I think I was nervous that you might not like the evening,' said Sam, 'and the inner disapproval took the form of "topical trash" and a "busman's holiday".'

'It may be topical, but I don't think extinction can be seen as a passing fad,' said Olivia.

'It could be seen as the ultimate passing fad,' said Sam.

'It's going to generate lots of fossils,' said Olivia, 'and I can't think of anything less topical than a fossil.'

'The Big Bang.'

'Initial Conditions,' Olivia overtrumped her.

'The Eternal Return.'

'Hang on; that's completely evidence-free.'

'Maybe, but we don't know what Initial Conditions were either.'

'Okay,' said Olivia, 'so, the Big Bang wins, but fossils are still seriously non-topical.'

'Well, I needn't have worried then,' said Sam with a sigh of relief.

'To be honest,' said Olivia, refilling both their glasses, 'I think I came up with this *Apocalypse* series because I was depressed. I was lured from Oxford where I had a research fellowship, to work for *Digitas*, but when I came back from maternity leave it had been sold. I got a golden parachute, but I would have preferred a smooth flight. I was left jobless in the middle of the countryside with a very young child during the pandemic, watching my husband go off to work every morning for an NGO started by a very rich, sexy, polyamorist philanthropist who he'd obviously fancied at some point. So, I was lonely, resentful towards Hunter for selling *Digitas*, jealous of Hope, envious of Francis, and creatively sterile.'

'That would do it,' said Sam. 'It must have been horrible, but in fact you weren't being sterile because you were beginning to imagine this series. The iconography of Melancholy is a stooped figure with its head in its hand looking downwards. It's a time for reflection, not a time for action, but now you can act on the reflections.'

'The absurd thing,' said Olivia, 'is that working on the end of the world has put me in such a good frame of mind I could pitch a series about Shirley Temple.'

'Slow down!' said Sam. 'There must be a middle way.'

The evening unfolded delightfully. They shared each other's main courses without having to put their choices in a conceptual framework. They drank their wine and talked about Silverline office politics; the interviewees on their wish list and the ones they had already secured. Any impression Olivia had that she was being seduced was dispelled by an update on Sam's current romantic life: she had a married man ('at least he can't propose'), a younger woman ('strictly non-Platonic . . . I kiss her the moment she comes through the door to keep the conversation to a minimum') and another woman whose name she couldn't reveal because she was a famous actress who chose to keep her sexuality hidden from the world in case it lost her a part in a Jane Austen drama, a romcom or a production of *Antony and Cleopatra*. Predictably, once Olivia was sure that Sam had no romantic interest in her, she wished the situation hadn't been quite so clear. She might have fought off any advances but welcomed an atmosphere of desire and special affection. They were two of the last customers to leave the restaurant, stepping out onto a subdued, semi-pedestrianised Exmouth Market, elated by the success of their first dinner together. Olivia saw that her Uber was waiting around the corner and Sam had to fetch her bike, which was chained to some railings halfway between the restaurant and the theatre, and so the two friends hugged each other, and Olivia thanked Sam several times before they managed to walk in opposite directions and start their journeys home. In the car, Olivia looked hastily at her messages, troubled by the image of the digital pigeons pecking at her attention, her location, her habits and her searches. She switched to airplane mode the moment she had thanked Francis for his reassuring message and thanked Sam for her generosity.

She was someone who always woke before it was time to get up, but the next morning she slept too late to catch her intended train. It was of no great importance, if she warned Francis, and he didn't waste his time meeting the wrong train. Downstairs, she caught her parents at the end of breakfast, about to set off to their polar offices, one in the basement and one on the top floor.

'Oh, you're still here,' said Martin. 'We thought you'd already left and that we'd missed you.'

'I was going to go early, but I overslept.'

'You never oversleep,' said Lizzie.

'I know,' said Olivia.

'Did you have a very relaxing evening?'

'Yes, it was lovely. That might explain it. Is it a sign of improving mental health?'

'Not if you miss an urgent appointment,' said Martin.

'Well, I didn't.'

'In that case, yes,' said Lizzie.

'So, are you catching the next one?' said Martin.

'Yes,' said Olivia. 'You seem . . .'

'No, no, just wanted to say goodbye,' said Martin, coming over to kiss her. 'Love to everyone and see you next week,' he said, opening the basement door and heading down for a preparatory ten minutes before his first patient.

'Do you want some toast or something?' said Lizzie.

'No thanks, I'd better go, or I'll miss the next train as well,' said Olivia.

Approaching Belsize Park Underground, Olivia saw Sebastian emerge from the entrance on the other side of Haverstock Hill. She had no time to stop, but she marvelled at the coincidence. She had been intending to write to Karen today and ask her for his number; now, if she'd had time, she could have asked him herself.

14

Hunter had been up since five in the morning, as usual, but instead of working on his investments and replying to his emails, he was trying to figure out whether it would be possible to create the ambitious installation he had half-dreamt and half-engineered during one of those patches of shallow sleep that sometimes took pity on his insomnia. He had imagined a tunnelled walkway rising gently through the centre of the highest hill on his property. On the ocean side there would be three apertures visible through tunnels of their own. The first would show a view of the Pacific; the second would be equally divided between sea and sky, and the third would open to the sky alone. How steeply would the path ascend? Could the openings be at a consistent right angle to the walkway, like a giant E, embedded in the hill, or would the first side tunnel have to point down, the second across and the third upwards, like a K with an additional horizontal bar in the middle? Should the third window in fact be the culmination of the path, emerging at the top of the hill? Or should the path simply stop when the third opening was displaying pure sky without it needing to be directly overhead? How would the tunnels be lit and how would the internal lighting affect the quality of the experience? Hunter had to go down to his study and get some paper and pencils, a ruler and a protractor.

He knew that he was being a hopeless, wannabee, kindergarten James Turrell, but he couldn't help it. He was fascinated by the great man's work, and it had started to sink into his dreams. A few years ago, he had finally managed to get a Skyspace on his land. Built of redwood, it stood on stilts raised among the trees, ten minutes from the house. A long external ramp led up to the entrance of a chamber with a rectangular opening in the middle of the ceiling. The simple fact of framing the sky intensified its colour. Interior lighting further modified its appearance, especially at dawn and dusk when the outside light was going through its strongest transitions. A bench, on which he and Lucy liked to sit or lie, ran around the room. The longer he stayed there, looking at the shifting colours through the opening, the more he realised that within the light-filled space that Turrell had designed, he was co-creating what he was seeing. For instance, it was obvious that the sky was engendered by light and that when the light disappeared the sky disappeared as well; so obvious that he had never really appreciated it until he lay on the bench at dusk one evening and watched the daylight fade. The protective blue dome of the sky gradually darkened and dissolved until he found himself looking into the black hollow of the star-encrusted universe. The Skyspace had become a no-Skyspace, and all that was required was for him to look through the same opening and let himself have the experience of 'wordless thought' that Turrell set out to offer.

Through the arrowhead of thick glass that formed the jagged modern edge of his panelled, red-leather study Hunter could see the dawn light begin to tinge the air. He knew that Lucy would probably be going to the Skyspace as she did most mornings. She didn't treat her visits as a formal meditation, but she knew that Turrell had been raised among Quakers and that the principal practice in their meetings was to sit in silence contemplating the light. Although the Quakers regarded art as a frivolity, Turrell's art had done more to disseminate the contemplation of light than any Quaker to date, and yet the contemplation of light in his work was only a prelude to the contemplation of seeing. Hunter had gone to Houghton Hall in Norfolk to visit *St Elmo's Breath*, an installation housed in a building which had previously contained the old water tank that supplied the house. After closing the door behind him, he felt his way down the dark corridor that led to a bench in a black room. He sat in total darkness for several minutes, wondering if minimalism could be taken any further, and then, slowly, slowly, the black wall in front of him started to emit a faint pink glow, like a private dawn, until gradually the entire wall was suffused with light. It had been there all along, but the darkness of the room was needed so that the cones in his pupils could expand enough to see what was before his eyes. Nothing had changed in the room; it was his seeing that had changed and by changing had transformed darkness into light. The light was of course 'out there' but its appearance depended on his continued presence in the room. Once he had started to see the hint of radiance at the base of the wall, he experienced a kind of yearning; reaching out to the light, as he might to an extended hand that was helping him to get up after a fall, feeling gratitude for the realisation that in this dark space there was something he could form a relationship with that was both astonishing and calm, and that it was growing stronger because his pupils were opening, not because the light was growing stronger on its own.

These two experiences of Turrell's work had changed Hunter's way of seeing the world. What he had fully appreciated in the old water tank in Norfolk was that there were not just facts of the case for him to look at, but that his looking changed the facts. This was to do with the process of seeing, not to do with 'pathetic fallacy' and the inevitable psychological traffic between an individual human sensibility and its surroundings. That would be going on anyway, of course, but was not the point. He didn't know enough about quantum mechanics to know how his experience of *St Elmo's Breath* related, if at all, to the famous 'observer effect' in which the superposition of two possibilities collapsed into the actual when they were measured or observed, but his experience of a participatory, co-created reality on the gigantic scale of his own body in a dark room certainly made him more sympathetic to the probabilistic and participatory world of subatomic particles he had sometimes read about and struggled to understand. What he became less sympathetic towards was the standard diagram about the nature of vision that he had been brought up on: the line of light hitting an object and then the dotted line of reflected light travelling to the retina: photons delivering information to the eye so that the brain could reconstruct it into a simulacrum of the outside world. For the viewer in the Neurology department, the moon was an electro-chemical occurrence in the visual cortex, while in the Astronomy department across the campus it enjoyed a robust existence as a celestial body with certain properties and characteristics originating a quarter of a million miles away from the dark and lonely cerebral incident generated by looking at it. This was not a war between a subjective, fallible, sentimental, anecdotal world, and a world of cold, hard evidence; it was a war between two forms of cold, hard evidence determined to exclude experience, the only real basis for either of them. Who could integrate these visions of the moon without becoming a lunatic? Were we really trapped in our skulls reading the light mail delivered through the letterbox of our eyes or, if we were in the Psychology department, *misreading* it thanks to the biases and prejudices and expectations unveiled by one cunning experiment after another? Or was vision, as Turrell had claimed, 'very much a feeling sense' with which we 'touch the light', as Hunter felt he had done in Norfolk, when his eyes took part in intensifying the glow that spread across the wall opposite him. Nobody who stroked a dog felt that they were alone in feeling the touch. Hunter also felt that when he touched a flower, the flower was touching him. There was no reason to believe that a raindrop landing on his cheek was experiencing a touch of its own, but there was no reason to deny that the raindrop was organised a certain way as it fell through the air and that it was drastically reorganised by shattering on his skin. Was the mutual relationship that was so clear in the realm of touch also true of vision? Was it in fact the only way to make sense of experience?

The sun would soon be rising and hiding its rival stars behind the blue lid of the sky. He must hurry down to see Lucy while other colours were still at play and before the glassy air was thick with photons. He folded his sketches and put them in his back pocket. He wanted to share a moment with Lucy in Turrell's ingenious space, and he also wanted to share his sketches with her. As a grown-up man, he felt a little fraudulent carrying his doodles of a completely derivative scheme, but he also felt like an excited child who is longing to show his parents his latest picture of a lopsided house with an outsized flower in the front garden, and a spiky sun radiating overhead. All he really wanted her to say was: 'That's beautiful, darling, I can't believe you came up with such a brilliant idea'; after that, she could bust him for bungling piracy, if he insisted on digging a trinocular tunnel system out of the top hill. Maybe he should just make another huge donation to Turrell's great work in progress, the Roden Crater in the Painted Desert of Arizona, an astronomical land art project that dwarfed the Pyramids of Egypt, rather than try to build his own optical barrow in Big Sur.

As he left his study to head for the Skyspace, Hunter saw Lucy descending the staircase, her hand sliding lightly along the banister beside her. She looked beautiful with the Mia Farrow hairstyle she had kept since her chemotherapy. Her hair had grown back light brown, and the new colour somehow suited her iceberg-under-the-water blue eyes even better than the more obvious blonde it had previously been.

'Hi, baby, are you going down to the space?' he asked.

'No, I was there yesterday evening, and I feel like having breakfast. Will you still love me when I don't look like a skeleton?'

'The more of you the better,' said Hunter.

'Within reason,' said Lucy.

'What's reason got to do with it?' said Hunter, resting his hand gently on her back.

They went through into the vast, cool kitchen. Raoul and the team were not yet in action, and although it was a luxury to have so much help, it was another kind of luxury to be alone together, knowing that nothing they said would be overheard and enjoying a moment of assertive competence in a life in which competence was so often delegated. Lucy sliced a papaya and arranged it with some berries on two plates. She also sliced up a mango for Hunter but didn't have any herself as it was too high in fructose for the diet she had been put on by her nutritionist. Hunter whisked some matcha in a bowl and poured the tea into two cups. It was Lucy's one caffeine shot of the day, whereas it was Hunter's first shot in a daily war between stimulation and tiredness, brightness and panic, dullness and cardiac symptoms. He was so impressed by his abstinence from most other drugs these days that he refused to consider the contribution of caffeine to his towering insomnia.

Lucy was leaving for London that evening, two weeks ahead of Hunter. After his visit to Assisi, they had spoken at great length about 'compassion burnout' and she had scheduled a cluster of medical appointments so that they would be over by the time he was back in England. Ash and Olivia and other friends of hers would be around if she wanted anyone to come with her to a scan or a consultation that might include alarming news. She knew that Father Guido had implanted in Hunter an aspiration towards infinitely self-renewing love, but being a realist and knowing that he was not very far advanced on the road to sainthood, she had decided to shield him from the routinely disturbing aspects of her condition, without putting on a show of insouciance and creating a false self for the sake of hanging on to Hunter. He had been almost excessively straightforward with her about his 'compassion burnout' and the trap of his desire to see himself as an honourable and generous man. In his case, financial generosity was cheap; it was the emotional generosity of helping someone else to carry so much suffering and fear that was pushing him to breaking point. When she had received all the possible treatments available to her, and was beginning to recover her strength, Hunter urged her to focus on living her life rather than being hypnotised by the prospect of death. Lucy had said there was nothing she would rather do and had shown great sympathy for the strain her situation put Hunter under, but as the discussion rolled on over several days, she eventually admitted to a more hidden layer of fury at being made to contemplate how difficult it was for other people to be close to something she never had a moment's respite from. They were tourists who could wander in and out of a diagnosis that had her nailed to the wall.

'I don't just have a gun held to my head, I have a gun inside my head,' she said, when he had spent a little too long describing the woes of co-dependency. In the end they had come to an equilibrium, and she was going ahead to London to get her tests out of the way.

Hunter carried the two cups through to a long, slim table, set in a rectangular alcove. He opened the doors that gave on to a terrace that ran the entire length of the ocean-facing side of the house. It was too cool to sit outside, but with the windows open there was an unobstructed view from the table to the horizon. On the three walls around the table were black-and-white seascape photographs by Hiroshi Sugimoto. Each was a study of the meeting of sea and sky. They were taken in different places around the world, under varied light conditions, but in all of them the horizon was the central line crossing the photograph.

Lucy came through with the plates of fruit and the two of them sat down to their frugal but delicious breakfast. Hunter, who couldn't contain himself any longer, took out his sketches and unfolded them on the tabletop, explaining the vision that had come to him in the night.

'Hmm,' said Lucy, 'it looks very intriguing, darling.'

'Thanks,' said Hunter. 'I'd love to ask JT how or whether it would really work, but I feel ashamed that I would be wasting his time. And besides, cultural appropriation is such an issue . . .'

'I think it's called plagiarism when it's two old white guys from the same country,' said Lucy.

'And that's bad too, right?'

'I'm afraid so,' said Lucy, smiling at him tenderly. 'To play devil's advocate for a moment: given how much digging and drilling is involved, couldn't we just sit on the top of the highest hill and look down at the sea, across to the horizon and up at the sky?'

'Sure,' said Hunter, 'but that wouldn't be a work of art – wouldn't be a mirror held up to nature. We can do that any time, but what I want to do is organise the experience so that it becomes more reflective, more deliberate.'

'You love having things organised for you, don't you, darling?' said Lucy.

'As long as they're organised by me first,' said Hunter, holding the back of her hand. 'It's like these Sugimotos. Why put a lot of photographs of horizons around a table from which we can see the "real thing"' through the open doors?'

'I've often wondered,' said Lucy.

'Too much teasing,' said Hunter. 'I've been thinking of my magnum opus all through the night.'

'And it could be great,' said Lucy.

'Anyway, the view and the photos resonate with each other, it's like playing the same note an octave higher.'

'Which is the higher note?' said Lucy. 'Why should the captured past be a higher note than the radiant present? Even if it's organising the experience for you . . .'

'That's a false dichotomy,' said Hunter. 'When you're looking at the photo, that's the radiant present; when you're looking through the window, same thing. The difference is that the photos make us think of the convergence of parallel lines. The horizon is a vanishing line made by our way of seeing. The sea and the sky don't ever meet.'

'But I could think that looking out of the window,' said Lucy.

'You could, but you don't have to . . .'

'Nor do I have to when I look at the photos.'

'Sure,' said Hunter. 'I guess it's to do with levels of encouragement. We *could* think everything that Hamlet thinks, but it really helps to hear him say it. In another way, we could sit on top of the hill and look down, across and up, but it would be a very different experience if we had just emerged from a space that encourages us to make each act more emphatic and reflective.'

'Absolutely,' said Lucy. 'So, let's excavate the "optical barrow". It could be sensational.'

She sounded more compliant than enthusiastic, and Hunter suddenly had an intuition that at some level she saw the excavation as a kind of cranial surgery on the uppermost part of the land, boring into the base and emerging from the crown of the hill, trying to get inside to find out what was really going on. Perhaps that's what he was doing as well – or all on his own. He had dreamt up this scheme during the night, just before she was tactfully leaving for London to avoid putting his compassion under too much strain. Perhaps his land art fantasy was an overwrought compensation for not accompanying her. There was also something troubling about the name. A barrow was a burial mound, a tumulus was a burial mound, a pyramid was a burial mound. Maybe 'barrow' was a bad choice of word.

'Let's not call it the "optical barrow",' he said. 'I can't think what . . . the "Trinoculus" doesn't sound quite right either.'

'That sounds like one of Noah's dinosaurs, one that went extinct before the rest. "Look, Lucy,"' she said, impersonating Noah's voice, '"it's a Trinoculus giganticus."'

'Okay,' said Hunter, 'maybe we'll just chuck a few beanbags on the brow of the hill. It would save a lot of trouble.'

'That could work,' said Lucy, smiling.

15

Olivia had already told Martin about the strange moment when she was about to cross Haverstock Hill as Sebastian emerged from the Underground station on the other side of the road. If she hadn't been hurrying back to Sussex, she would have pursued him and struck up a conversation. As it was, the near encounter had made her determined to overcome her annoyance with Karen and ask for Sebastian's phone number. Martin had imagined the scene at the tube station so many times that it had taken on the frantic quality of an anxiety dream or an early silent movie, in which a concerned sister emerges through one door as her disturbed brother disappears through another, until eventually they crash into each other in the corridor, in a flurry of confusion. He imagined Sebastian's caption, accompanied by rumbling piano music: 'Olivia! My Bio Sis! I'd love to shoot the breeze, but I'm off to see my psychoanalyst, the famous Dr Carr!' Close-up on Olivia's astonished and heavily made-up face. 'But he's my father!' The two protagonists pace in tight circles, until Sebastian exclaims, over a crescendo of crashing keys, 'You mean we have the same Psycho Dad as well as the same Bio Mum!'

Sitting alone in his sunken armchair, next to a half-finished cup of coffee, Martin's frenetic fantasy was replaced by the sense of doom it was designed to distract him from. Letting Sebastian down was as unthinkable as it was now inevitable. It had the melancholy but irreducible shock of something long expected but partially denied. However proudly displayed on the desk, a skull remains a *memento* of a *mori* the collector has so far avoided, especially if he can spare the time to be painted standing solemnly beside it. Since Martin had watched Sebastian's unwitting interaction with Olivia at the Happy Helmets launch, the anguish he felt that evening had faded, without ever disappearing entirely. The trains he had been watching from a high hill, as they moved towards each other along the same track, were about to crumple into each other, as they were always going to, albeit with agonising slowness, and yet he couldn't quite believe it was happening at last.

Meanwhile, in their sessions, Sebastian made references to Olivia which Martin had to respond to without saying anything about her that Sebastian had not told him. In a sense, it was always his mission to stay within the frame of reference provided by his patient and to import as few of his own attitudes as possible, but excluding extraneous knowledge was so much easier when he didn't have any. Martin's vision of Sebastian's 'fake' parents, of Helio or Simon, or of the staff at Heron House, was built entirely on his patient's own associations, whereas Martin's vision of Olivia was stubbornly rooted in being her father. He dreaded Sebastian, like a detective who catches out his opponent, saying, 'Who told you her eyes are blue?' or, 'I never said that she was working on a radio series,' or, 'How did you know she had a four-year-old son?' Martin also caught himself imagining his responses being judged by Sebastian in the future light of his discovery that Olivia was his therapist's daughter. How disingenuous or misleading he might seem when Sebastian looked back on Martin's feigned ignorance and withheld interpretations. He even wondered if his silences, which were a natural part of their dialogue, leaving room for Sebastian to have his own insights or associations, were too frequent when they surrounded the mention of Olivia – not that he should overcompensate – and might make him seem ridiculously indifferent to what had naturally become one of Sebastian's main preoccupations.

Given the steep gradient he was facing by analysing his daughter's brother, Martin couldn't help marvelling at the cliff face that Freud must have confronted when he analysed his own daughter, Anna. At least Freud could have said, 'Well, I'm not giving her to Adler; he's too preoccupied with aggression and class; and I'm not giving her to Jung, now that he's gone fuzzy on us; I suppose I'm the only one who can be entrusted with such an important task!' Martin couldn't make the same claim, but he had something of the same feeling of possessiveness. To lose Sebastian at this point would be such a waste of the knowledge and loyalty accumulated over five years of work. It was like abandoning a dictionary when they were only halfway through words beginning with M. Why had he chosen M? Mother? Middle? Martin? Did he feel he was only half the analyst he should be? Sebastian had recently met his mother, it was true, and M was not only the middle letter of the alphabet but, as a letter, had such an emphatic middle to it, like the cross-section of a V-shaped valley. That's where he must feel he was, in a deep valley, between the steep slopes – there they were again – of familial and professional responsibilities. Perhaps he wished they had reached V; perhaps it would have been almost bearable to abandon the dictionary with only four letters to go – two of them frankly marginal. Sebastian could probably get by without Xylophones and Ziggurats – in fact, Martin could almost hear him saying, 'I've given up Ziggurats on doctor's orders.'

It was natural for him to think of a dictionary since psychoanalysis was a science so deeply rooted in literature, in both Freud's experience of literature and his contribution to it. There had been no scanner available to get a snapshot of Oedipus's brain while he killed the stranger he met on the road to Thebes, let alone a control group which killed old men who were not their fathers; nor was there any meta data searching all the scans ever taken to find cerebral correlates for the id, the ego and the superego. Hamlet had not been strapped to a lie-detector by Ernest Jones to see if he felt any inhibitory guilt caused by his incestuous attachment to his mother. Nor, if it came to that, was there any CCTV footage of the young Wolfman admitting that he had developed castration anxiety after being read the story of Reynard, the fox who lost his tail when he used it as bait to catch fish through a hole in the ice.

'Hello, darling,' said Lizzie, coming into the drawing room with a soothing cup of camomile tea and taking in the uncertain atmosphere surrounding Martin. 'Are you staring into space vacantly or pensively?'

'Pensively, I'm sorry to say,' said Martin.

'Oh dear,' said Lizzie.

'Well, it's bound to happen now and again,' said Martin, 'even with someone who has such a strong preference for vacancy.'

'It must be a shock to the system,' said Lizzie, smiling at him as she sat down.

'It is,' said Martin. 'In fact, that's part of what I've been thinking about: the way inevitability has its own power to shock the system. We expect the unexpected to be shocking, which of course it is, in its brassy and sometimes traumatic way, but inevitable things are also shocking when they finally happen, partly because we think we've outmanoeuvred them with anticipation whereas, in reality, we may have been secretly building up their impact.'

'Or displacing and prolonging it,' said Lizzie, 'like deflecting one of Olivia's asteroids into the sea so that everyone can drown in a tsunami instead of being incinerated by an explosion.'

'Something like that,' said Martin, now seeming more vacant than pensive, if only because he couldn't really talk about what was on his mind. Lizzie was used to this vague but charged state in which they sometimes spent the early evenings, among the shadows of patients Martin could neither discuss nor dismiss. He was not easily perturbed, but his cheerful equanimity seemed to have been ringed with cloud for a good while. She missed the sunlit snow but knew better than to ask what had been obscuring it for so long. Her own approach to the hangover of a difficult session was much more direct and she would sometimes open a conversation with remarks like, 'If you had a patient who saw her father die of a heart attack during her sixth birthday party . . .' while making every effort to keep the example confidential.

'By the way,' she said, 'I was thinking that next Thursday I might save Olivia the trouble of getting a babysitter and look after Noah myself.'

'Amber is always happy to step in,' said Martin.

'I know,' said Lizzie, 'and I hate to deprive her of the pocket money, but I'm always happy to step aside, when it comes to one of Hunter's bashes.'

'Hmm,' said Martin, 'do you remember when "smashing" was a term of praise? One of Hunter's smashing bashes.'

'Exactly.'

'I like his rather belligerent hospitality,' said Martin. 'Perhaps it's infantile of me but everything is so thoroughly planned that the torments of choice disappear.'

'Yes,' said Lizzie, 'there's a kind of simplicity to having every detail decided in advance, like the "ultimate cocktail" which Hemingway asked the head waiter at Harry's Bar to make as overwhelming as Montgomery's forces in the deserts of North Africa.'

'Frozen gin in a frozen glass, with a slither of lemon shivering in the stainless pool,' said Martin. 'You've got to admit it's pretty ultimate.'

'Well, I suppose I end up feeling like the shivering slither of lemon,' said Lizzie, 'whereas you feel like Hemingway after his third Montgomery.'

'Fair enough,' said Martin.

'I would rather bring Noah a mug of warm milk.'

'Grandmother's milk,' said Martin.

'Yes,' said Lizzie. 'It's a great privilege being a grandmother: at a safe distance from the poor mother with her good breast and her bad breast doomed to turn her baby into a paranoid-schizoid wreck. Instead, my only job is to heat up some cow's milk and put it in Noah's favourite mug and help make sure he's having an integrated depressive experience.'

'It's disconcerting to look back at what people were allowed to make up in the early days,' said Martin. 'The fairy stories about infancy. On the other hand, there's so much split consciousness of one sort or another in the world, it must come from somewhere, and,' he added, more pensively, 'it will always come back under pressure.'

'Yes, if only we could remain ordinarily unhappy, reality principled people, firmly rooted in our integrated depressive phase, but splitting has a horrible way of breaking back into that nirvana of sanity . . .' Lizzie trailed off, seeing that Martin was worrying again about how to look after his mysterious patient.

'Still, we must be allowed our fairy stories, especially with infancy,' said Martin. 'I mean, if we weren't allowed to infer causes from consequences, we wouldn't be able to do science at all, or only a science of axioms and tautologies, which would have the disadvantage of never telling us anything we didn't already know.'

'Darling, you're getting terribly abstract,' said Lizzie, 'you must be very worried about whoever it is you're worried about.'

'I am,' said Martin.

'Do you want to talk about it – in a general way?'

'I really can't,' said Martin, 'except to say that I feel I am going to be letting down my most vulnerable patient and there's nothing I can do to stop it.'

'It's hard for me to imagine you letting down any of your patients,' said Lizzie.

'Well, it's even harder actually doing it,' said Martin.

'I'm so sorry,' said Lizzie. 'It must be a real gridlock if you can't find a way through. I don't know if it'll help cheer you up at all, it's obviously nothing to do with your problem, but Olivia rang me today to say that she's had a reconciliation with Karen and has got hold of her brother's number.'

'Really?' said Martin. 'That's sooner than I expected.'

'I know; Olivia can be so stubborn, and I also thought she would take longer to reconcile, but it's basically good news.'

'Yes, yes, absolutely,' said Martin, 'very good news.'

'Olivia seems to feel protective towards him, which is sweet. I mean typical, but it could have gone the other way.'

'Maybe Sebastian is just someone who arouses sympathy,' said Martin. 'As you know, Winnicott said that you can tell when someone is truly mad because they make you feel profoundly bored, and you can't wait to get away from them. He didn't mean at a drinks party, of course, where the numbers would get out of control, but in a clinical setting. There's a level below that, where people are quite mad enough, but not at all boring, much less boring in some ways than a clever neurotic. Perhaps he's one of those.'

'Yes, I know what you mean,' said Lizzie. 'I suppose we'll find out if we ever meet him.'

'Quite,' said Martin. 'It's much more likely to be Olivia's natural kindness and her feeling of connection with her brother.'

'Exactly,' said Lizzie, 'but the other thing she said was that she really wants to help him get some psychotherapy. She's very conscious of having had a better deal than him when they were separated, and she feels that fate has thrown them together – I mean, you know she wouldn't put it in that sort of language, but that's what she essentially means – and that she ought to, or wants to at any rate, help him. Obviously, it can't be either of us, that would be too bizarre, but she wondered if we could think of someone who would take him on.'

'Yes, I've been thinking about that,' said Martin. 'I mean, obviously I haven't been thinking about it: I *will* think about that. Give it some thought,' he said, finally settling on the present. 'Ask around. Is she proposing to pay for him?'

'Well, I don't suppose he has any money.'

'Probably not,' said Martin, 'but neither does Olivia. So, we would have to find someone who would give him scholarship rates.'

'Yes,' said Lizzie. 'And we could all contribute. I mean, "all", I can't speak for anyone else, but I would be prepared to do something. He is part of the family in a rather unusual but very real sense: a complete stranger who happens to be our daughter's brother. Apparently, he's been in some serious trouble. He was in a psychiatric unit earlier this year.'

'Really?' said Martin. 'Well, listen, I'll join in and do what I can. Maybe we could contribute to one session each.'

'Wonderful,' said Lizzie. 'That sounds perfect.'

16

Months went by or, to be honest, it was sometimes years, without Seb being asked to what you might call a 'social occasion'. There was always the TV room at Heron House, but that wasn't exactly a social occasion, with the usual suspects talking to the people behind the screen more often than to the ones in front of it, except to tell the ones in front to stop talking to the ones behind because they couldn't hear themselves think. This week was a real exception: he had been invited next Saturday by Olivia for a walk on Hampstead Heath, and a bite to eat at a café she knew; and not only that but tonight, on top of it all, he was going to a proper party, a gallery opening Helio was beside himself with excitement about, because the gallery was thinking of taking him on as one of their artists. The work they were showing tonight was by one of Helio's 'absolute heroes'.

'To me he's like a god,' said Helio, 'I mean, the idea that we might one day be represented by the same gallery – it totally blows my mind. Sorry, man, I know that's one of your bad phrases.'

'No, no, not at all, I didn't bat an eyelid. "Blows your mind". Excellent. It blows my mind too,' said Seb, and to show how unperturbed he was, his hands expanded in the air around his head, and he made the sound of a gigantic explosion.

When Helio told him he had been given a 'plus one', Seb had joked that 'plus one' would not have been nearly enough for him, even if he'd been going on his lonesome. Helio threw his head back and laughed, sweeping his hair behind his ears at the same time.

'That's a good one, man,' he said. 'You know, jokes are the best medicine because they are about things being out of place, out of context or, you know, upside down. That's what drives people crazy in the first place, right? But with a joke, it's deliberate, so it can help you relax. You know what I'm saying?'

'Yeah, yeah, I think you're bang on there,' said Seb. 'I always told Dr Carr that I wanted to work on my jokes, and I think what you said is why it seemed so important.'

Naturally, Helio's 'plus one' was going to be Isabella, but she had tested positive (Seb always thought 'negative' would have been a better term, because it wasn't exactly good news, was it?) for the new strain of Covid, which was more transmissible but less lethal, or more lethal and less transmissible, or more transmissible and more lethal; anyway, not positive. Helio had told him her response.

'Why don't you take Seb?' Isabella had said. 'He was so appreciative of your work. I think he really gets light art.'

After that, Seb was even more hopelessly in love with her than before. To be honest, he would have preferred to spend the evening with Isabella and get the new strain of Covid. They could have been quarantined for five days and he could have put his head in her lap and let her play with his hair, or she could have put on some Brazilian music and taught him one of their famous dances, or they could have watched TV and stayed together on the same side of the screen. Magic.

As it was, he was going to meet Helio at the Hare and Tortoise, a pub near the gallery, to make sure that they arrived together on time. Seb had been googling his head off trying to work out what to wear. He had an old blue suit, but he didn't want to look boring among all the artistic types. His other clothes, though, were just dead ordinary and he thought they might be a bit too sloppy for a party. The truth was that he didn't have any party clothes as he never went to any parties. When he looked at pictures of people at gallery openings, some were formal, some were artistic and dressed like Boy George, or whatever, and some were very street, but not in the way that people in the street were. They had T-shirts and big boots, but then they had cheeky little hats and pre-torn jeans. Their street clothes were somehow different, specially tailored rubbish, whereas Seb's clothes were, well, just good old rubbish. In the end he decided to wear the jacket of his suit, his better trainers, a pair of black jeans and a white shirt he had found at Oxfam with rows and rows of stick men encircling it.

After that, he'd googled the work of the artist who was being exhibited tonight. He was an American bloke with a big white beard. If there had been a wise old cowboy in the Bible, he might have looked like him, a sort of Desert Father, but more into surveying and building than fasting and castration, and probably quite fond of a steak by the campfire under the stars, rather than writing in double Dutch in the baking sun, using a skull as an inkwell and keeping a lion as a pet. Looking at his stuff, he could see that Desert Dad was into some of the same sorts of thing as Helio: light and land and space, but the internet being the internet, after a few glimpses of his work there was lots of stuff about Kanye West, because you couldn't expect a light artist to stay at the top of the click league for long if he was somehow connected with a controversial celebrity. Kanye turned out to be a bit of a religious nut who was totally obsessed with Desert Dad's work and often borrowed from it for his sets. He had made a recording of a very catchy song for one of his Sunday Services, with a choir swaying under what looked like a perfect oval of brilliant cloud seen through an imaginary skylight. Seb found himself swaying along with them, playing the song again and again with his headphones on, dancing alone in his room. The more meaningless the words, the less they interfered with the music. Seb's favourite line, as far as he could remember, was, 'He's the king of the kingdom,' because you couldn't have a king without a kingdom, and the monarch was bound to be a king once you said 'he'. So, the words were pretty much equivalent to humming which, to give them their due, the choir started doing as soon as possible, given that there wasn't any mileage in verbal nonsense when the meaning was all in the musical feeling. Seb sometimes thought he was serving a life sentence a bit like 'He's the king of the kingdom', in which nothing really happened at all. Superficially, it sounded as if people were telling you something important, but on closer examination, what they were saying was circular, like a little racecourse with a hollow centre and only one horse in the race.

'And the winner is the loser!' Seb announced to the empty room.

At other times, when he cut down on his meds, and started surfing the multiverse, it was the opposite, with meanings branching out all over the shop. There was a third option that came over him when he was sad and he felt that whatever happened, or whatever was said, it depended on the death of all the things that hadn't happened and hadn't been said, and that 'the facts of the matter' were like the last bloodstained soldier left standing in a field of corpses. The present was one of those victories where you won the battle but lost all your troops. When he went off his meds it was because he wanted to get the army of possibilities back. It was like having a private party, the only sort he usually got asked to – until tonight, that is, until tonight.

Gallery openings, charity auctions, fundraising dinners, being a philanthropist, joining the Platinum Circle, accepting a place on the Board of Trustees; more patronage, more pressure to buy or contribute or donate. How much did he mind? If someone only loved Hunter for his money, at least he had the consolation of knowing that they must be besotted with him. It would be so much bleaker if they were keeping their love for someone who had managed to plant a flag on the summit of Mount Everest or played the lead in *La Fille mal gardée* or in the Sri Lankan ice hockey team. The areas of human endeavour in which he was relatively unqualified, compared to being rich, were legion. In any case, although he accepted the theoretical distinction between the 'qualities' that emanated from his inner life and the 'attributes', which were the things that could be said about his circumstances and background, he found that even in introspection these different types of characteristics tended to become blurred. His diet was rich, his clothes were rich, his expectations were rich, his actions were rich; his dreams sometimes insisted on other dimensions of life, but they usually evaporated as the blackout blinds purred up to reveal the reassuring contours of one of his immense bedrooms. All his investments might crash overnight, but then he could have battery acid thrown in his face and change his appearance even more suddenly than his net worth, or he could have a stroke and lose any memory of his former mental habits. His blood group was extremely unlikely to change but how big a part did that play in his social interactions, unless he needed a transfusion from a plastic bag? If he couldn't separate the supposedly distorting lens of his great wealth from his own sense of identity, wasn't it pretentious to expect other people to do so? The word 'generous', so often deployed by guests, campaigners, godchildren, alma maters and corporate beggars, sometimes irritated him because it took the distinction between his situation and his values more seriously than he did himself, attributing a moral intention to what was often just the inevitable side effect of spending time in his world. There seemed to be a firm distinction between including people in his fabulous lifestyle and giving them a fabulous lifestyle of their own, but even then, the term 'generosity' was only warranted if there was an element of sacrifice on Hunter's part. His time, attention, love and compassion represented the real sacrifices. The paradox of being extraordinarily rich was that it effectively eliminated one form of generosity while making it the centre of other people's attention. A gift from him could transform someone else's life without making any difference to his own. Strictly speaking, any gift reduced his range of choices, but it was not a sacrifice if he was eradicating choices which he had no interest in making. If Hunter had longed to colonise Mars, he should never have wasted his money buying anyone a milkshake, let alone an apartment, but he was mercifully free from extra-terrestrial whims, and there was nothing he wanted on humanity's home planet that he was unable to buy.

Thanks to its system of tax-exempt philanthropy, rich Americans could ride their hobbyhorses into the sunset, being mad about Sonoran Desert toads, mad about opera, mad about rabies, or mad about the mental health of Greek-American adolescents in the Des Moines area, while leaving ordinary taxpayers to strengthen bridges and fill potholes, and provide the metal detectors and heavily armed elementary school teachers guaranteed by the Second Amendment, not to mention the excellent surveillance systems needed by television stations all over the nation to broadcast footage of a disgruntled former student returning to his school in a black hoodie with the assault rifle he had picked up at the local candy store, despite his troubled psychiatric history, and of the brown-suited law enforcement officers who quite understandably prevaricated in the corridor, pistols in hand, while the thud of one gunshot after another in nearby classrooms deterred them from going any further into the building. Everybody knew, or else should know, that these culture wars were polarised and paralysed and that the richest people in the country were better off making sure their names were screwed to the back of a chair in Carnegie Hall than getting involved in those uncivil civil wars. Hunter persisted in trying to make a political difference, focusing his efforts on the mayoral level of elections, where he felt that there was sometimes more room for creative ecological or educational solutions, but in the vast range of his philanthropic projects, what was making a difference to this particular day was that years of enthusiastic support for Turrell meant that he could bring a large party of guests to the show tonight. He was even flying in Father Guido, to thank him for the time they had spent together in Assisi. The artist and the abbot had both thought a lot about light, and he liked the idea of bringing them together. He had lured Guido with the promise of paying for the repair of the monastery roof, saying that there were papers to be signed and witnessed. It could all have been done electronically, but the truth was that he liked seeing Guido now and again. He was such a sweet guy.

'Do you know anything about this show?' said Martin.

'As I'm going to be looking after Noah, I haven't exactly been mugging up on it,' said Lizzie. 'My research has been more *Pingu* versus *Incredibles 2*, but I do seem to remember Francis saying that Hunter had bought a building with a hole in the roof – the sort of thing a surveyor would warn you against strongly – and that he had a lovely time sitting there gazing at the sky.'

'I suppose the Pantheon started the craze for holes in the roof,' said Martin.

'There could be all sorts of reasons for exposing your shelter to the elements,' said Lizzie, 'although I doubt that "a lifestyle choice" is one of them.'

'Not being a shelter in the first place is one thing they have in common,' said Martin. 'The Pantheon seems to be about an interior dome resonating with the outer dome of the sky and the ultimate dome beyond the sky. The ceiling is like a visual bell reverberating through space. An inspiration to aspiration. Something like that. It's also like a womb with a narrow aperture through which we emerge into a wider world. The constraint without which we can't have freedom.'

'You do love an interpretation, don't you, darling?'

'I'm sorry,' said Martin, 'I just can't stop.'

'I know; it's one of the things I love about you,' said Lizzie. 'Maybe the artist Hunter collects has quite different reasons for making an opening in the roof of his buildings. You can tell us tomorrow, and we can give you a multifaceted interpretation of *Pingu*.'

'Or *The Incredibles*,' said Martin. 'I like the sound of them.'

'Yes, I saw the first one,' said Lizzie, 'and of course it worked because they are so credible, as a family – apart from their superpowers, of course. Still, having superpowers beats coming from the average family in which you kill your father, marry your mother and then blind yourself with the brooches she was wearing when she hanged herself in the incestuous bedroom.'

'Well, we all need to escape from ordinary life now and again,' said Martin, 'however incredible those little holidays might be.'

It was almost always a joy to spend time with a priest or a nun, another person who had received the calling and dedicated their lives to the contemplation of God, and to the relief of human suffering. In Guido's long history of such encounters, only Cardinal Lagerfeld had been a persistent exception, darkening every meeting with his choleric nature, his craving for wealth and power, his monstrous pride, his ingratitude . . . Guido stopped himself from extending this list of harsh judgements on his very superior superior, shaking his head sadly at his own failings, as he got out of the gigantic electric taxi which had driven him with such hushed potency to the gates of the Brompton Oratory. The essence of charity was to go to where it was most needed and among his colleagues it was impossible to think of anyone who needed it more than the Cardinal, may he rest in peace. It was all too common for people to extend their compassion to children who had been extracted from the rubble of a collapsed building after three days of meticulous excavation, children who had become the darlings of a global audience of devoted viewers, and then to withdraw it abruptly at the mention of Vladimir Putin or Donald Trump, a noisy neighbour or an angry dog, as if hatred could suddenly acquire moral stature by selecting the right target, when all that had really happened was that compassion had disappeared when it was no longer aligned with pleasure, with a gratifying orgy of tears or an ostentatious display of sensitivity, and been asked instead to turn into an unwavering and often strenuous commitment to helping people who were in the deepest trouble, like *I due amici*, Putin and Trump. Guido was mystified by the number of vaguely decent people who thought it made sense to love Tibetans because of their charming religion but to hate the Chinese because some of them had behaved aggressively towards Tibet. Even within their own picture of what was taking place, it was clearly the Chinese who were in the greatest need of loving kindness since they were the ones who had harmed themselves by behaving violently. As he could see from observing his own thoughts at the end of the taxi ride, one's first obligation was to clear the mind of hatred, whatever its object, rather than luxuriate in hatred once its passport had been stamped by indignation. Even hating sin was a perilous mentality. Manfredi had suggested the other day, in a discussion of the Seven Deadly Sins at one of the monastery's *Dibattiti del Giovedì*, that although gluttony was usually characterised as a pig in the trough of unrestrained appetite, it should be seen as a more general obsession with food and drink which included the opposite behaviour, the explosion of dietary restrictions and eating disorders. Anorexia nervosa was a form of gluttony masquerading as a fanatical rejection of its more familiar caricature. The morbidly obese and the morbidly emaciated belonged side by side on the same bench in the emergency room. What good could come from hating their fatal fascination? Cardinal Lagerfeld, may he rest in peace, had himself died during an overzealous condemnation of what he took to be a transgression. A young priest had written an article in a popular newspaper, questioning whether celibacy had done more harm than good over the centuries. Although the unauthorised author recognised it as a noble gesture of renunciation, he suggested that perhaps celibacy should be a voluntary addition rather than a prerequisite to the priestly vocation, arguing that faith and kindness were indispensable, but celibacy was a 'matter of taste' since marriage was after all a holy union. Lagerfeld had summoned the rebellious young priest to his magnificent apartments in the Vatican and while screaming abuse at the advocate of what the Cardinal regarded as a Protestant heresy had worked himself into such a state of dogmatic rage that, despite its long training at coping with his temper tantrums, his poor old heart had seized up altogether. It was not clear to Guido why the subject of celibacy, among such a vast herd, should be the particular bête noire to have fatally gored the Cardinal, but he could only imagine that for a man who had dedicated his life to the service of the Church, as an institution, perhaps occasionally losing sight of the fundamental reasons for its existence as a spiritual endeavour, that for a traditionalist who had barely reconciled himself to the Bible being translated into Latin, let alone into the vernacular of the multitudinous countries in which it was recognised as a sacred text, the idea of a priest who was not prepared to sacrifice his sinful desires, as Lagerfeld would have seen them, on the altar of his career was simply too preposterous a pressure for his cardiovascular system to bear, already strained as it was by his enormous financial responsibilities and his innumerable trips to Mexico, the Philippines and other developing nations where the flame of faith often burnt most brightly, and where every seminary was filled almost to bursting point with his fresh recruits. Guido knew the story of Lagerfeld's demise because the rebel author, Stephano, had come to Assisi to contemplate his future and to recover from the trauma of being implicated in the death of such a prodigious cleric. He had described how the Cardinal, who had been towering over him 'like a scarlet skyscraper in a controlled detonation', had collapsed in a crumpled heap of silk and lace at his feet. He felt doubly guilty because he had experienced a moment of 'blissful relief' when Lagerfeld, may he rest in peace, had finally stopped screaming at him. The full story emerged when Stephano admitted that he wanted to marry his childhood sweetheart and that she wanted to become 'a priestess'. Guido, although he felt it was a great loss to the Church, had encouraged him to follow his heart. The happy couple had written to him from 'the poorest neighbourhood' of a Belgian city where they were running a soup kitchen and bringing up their young daughter, whose birth had occurred rather less than nine months after Stephano's interview with the Cardinal.

Today, Guido was visiting a very different kind of colleague. He had met Father Thomas in Rome at a conference on mysticism. He had enjoyed what little he was able to understand of the Englishman's erudite lecture on *The Cloud of Unknowing*, and his warm congratulations after the event had resulted in an invitation to lunch, with the proviso that Guido come to fetch Father Thomas from his borrowed apartment in the *centro storico* of the city and book a table at a nearby restaurant.

'I have a genius for getting lost,' Thomas had explained, 'and if I agree to meet you in a restaurant for lunch, we would be lucky to have dinner there on the same day.'

Guido arrived the next day only to find that Thomas was still wearing a pair of pinstriped black boxer shorts, a white vest and some impressively long black socks.

'I have misplaced my cassock,' said Thomas, in a high state of agitation. 'I was dancing on the rooftops last night from the relief of having delivered my lecture, and I'm afraid that I have a somewhat imperfect memory of the last few hours of the evening, although I can say with moderate confidence that I did not disrobe myself in a Roman bar, if only to avoid the unwelcome attention of the *carabinieri*, or indeed the somewhat less unwelcome attention of the Swiss Guard, who might have come to my rescue and spared me whatever banal retribution a secular society visits on a person who undresses in public and dragged me across the frontier to the Vatican City where I could have been given the cruel and unusual punishment I so richly deserve; not a crucifixion perhaps, that would be asking too much, but at least a public flogging.'

'Please, my dear Thomas,' Guido began, '*calmati*.'

'You see before you a broken fool,' Thomas continued, immune to interruption or sympathy. 'Alcohol is the poor man's mysticism, and although I could recite to you verbatim *The Cloud of Unknowing*, I have all too often taken the shortcut of Gin Alley to an artificial paradise, fabricating a simulacrum of the state described in a text which I admire precisely because of its absolute rejection of fabrication and simulation – as if the refusal to reduce union with the Godhead to any name, or analysis, or formulation could be compared to the blackout of a drunken sot, as if the glory and the profundity of the *Via Negativa* were no better than this nest of scorpions breeding in my mind and racing down the branches of my nerves. I am a fraud, my dear Guido, a man of the cloth who has lost his cloth – I have been defrocked by God because I am unworthy of my office.'

'This is not necessary,' said Guido, alarmed at the stream of gin-laden tears coursing down the cheeks of his repentant acquaintance. 'My dear Thomas, you were naturally delighted by the success of your *magnifico* presentation, and perhaps your celebration was a little too *entusista*, but it is not a problem for me to go around the corner to Barbiconi – it is only a few hundred metres – and fetch you a new cassock.'

'Off the peg?' wailed Thomas, despair and hysteria competing for dominance of his quavering voice. 'Off the peg!'

'I am sorry, I do not understand,' said Guido.

'I have a tailor,' said Father Thomas, abruptly regaining his composure as he wiped his wet cheeks with the back of his black-haired wrists, 'who it is no exaggeration to call a genius. I would not insult him by wearing a mass-produced ecclesiastical garment, laced with polyester, and sewn together with nylon threads by frantic machines. If we were to find my old cassock sinking in the filthy waters of the Cloaca Maxima, I would fish it out and pull it over my head with joy rather than wear the sort of garment you have kindly offered to pick up for me from a local shop.'

'And yet,' said Father Guido, who was growing hungry, having skipped breakfast in the expectation of an unusually copious meal at Fortunato al Pantheon, 'it is not possible to go to a restaurant in your underwear . . .'

'There are points on which I cannot compromise,' said Thomas.

'In that case,' said Guido, removing his glasses and polishing them on the somewhat threadbare sleeve of his own outfit, 'we must pray to St Anthony for the restoration of your hand-made clothing.'

He lowered himself painstakingly onto the cold terrazzo floor, just as the bells from the towers of the numerous surrounding churches started to toll the hour and remind him that they were already late for lunch.

'One moment,' said Thomas, striding across the room,

jerking down the chrome handle and pushing open the two halves of the nearest window, 'let us clear the air first to help us clear our minds.'

The reverberation of the bells and the light breeze of the spring day flowed unimpeded into the room. Guido clasped his hands and closed his eyes.

'My cassock!' cried Thomas before Guido had begun to formulate his petition to the patron saint for the recovery of lost items. Guido raised himself from the floor with the aid of a nearby armchair and hobbled over to the window. A black cassock lay neatly folded on the terracotta tiles of the windowsill.

'I must have put it out there to air overnight,' said the astonished Thomas, as relieved to fill his blackout with rational intentions as he was to have found something to wear. 'You must have a very powerful connection with St Anthony,' he said, beaming at Guido as he lifted the black cloth from the sill.

'I hadn't started to pray,' said Guido modestly.

'That's what I mean,' said Thomas, 'you didn't have to!'

When they arrived at Fortunato, their table was still available.

'We must celebrate,' said Thomas. 'A bottle of Cervaro and two Negronis to kick us off,' he said to the waiter.

'No, no,' said Guido, too late to stop the order. 'I do not drink cocktails – or very seldom at least, and not quite intentionally. A little wine, *certo*.'

'Oh, come, come,' said Thomas, 'it's not every day that you see the intercession of saints imprint itself so unmistakably on ordinary life.'

'Surely it happens all the time,' said Guido.

'Of course,' said Thomas, 'in principle . . . Ah-ha, here they are!'

Thomas dispatched the two Negronis with the relief of a man chucking a couple of overdue thank-you letters through the slit of a postbox. He seemed to relax, not from the cocktails, since it was too early for them to have reached his bloodstream, but just from the knowledge that the cloud of unknowing was on the horizon.

'So, what's your position on free will, Guido?' he asked, with the same mechanical brightness with which someone else might have said, 'Do you come here often?'

Guido gave a surprisingly prompt answer to such a vast question.

'I do not think we can pick things,' he said, 'there are too many causes leading to every moment, but I think we can unpick them – otherwise there would be no confession.'

'But surely the unpicking is a form of picking,' said Thomas.

'No, because what we are unpicking has already happened. It is a lower order; it is the human playground. My English is . . .'

'I like that, I like that very much,' said Thomas.

Guido was about to thank him, but then saw that Thomas was smiling at the waiter who had just poured him a sample of white wine.

Whoever he was complimenting, it was during that merry lunch that the two men had promised to visit each other if they ever found themselves in the same city, and in keeping with that promise Guido was now crossing the courtyard adjacent to the Oratory, approaching the impressive-looking building where Thomas had invited him for some 'Brompton coffee' (a drink unknown to him) and a tour of the church.

Francis remembered visiting the Skyspace at *Apocalypse Now*, but for some reason the thing he remembered most from Hunter's stories about Turrell's life and work was his love of flying. His father had been an aviator who had died when Turrell was still a child but not before they had been on a flight together. Turrell acquired a pilot's licence exceptionally early and when he became a conscientious objector during the Vietnam War showed that his refusal to kill other people didn't come from any disinclination to put his own life at risk. Instead of fighting in the jungle, he had flown over the Himalayas in a single-engine plane to extract Buddhist monks from Chinese-occupied Tibet. In retaliation, the Chinese had mined the dense canopy around the secret airfield he used in Laos, draping the foliage with explosive-laden nets. On one of his steep descents, his wheels grazed some leaves and detonated a grenade that blew the wing off his plane. As it burnt and pitched and crashed its way onto the airfield, Turrell's attention was absorbed by the swirling colours of the sky, the flames, the forest and the failing machine, magenta, green, orange, black. He had also flown a U2 spy plane at over seventy thousand feet, more than twice the height of an ordinary commercial flight. At that altitude you could see the bright blue band along the curve of the horizon gradually turning into a deep blue before surrendering to the encompassing blackness of space. So many experiences of flight had informed his work, the covert iridescence of clouds, white until the right angle made them glint or glow with colour, the disorientation of flying into them, on 'instrument flight', with no reference point outside the plane to measure height or direction; the hours he spent criss-crossing the South Western deserts until he found Roden Crater, the giant eye socket for his sky-gazing and walking meditations, for his Stonehenge of engineered astronomical alignments. Francis liked the fact that this artist was also a pilot, a student of perception, a lover of wild land, a thinker who was curating experiences for anyone who turned up to have them, rather than flogging expensive objects to the few individuals who could afford them. He felt an affinity with this stranger who he would very probably never meet, but who seemed to be deeply cool. There was something about him that only America could have nurtured, and only an America that seemed to be fading relative to some of its other national characteristics, an America of directness – why use paint to mimic the effects of light when you can use light itself? – of gigantic ambition and optimism – his *objet trouvé* was not a sheet of newspaper or a bottle top, it was an extinct volcano – and of an easy-going but faithful marriage between the inner light of contemplation and the natural light of the world.

'So, you mostly remember him being a pilot,' said Olivia. 'Okay, well that's helpful. I don't know anything about him, but I'll start in the cockpit.'

'Well, I remember lying on the bench in the Skyspace . . .'

'That was installed after my last visit,' said Olivia, 'when you went to Big Sur alone from Ecuador.'

'Yes,' said Francis, 'I'm sure you'll see it sometime, now we can all travel again.'

'Not before tonight,' said Olivia. 'On the other hand, that will leave Hunter the chance to explain everything to a novice. He'll like that.'

'Exactly,' said Francis. 'It's a huge asset that you don't know anything about Turrell, whereas I remember a few things that Hunter told me in the first place and won't be interested in being told back.'

'Who's a pilot?' said Noah, looking up from his book.

'The artist whose show we're going to tonight,' said Olivia. 'Apparently he likes flying.'

'Are there going to be planes, like in the Science Museum?' asked Noah. 'If there are going to be planes, I want to come.'

'No, no, there won't be any planes,' said Olivia. 'I'm not sure what there will be, but there won't be any planes.'

'If you're not sure what there will be, how do you know there won't be any planes?' asked Noah.

'Good point,' said Olivia. 'But I think he uses planes to get ideas and to have fun – and to travel, I suppose, but he doesn't actually put them into galleries.'

'But you *could* put a plane in a gallery,' said Noah.

'Yes,' said Francis, 'you could put more or less anything in a gallery, as people have gone to great lengths to show over the last hundred years, but he's not interested in making that kind of point. Anyway, you'll be watching a film with Granny at Belsize, so you'll be having a lovely time.'

'Are we nearly there yet?' said Noah.

'Two more stops,' said Olivia.

Seb had danced around for hours, humming along with the swaying choir under the radiant artificial sky. Kanye's song was more contagious than Covid. It was gain-of-function infectious. They must have been working on it in a Biohazard Level Four studio on Sunset Boulevard, or the Wuhan Institute for Virology to make sure it was as catchy as bats in a belfry. Then he realised, with one of those accordion-squeezing rushes of shame that suddenly blared at him out of nowhere, that he knew next to nothing about art and that he was going to be in a room full of art collectors, art lovers, art critics, art types, artists and art. They were bound to be talking about Leonardo da Vinci, lifting their specs to have a closer look at the brushwork, or the light bulbs, or whatever, while he stood there with a canapé on a toothpick, sticking out like a sore thumb. He had better google Leonardo asap. What if the culture vultures asked him if Desert Dad was better than Leonardo and he just stared at them with a stupid expression on his face? What if Helio had to ask him to leave because he couldn't tell the difference between a Picasso and a pork pie? It didn't bear thinking about, but before he left the page he was on, he saw a picture of Kanye and Desert Dad standing together in a field of magenta light. It must have been a room designed to look like infinity. It must have been an illusion created by the light being so evenly spread, and so perfectly absorbed into the walls and ceiling and floor – there must be a floor, or they would be falling – that they seemed to melt away.

After all the trouble he had been through, trying to establish boundaries between what was real and what was not, where he started and where he stopped, Seb was not sure he wanted to be in that sort of space. Then again, maybe it was like what Helio had said about jokes. When you didn't know an illusion was an illusion, it was madness, but when you made the illusion that you set out to make, it was art.

Art! The thing he knew nothing about. He hit the red dot, nuked the magenta field, and searched for Leonardo.

He started scrolling through Leo's pictures and found some of them a bit murky and disappointing. To be honest, they were crying out for a fresh coat of paint. Becky at Heron House had told him that on average the front of a building needed to be repainted every seven to ten years. On that basis, Leo's *Last Supper* was long overdue. The way things were heading, the poor old Apostles wouldn't have anything left to eat soon, their bread was so broken. Seb raced through more images, shaking his head in disbelief until he came across a painting called *The Annunciation* which was in relatively good nick. What were the chances? Leo had seen an angel. He must have been well off his meds. Seb had seen an angel once, but it was more transparent, like the light from cut glass floating on a wall. Leo's angel was as solid as anything, with feathers on its wings and layers of complicated clothing and a thick head of curly hair. It was kneeling and holding its hand in a way that reminded him of Dr Spock – it looked like it was straight out *The Vulcan Book of Sign Language*, as if the angel was saying, 'Live long and prosper', or 'God says hello', or whatever. Anyway, Seb read up about it, and it turned out that Gabriel, the angel, had come to tell the Virgin Mary that she was going to be the mother of Jesus. Mary's hand was held up as if it was about to have a nail driven through it, but she looked very serene, not like the women in modern films who have pregnancy test kits instead of angels and were generally on the floor of their bathrooms clutching their heads and swearing because the test was positive, in a negative way. You never saw the test scene if they *wanted* to be pregnant. If that was the case, they told their boyfriend or husband they were pregnant, and he gave them a big, long hug. That would have been a hard scene to paint in Mary's case, given that she'd never had sex: Joseph throwing a soup bowl at her halo, shouting, 'What do you mean, you were visited by the Holy Spirit?' Nobody had ever painted that scene, as far as Seb could make out, but there were tons of Annunciations, so it seemed that everyone in the art world at one point was seeing angels left, right and centre. He hopped from one to another and it was true that Mary didn't always look as relaxed as she did in Leo's version. She must have been thinking, Oh, no, I'm going to be up the duff when I go up the aisle; or, What was the point of all that sex education, if I'm going to be overshadowed by the power of 'The Most High'? Or, Why can't I have a son who plays for the Premier League instead of getting crucified? Just my luck. At some point, she obviously adjusted and realised she had been given a very special young lad to look after. Seb couldn't help wondering if Karen had been visited by an angel and told she was going to have a very special boy to look after, or whether it was more a case of swearing and head-clutching on the bathroom floor.

It was somehow typical of her life that instead of having lunch Lucy was about to have a Zoom call with her nutritionist. Janet was a Boston-based Mormon, a cutting-edge brain-cancer specialist with two PhDs, a best-selling book and another in the works. Lucy knew that there was no point in grilling some asparagus only to be told that she might as well be inserting plutonium rods into an unstable nuclear reactor as allow those barbed spears to slip down her throat. It simply wasn't worth setting off on the path of hackneyed dietary virtue, only to be told that coffee was in fact her friend and that yes, if she had colon cancer Janet would be advising against red meat but with her condition, beef was also her friend: reliably sourced, organic, grass-fed, antibiotic-free beef had more Omega-3 than wild, line-caught sockeye salmon. Despite her hunger she had resisted pouring organic olive oil over steamed broccoli in case she should have been pouring it over purple-sprouting broccoli and not the banal green variety delivered by Pure Planet before Janet had been given the chance to analyse her latest blood work. Phytonutrients were so important. 'Work the rainbow,' as Janet liked to say. Green foods were rich in cancer-blocking chemicals like sulforaphane and indoles, but blue and purple foods contained powerful antioxidants that Janet might want to foreground after she had worked out how to maximise the optimal diet for this exact moment in Lucy's healing journey. 'Work' was undoubtedly Janet's favourite word and Lucy already felt a little breathless at the prospect of the upcoming call. She had read Janet's book *Working Together*, which was based on several decades of 'my work with over eight thousand patients'. Lucy couldn't help thinking that quite a lot of them must have died to free up so much time in Janet's schedule, but then again maybe Janet just never took a holiday. They only talked once a month, after all.

Lucy was the one who needed a holiday, a holiday from being a patient. She had scheduled her call while Hunter was out to lunch with a 'pharmaceutical giant' – he sounded as if he needed Janet's help at least as much as she did. She had intended to spare Hunter the tedium and stress of her blood tests and scans by coming to London well ahead of him, but things hadn't quite panned out that way.

'Well, at least you got several years of compassion before the burnout,' said Olivia, when Lucy rang to pass the time until her consultation with Janet. 'Hunter has been pretty good. Some people rush straight to burnout without letting a drop of compassion escape on the way.'

'Yes, like Alexis Biedermeier,' said Lucy. 'She burnt out on contact with the news and ran from the room leaving me with the bill for her pink champagne.'

'After drinking it?'

'Of course, it wasn't the champagne she was running away from, but she was in such a hurry she knocked it back like a child having her first glass, with the bubbles surging up her nose – which helped her to look distressed. Then she heard I was going out with Hunter, and she tried to revive our friendship. It was like a crocodile impersonating a puppy. Not entirely convincing. Are you on a train, by the way?'

'Well, actually we're just getting off,' said Olivia.

'Oh, okay,' said Lucy. 'I'm sorry to bang on about compassion burnout or, in the case of Jody Gap, the current record holder, the bonfire of compassion.'

'Oh, yes,' said Olivia. 'The supermodel I'd never heard of who Hunter said he'd had an "absurdly long" one-night stand with – before your time, of course.'

'Exactly,' said Lucy, 'they fell into conversation at the end of a late party, but he's such a gent he still offered her breakfast, which he likes to have at about six thirty.'

'Very old school,' said Olivia. 'What was it she said when she finally asked you to dinner? It was so disgusting I've sort of blocked her as a memory.'

'"Hunter, shu-ga,"' said Lucy in a caricature of a Southern drawl, '"you've put on so much weight! There's no need to comfort eat just because your girlfriend's got a brain too-ma."'

'Jesus,' said Olivia. 'No wonder I'd suppressed it.'

'And then she tore off my headscarf,' Lucy went on, 'saying, "We've all been longing to see what's going on under there." It was after my chemo and radiation, when Hunter had shaved my head to help with my hairstyle crisis. Of course, there was a dent in my head because of the biopsy. The trouble with brain tumours is you can't get a sample without drilling into the skull. That's what makes the scans so important.'

'What a bitch,' said Olivia. 'Talking of scans, did you get the latest results yet?'

'Yup.'

'And?'

'Let's talk about them this evening,' said Lucy. 'You have Noah and everything.'

'Okay . . . but . . . okay.'

'Don't worry, it's fine. There's a plan. I'll tell you later.'

'I'm feeling like Alexis Biedermeier,' said Olivia. 'Without the champagne.'

'Oh dear,' said Lucy. 'I should have had a bottle waiting for you at the station. Anyway, there's an underappreciated counterpart to compassion burnout: sympathy burnout. Always being the one who needs help.'

'Some people never seem to get that,' said Olivia.

'Well, I've grown to dread people saying, "Of course this is nothing compared to what you're going through." Their lives matter as much to them as mine does to me, perhaps more. I've had to cultivate a certain, whatever Francis would call it, "non-attachment", I suppose – not that I'm doing too well; I've still got training wheels rather than a monocycle. At some point my emergency subsided into a condition. In a way I was relieved when the WhatsApp group dissolved, in a firework display of stellar and cardiac emojis, after all the "Go Girl"s and "I'm in awe at your courage and resilience" – not that I wasn't immensely grateful for them in the first year or two.'

'It dissolved partly thanks to Ash's excellent summary of where you were in your treatment, and the benefits of the immunotherapy you were about to embark on . . .'

'Hmm,' said Lucy.

'I know, but still, he was right at the time . . . Listen, darling, I'm going to lose the signal in the Underground. We'll speak about all this at the party.'

'Can't wait, but remember, I won't have told Hunter, so don't talk to him assuming he knows, or tell anyone else.'

'Got it,' said Olivia, just before the connection was broken.

Ash had been 'right at the time' and for some time after. Ipilimumab was part of the immunotherapy revolution that was sweeping through oncology. Originally designed for premature infants as a kind of liquid immune system that could be injected into their incubated bodies, it turned out to have radical benefits for patients with the worst kind of skin cancer, melanoma. Lucy became involved in a twelve-month trial to see if it could help with brain cancer, whose treatment hadn't changed for forty years: radiation followed by chemotherapy, with surgery only sometimes being an option, because so many areas of the brain could not be safely resected. The effect of therapeutic drugs was also severely depleted by the blood–brain barrier. The idea behind immunotherapy was that everyone carried cancer cells in their bodies but only some of them formed tumours. The immune system would normally identify and destroy cancer cells, but a tired immune system could start losing track of them while they, in turn, developed deceptive appearances, becoming like that slightly odd but seemingly harmless man-next-door who later stars in a depressing documentary about a serial killer broadcast on a minor channel in the middle of the night. If the immune system could be reanimated, it could return to its job and start to destroy the cancerous cells. A tumour was not entirely homogenous; it contained some healthy cells as well as being surrounded by them, and so it could be attacked simultaneously from inside and out by a retrained and reinforced army of T-cells.

The first eleven doses of 'Ipi', as it had become known, went well, and the scan results were promising, but after the final dose Lucy woke up feeling strange. She called Ash to ask for his advice. Luckily, he suggested she go to the hospital in charge of her treatment. By the time she arrived she was struggling to breathe and feeling seriously unwell. It was during the pandemic, so it was assumed at first that she might have Covid, but the test proved negative. Her respiratory difficulties became more acute, and her oxygen saturation plummeted from the high 90s where it belonged, through the 80s, into the 70s, while at the same time her heart had started to beat arrhythmically. She was rushed to the Intensive Care Unit. Her final dose of Ipi turned out to be an overdose, pushing her immune system into a kind of auto-immune psychosis. Instead of attacking viruses, infections and cancer cells, it had started to attack her own organs, first her lungs and then her heart. What would be next?

By the time Hunter arrived, Lucy was sedated with the most adhesive possible mask sealed to her face and a hundred per cent oxygen being blown into her at maximum pressure. Her arms and hands were full of cannulas channelling various bags of dripping fluids into her bloodstream. There was an X-ray machine directly above her bed, and an especially complex and sensitive monitor next to it. A doctor took Hunter aside and said that Lucy had refused to give permission for intubation, which might be needed to bypass the effort of breathing and pump oxygen directly into her lungs. A general anaesthetic was needed to suppress the gagging reflex and force the tube down her throat. Lucy had a long-standing fear of never waking up from a general anaesthetic, which Hunter promised the doctor he would try to overcome. A nurse woke Lucy and removed her mask; her nose looked bruised, if not broken by its frame. Hunter had been warned he didn't have long. He watched the oxygen saturation number fall precipitously as he said hello.

'About the intubation . . .'

'They give to people who are dying.'

'To stop them dying.'

'I don't think I will wake up . . .'

'You will, baby, you've just survived on high vigilance and super-intelligence all your life and it's hard to volunteer to have them taken away.'

There was a grey pallor to Lucy's face as she sank back onto the pillow and took a few more breaths from the mask.

'I trust you,' she said. 'If you think . . . Fine.'

Her oxygen saturation was already so far down that she was having trouble making sense. The nurse reattached the mask and switched off the alarm on the monitor. Lucy closed her eyes again and passed out after her brief conversation. Over the next two weeks Hunter spent in the ward, he found that one alarm or another was beeping or squealing most of the time. There was an atmosphere of highly regulated horror, which he had never encountered before. He came to admire the staff who worked every day in a place which he could barely tolerate for the brief period he was forced to be there. The other half-dozen patients were in various forms of extremity, some occasionally screaming, several groaning in the twilight zone, others apparently dead but attached to machines that claimed to know better. He sat for hours a day watching Lucy sleep, and sometimes talking to a doctor about her situation.

On the second day a doctor had come in from the immunotherapy team to say that he was going to have to administer a drug to rein in the delinquent effects of the Ipi.

'And will that reverse the long-term benefits as well?' said Hunter.

'No, no, not all of them,' said the doctor. 'If this storm goes on, we can give her something stronger, but we'll start with the lowest possible dose. The long-term benefits will still be very significant; it's just that for the minute her system has gone into overdrive. It's such a pity . . .'

'Yes,' said Hunter, who was close to despair, and felt that 'such a pity' sounded as if rain had spoilt a picnic and didn't cover the case of a life-saving treatment that appeared to be killing the woman he loved.

That fortnight in the ICU had been a watershed in Hunter's engagement with Lucy's illness. He turned from being something like a war correspondent embedded among the troops to something more like an editor in a corner office who decides how many front pages and leading articles should be allocated to the war. It could not be ignored, nor could it be the only headline of their lives. Lucy was in many ways grateful for this realistic reappraisal of the attention paid to her illness, but at the same time she envied that corner office since her body was stuck on the front line whether she wanted it there or not.

A Zoom invitation appeared on her screen. 'Let's get to work,' she muttered in a parody of Janet's irrepressible vigour, before she pressed Accept.

'Hi, Janet,' she said.

'Lucy! It's great to see your beautiful face.'

'Oh, thanks,' said Lucy.

'I know some of these results are a setback,' said Janet, 'but we're going to work together to set the setback back.'

'Wow! What a tongue-twister,' said Lucy. 'Did you have to practise that, or do you say it all the time?'

Janet laughed so loudly that Lucy unobtrusively turned down the volume.

'No, I do not!' said Janet. 'Listen, it's only a millimetre here and there, so I'm thinking more mushrooms, garlic, cauliflower, onions: white and brown foods are full of allicin with great tumour-fighting properties . . .'

For some reason Lucy had not turned the volume back up.

She smiled with real affection at Janet. She was so grateful for all the people she had been working with. Only last week her GP had said, 'We're living in revolutionary times. Every few months a drug comes on the market that's as important as penicillin.' For the moment, though, she had tuned out of Janet's manic if muted discourse. She realised how far she had moved from her terror of general anaesthetic. She pictured the first drop from the tip of a syringe, an artificial tear that would bring an end to pain and sorrow. It was not what she wanted, nor what she dreaded. For a moment she was in a state of perfect equilibrium, neither grasping at life nor rejecting it. It really didn't matter, not from indifference, but from something she hadn't really experienced before and couldn't put a name to.

'Right,' she said absently, turning up the volume and landing back in a busy and crowded world of shitake and lion's mane and garlic extract, and herbs and more herbs and cooking instructions.

'Lucy, are you okay?' asked Janet.

'Yes, yes,' said Lucy, realising that she must look as if her mind was not firmly rooted in the conversation. 'I'll eat all the mushrooms and everything, but maybe I'm really okay. Everything seems so beautiful. I can't explain . . .'

'Oh, Lucy, honey, I get it; I totally get it,' said Janet, putting her hand on her heart and starting to pound her chest empathically. Lucy saw that, against the odds, it was Janet who was crying, not her. She could not tell whether Janet was crying on her behalf, for some completely different reason or simply because she couldn't face talking about mushrooms any more, but she had no interest in finding out. She felt that for the first time she could do without working together, without being understood, without being treated with special care, and although she would no doubt need all those things again one day, just for the moment she had never felt stronger. It was a strength that refused to be anatomised as acceptance or transcendence but just seemed to have arisen, like a phoenix from the ashes of her sympathy burnout and Hunter's compassion burnout and all the other burnouts. The feeling was both fleeting and indestructible; she knew she couldn't hold on to it, but she also knew that she would never forget it.

'Do you know what?' said Lucy. 'Would it be okay if we wound things up for today? Please send me the Word document, which I will follow to the letter, and we can have a proper talk next month. Is that okay?'

'You got it,' said Janet, pulling several tissues from a box, while Lucy smiled at her kindly before ending the call.

Everyone knew that T-rex was the scariest creature in the whole history of the world, apart from its silly little arms which made it look as if they would lose a boxing match against a big boy of eight or nine, but what a lot of people *didn't* know was that T-rexes ate other T-rexes, which was how Noah had learnt about cannibals the day before yesterday. When Mum first told him, he thought she had said 'cannon balls', and he had said that he didn't know dinosaurs had cannons and he thought that gunpowder had been invented much later. And then, when they had cleared that up, Dad had muddled him again, catapulting Noah sixty-five million years from an extinct extinction to a living extinction, by saying that there were human cannibals and that some of them were still around.

'Where?' Noah had asked nervously.

'General Power, the banking industry . . .'

'Don't confuse him,' Mum had said, and then Dad had listed lots of places that Noah had never heard of, except for the Solomon Islands, because he remembered Solomon being talked about by Miss Foster. He was an old king who had suggested cutting a baby in half, which was the sort of horrible thing a cannibal would do, although the point of the story was something to do with working out who the baby's real mum was. It turned out she was the one who didn't want the baby cut in half, which didn't seem to Noah like an incredibly high standard for mothering, but probably among cannibals it was thought of as totally amazing, like not wanting extra ice cream or something.

'But why do they eat other people?' he had asked.

'To discourage tourists,' Dad had said. 'Not everybody wants their beaches littered with sunbathing holidaymakers.'

'But that would be a cannibal's dream!' said Noah.

'Easy pickings,' Dad had said, ruffling his hair and smiling.

Anyway, since then Noah hadn't been so sure that T-rex was the scariest creature ever. That night he had got into his parents' bed, saying he was having a nightmare about cannibals, which wasn't strictly true, but he had been staring at the ceiling thinking about them a lot. His dad had said not to worry as the Solomon Islands would soon be under water because of global warming.

'So reassuring,' Mum sighed.

'But what if we meet them in our ark?' he had asked.

'It's a long way away,' said Dad, 'they will have all eaten each other by the time their boats get anywhere near us.'

'What will the last one do?' Noah asked. 'Will he eat himself?'

'Well, oddly enough there's a phenomenon called autoph—'

'Shhh,' Mum had said. 'Anyway, our ark is for bobbing around Sussex,' she said in her sleepy voice. 'Even if all the ice melts and the waters rise, we'll still have our lovely bedrooms and we'll just use the ark to go shopping instead of the car . . .' And then he had fallen asleep, curled up next to his mum, quite pleased to have tricked his way into the bed.

The next day he was determined to perform a scientific experiment, because he was still a bit worried about the cannibals. So, when his bath was run, he made several marks just above the waterline – those were the Solomon Islands – and then he took a lump of ice from a bowl in the kitchen and dropped it into the bath – that was the Antarctic melting into the sea. To his disappointment the Solomon Islands were still above the waterline, so he went and got the bowl and threw all the cubes into the bath. When Mum asked him where the ice had gone, he said he'd been doing an experiment and instead of being proud of him, she was quite irritated, saying that Emma was coming from the big house for a drink, and she liked to put lots of ice into her white wine and that *someone* had put the ice trays back in the freezer without refilling them after *someone* had performed another science experiment, and the new ice was not fully formed yet.

Anyway, it had turned out all right because Emma was late, and the ice was made by the time she arrived. She said she thought it was an excellent experiment, but they should repeat it under more scientific conditions. So, she asked Mum for three glasses of white wine, put lots of ice in one and started drinking it, which didn't seem to Noah especially scientific; and after marking the level of the wine in the second glass dropped an ice cube in and marked where the new level was, and left the third glass with just wine in it – she said that was the 'control group', which made it a 'double blind' experiment, and because they were all there to witness the results, it was being 'peer reviewed', whereas if he had just reported his findings from the bath, the claims might have become part of the 'replication crisis', when nobody else could get the same results and started to question his 'methodology', saying he hadn't taken account of evaporation, or had used the wrong sort of plug. Mum and Dad were smiling away, as if she was being funny, but all Noah wanted to know was whether the Solomon Islands had disappeared.

'Definitely,' said Emma. 'That was just the Alpine glaciers. This,' she said, filling the other two glasses with lots of ice, 'is Greenland and the Antarctic. No more cannibals!' she declared, raising the second glass.

'Hurray,' said Noah, jumping up and down in his polar bear pyjamas. They were dark blue with white bears on them that glowed in the dark.

And Emma had said that 'Eureka' would be even better than 'Hurray' because an Ancient Greek had shouted it when he realised that he could work out how big he was from how much the water level rose when he got into his bath, and so Noah had run upstairs and plunged into the bath to see how far the water rose over the old marks, and shouted 'Eureka' down the stairs. And then he suddenly felt sorry for all the people who were going to lose their islands and asked if he could sleep in his parents' bed again, but Mum said that his concern was just proof that he was a nice boy, which wasn't the sort of emergency, like an electric storm or a terrifying nightmare, that justified being allowed to sleep in their room.

'We're here,' said Mum, jolting Noah out of his daydream, as the train pulled into the white-and-brown-tiled Underground station.

'We're always "here",' said Noah grumpily, 'that's what "here" means: where you are.'

Mum didn't say anything. He knew he was being annoying; the reason was that he wanted to go to the light show with them this evening, so he was refusing to enjoy anything openly. It wasn't as if he hadn't been to a light show before, but Mum said that had been during the day and he was too young to remember as she had taken him around in his stroller and he had fallen asleep, but he remembered the whole thing when he was shown the website: the coloured lights drifting on the wall, the stroller, being very young. Sometimes when he was asleep, he could see the room he was in without it being a dream. He could see Mum open the door to check whether he was asleep when he was asleep, so why couldn't he have seen the light show just because in her boring way Mum assumed that it wasn't possible because he had his eyes closed?

There were two hundred and nineteen steps between the platforms at Belsize Park Underground and the street, so they took the lift, although Noah had once been down the whole staircase with Mum, who had done it quite often when she was a child, and it was the longest staircase he had ever been down in his whole life. His grandparents' house was huge, and the first thing everyone did when they arrived was to settle into their rooms. Mum had her old bedroom, which was quite grown up, because it had been redecorated when she was at university, but he had his Uncle Charlie's childhood bedroom right up in the roof, because Uncle Charlie had moved to a bigger room when he was a teenager – the bigger room was now Granny's consulting room. Granny and Grandad helped people who had emotional problems, so they were always extremely busy. Anyway, they had never bothered to change Uncle Charlie's small room, so it still had giraffes and zebras on the wallpaper and some *Star Wars* stickers on the bedhead, and Noah loved staying there. He hardly ever saw Uncle Charlie since he had gone back to America with his girlfriend, but Noah felt close to him because he got to use his childhood room in London. They had both stared at this wallpaper so much that they could sort of meet there on the grasslands, like in a David Attenborough documentary, both dressed in khaki shorts and khaki shirts, with giraffes curling their muscular tongues around thorny acacia branches to get to the juicy leaves, and zebras galloping by, being chased by cheetahs and lions.

'Hello, Uncle Charlie.'

'Hello, Noah, my friend.'

'Who were you talking to?' said Mum, putting her head around the door.

'Oh, just Uncle Charlie,' he said. 'We ran into each other in the wallpaper and were having a chat, until you interrupted,' he added, remembering that he was supposed to be grumpy. The thought of Uncle Charlie, though, who was always so warm, and good at playing games and climbing trees, made it hard to keep up being grumpy. Charlie had always talked to Noah seriously about his feelings whereas some grown-ups talked to children as if they were addressing the other grown-ups in the room, or other grown-ups who *weren't* even in the room, and behaved as if children were always being typical – naughty, or silly, or adorable, or whatever. That way, they didn't need to take them in as a particular child, who might be a special mixture of things that hadn't ever happened before in the entire history of the world.

'I miss Uncle Charlie,' he said.

'So do I,' said Mum. 'Do you want to come down? Granny has made us lunch.'

'I don't want lunch,' said Noah. 'I just want to come to the light show with you. I've been to one before.'

'Yes, that's true,' said Mum, 'and that's why I brought you your Little Sun. I've been recharging it on the windowsill at home.'

His Little Sun was a solar-powered lamp from that exhibition he had been to years ago and which he distinctly remembered being given by his mum in the museum shop. It was based on a yellow flower from Ethiopia, so maybe he could find some if he went into the wallpaper later to have a proper chat with Uncle Charlie. The inventor, who had a name like a Viking, had made it because millions and millions of people didn't have electricity in their homes. Now, thanks to Little Suns all around the world, lots of children who used to be able to say, 'Sorry, miss, I couldn't do my homework because it was too dark at home,' had no excuse. Mind you, their parents could read them bedtime stories, and cook without using paraffin lamps which were bad for your health and contributed to global warming and meant that the Solomon Islands would disappear faster.

*

Guido gently put aside the Brompton Brew Thomas had offered him almost before he had time to sit down. As he lifted the cup to his lips, he realised that the delicious aroma of coffee he had been expecting was entirely overpowered by the fumes of brandy curling off the steaming surface of the dark liquid.

'It's the most restorative and stimulating beverage,' said Thomas. 'I drink it throughout the morning and there's no doubt that my best ideas come to me at that time. If only our formal lunches were restored. Readings from the scriptures and from the life of our founder, St Philip of Neri, are just what I am in the mood for after a couple of pots of coffee, but we only have formal dinners these days, when I am often invited out or find myself far less receptive by the end of the day to the inspiration of the holy texts.'

The invigorated Thomas took Guido on a tour of Brompton House, showing him the common rooms on the ground floor, where the residents could read, converse or entertain while overlooking an immense and peaceful garden. He told Guido that during the Second World War a bomb which had been hurtling its way sacrilegiously towards the magnificent dome of the Oratory had been harmlessly absorbed by the soft lawn they were admiring through the French windows. In some sense, Guido felt that the bomb had fallen where it fell, but he also sympathised with Thomas's impersonation of providence, as he snatched it from the air and cast it down onto the imaginary lawn at his feet.

'Bravo,' said Guido quietly.

After passing through an antechamber full of worn copies of *Who's Who* and *Burke's Peerage*, they entered a high-windowed library and strolled past stacks of ancient books, so tightly packed and beautifully matched that they looked as if they might never have been taken from their shelves. They also visited the private chapel, with its chequerboard floor, dark wooden pews and red velvet chairs, and went on to the sacristy where Thomas opened one slim drawer after another, filled with exquisite vestments of deep red, bright green and other jewel-coloured silks, embroidered with thick bands of gold thread. Although the bell sounded for lunch, Thomas insisted on quickly taking Guido around the Oratory itself. The relatively flat and simple modern chapel dedicated to Cardinal Newman was the only one that Thomas had any aesthetic reservations about, but Guido extolled the Millais portrait of the excellent and canonised Cardinal and, in the hope of offering an easy solution, said that perhaps the reddish stone background to the altar might detract from the scarlet of Newman's cassock.

'I had no idea there was an interior decorator lurking inside the little abbot,' said Thomas exuberantly. 'Yes! A black marble or Malachite *mise en scène* would bring out the scarlet to perfection.'

Thomas continued the circuit of more ornate, traditional and Italian-looking chapels dedicated to Mary Magdalene, St Patrick, St Joseph and to 'our old friend', as Thomas called St Anthony, smiling complicitly and even allowing himself a little wink as he tapped the donation box next to the statue of the saint.

'I thanked him for my cassock,' he whispered.

Eventually, their clockwise journey took them to the Altar of St Philip, the sixteenth-century Roman founder of the Congregation of the Oratory. Guido had been sitting in front of that altar ever since Thomas had left him to join the other residents in the refectory. St Philip used to dispatch missionaries from the Venerable English College in Rome with the words 'Hail the Flowers of the Martyrs' since their return to England would in all probability lead to the operating table of a hideous public execution. 'Hung, drawn and quartered,' said Thomas, with a certain complacency, as if recommending a famous hotel on the outskirts of Paradise. Guido had been shocked by the extreme heroism of these young priests, leaving the sweet life of Rome to live in a priest hole in a cold country, saving the souls of the Elizabethan gentry while inviting the most disgusting retribution onto their own fragile bodies. He said a quick prayer for them before his thoughts drifted back to his more immediate circumstances. With the winter solstice approaching, the days were so short he probably ought to start heading back to Hunter's apartment before darkness enshrouded what was already to him an unfamiliar city. It was the first time he had stayed in Hunter's London home, and he had not yet entirely adjusted to the contrast between being on retreat until yesterday afternoon in the Blessed Fra Domenico's old hermitage and his arrival later the same day in one of the guest rooms on the lower floor of Hunter's triplex penthouse overlooking Green Park. He struggled to remain unimpressed by the luxury of his room, especially the bathroom whose backlit alabaster walls and counters glowed with the amber, honey and pale-yellow translucence of a stone which until then he had only ever seen reflecting light from its surface. Through the double-glazed windows at the end of his long bedroom he could make out Buckingham Palace beyond the leafless plane trees, and on the other side of the park, the receding red brake lights and advancing white headlights crawling silently along Piccadilly. Only a few hours earlier he had been aching from the cold and damp of the hermitage but had also been feeling the lightness and clarity that came from two weeks of solitary reflection.

The core of the hermitage was a cave embedded in the forests near the monastery. A wooden extension, camouflaged by moss, provided enough shelter for a pallet bed, a small table and a single chair. There was no heating or electricity, and only a basin where water gathered from the weeping stone at the back of the cave. The immediate relief of being set free from the burdens of office was soon replaced by a battle with boredom and inconvenience. After a week of solitude, Guido had been sitting just outside his warped and ill-fitting front door, wrapped in an overcoat, staring at the woods yet again, his formal exercises and prayers done for the morning. During what was frankly an idle daydream, he remembered being a four-year-old child at a cousin's wedding. After the ceremony and the endless lunch, which he had found as tedious in its own way as the week he was currently spending in the hermitage, he could remember walking past the half-open door of a bedroom and seeing his sister unzipping the back of his mother's long, formal dress. Sophia had spotted him and had closed the door with a murmur of reproach, but he would never forget that little shake of his mother's shoulders and the dress falling in a heap at her feet.

For the last week he had been an ageing and balding man gazing at ageing and balding woods, noticing that the leaf litter on the forest floor was at the most melancholy point of its return to the soil, no longer vividly coloured but not yet completely transformed into the mulch through which new shoots could push; thinking that the wintry woods needed a rest before the hectic spring just as he needed a retreat before his spiritual renewal, but finding the prospect of that renewal more and more remote as he groaned his way into or winced his way out of a narrow bed of such hyperbolic discomfort that even the pious thought that it had once belonged to a beatified mystic couldn't prevent him from wanting to donate it to the monastery's collection of holy relics and replace it with a more accommodating mattress. And then he remembered, because there was always a moment when this happened, but he always forgot about it until it happened again, that almost all his thoughts were made up of mingling his preoccupations with his surroundings and then receiving impressions that echoed his original preoccupations, like a paralysed bat confirming its immobility with a series of little squeaks. As he recognised the system of self-imposed staleness in which he was trapped, the engrossing but entirely futile traffic between his feelings and his perceptions paused for a while. He sat in the tilted chair on the uneven ground and noticed that the dull scene before him was acquiring a certain brightness; the woods were a little more naked now. That's why he had thought of his mother's dress! It was the overture to this initial release. He was like a man who clutches his head to contain his growing sense of insanity only to find that the glasses he has been searching for frantically have been perched there all along.

After that, things started moving quickly. Birds landed on his chair and on his knees; a *cinghiale* with tusks and her five piglets came and foraged unconcernedly a few metres from where he sat. Instead of looking enquiringly, impatiently, jadedly, greedily at the woods, he was being in the woods, along with everything else. This subtraction of himself as an indispensable and demanding witness was an unqualified relief. There was no need for him to witness anything. The sound of a falling tree would be the same whether he heard it or not. The sound he would make if the tree fell on him was another matter, but putting that aside, he felt he had arrived at the hermitage wanting some sort of mystical experience worthy of the great Domenico and by giving up that immodest ambition he was having the gentler experience of being on equal terms with the world, of being a form of life among many other forms of life. On the one hand, the hard-edged individuality of things seemed to have been softened and distributed, like sugar cubes dissolving in a swirl of melting granules, but paradoxically, at the same time, the individual vividness of the things around him – like the silver-green lichen growing on the dark rain-soaked branch of the tree nearest to his chair – had become more emphatic. The less he asked of things the more they gave and the less he imposed himself on them the more they revealed their own nature.

During the first dreadful week of his retreat, Guido had been so distraught that he had started to regret having left behind the

Capo Santo that Hunter had been kind enough to give him years ago but which he had always resisted trying out. When the little family of *cinghiale* turned up, he suddenly realised that they were standing exactly where Hunter's former colleague, the boisterous Saul Prokosh, had set up his equipment for scanning Fra Domenico's brain. What a strange occasion it had been, struggling to this remote part of the forest with millions of euros of sophisticated equipment transported in a truck that looked as if it had been designed to bounce over the broken pylons and heaped rubble of a war zone while under fire. The *Capo Santo*, which was the result of that perhaps impertinent scan of Domenico's brain, languished untested in his private quarters in the monastery. The idea that he might instantly experience the mystical profundity that Domenico had acquired through decades of discipline in the inhospitable refuge that Guido found it hard to tolerate for even a week seemed irreverent and slothful. He felt he should work to attain whatever small revelations lay within his own capacities. Domenico had deprived himself of human conversation to facilitate a deeper conversation with God. Left alone for a week, Guido was finally talking to piglets and sparrows. Why should he be allowed a shortcut to the profound communion which Domenico had made so many sacrifices to achieve? On top of that, he didn't want to disappoint his friend Hunter if it turned out that his machine didn't work; nor did Hunter ever interrogate him about the results. They seemed to have tacitly agreed not to discuss the matter and consequently Guido only had a faint understanding of the science behind Happy Helmets, of which the *Capo Santo* was the religious subdivision. Despite Saul's generous attempts to put him in the picture, Guido did not understand how the helmets were supposed to reverse-engineer a magnetic image of the sublime state in which it was assumed the great contemplative perpetually dwelt and reproduce it in other people by trans-cranial stimulation. For a start, cerebral cartography seemed to be unlike other kinds of map-making. A year after poor Father Giorgio had been struck down by a ferocious stroke that robbed him of the power of speech, he was praying again fluently, although the doctors said that some of the damaged parts of his brain remained inactive. The brain seemed to have a strange plasticity; no doubt limited but nevertheless remarkable. Nobody thought, as far as he knew, that if the United States were wiped out by an asteroid or a nuclear catastrophe, that the Empire State Building would reappear a year later in Pondicherry or that the college of cardinals would be empowered to rewrite the American tax code.

There was also the question of whether there was something unique about Domenico's frontal lobes, to name the only region of the brain that Guido could remember despite Saul's crash course in brain parts. If his own humble frontal lobes were stimulated would that be enough to recreate similar experiences? He had worried at the time of the original scan that Domenico's mystical state might have been interrupted by carrying the poor man from his dim cave into the noisy tunnel of an fMRI machine, but had submitted to Cardinal Lagerfeld's insistence that in the modern age the faithful should be provided with an 'instantaneous technological relic' and not wait 'to admire Fra Domenico's skull in a glass case', but even supposing that the mystical state had remained completely stable, where were the memories and accumulated expertise stored? He had asked Hunter about memory and, to his surprise, it turned out that it was impossible to locate any material traces – any relics, so to speak – of memories in the brain. All the evidence was negative: certain types of damage to the brain impaired memory, but even when memory was treated as a creative global process, involving collaboration and integration between many regions, Hunter had said that the cause and nature of this process were not properly understood. If Guido's brain had been scanned while he had been remembering his mother's dress falling to her ankles sixty-five years ago, he found it hard to believe that any helmet in the world could induce Manfredi to have the same experience.

He was thinking of Manfredi because it had been his tireless assistant who had driven him yesterday to the little airport where Hunter's plane was waiting to whisk him to London. He did not have to explain to Manfredi that he was barely able to make conversation. The transition from a retreat to the outer world was always fraught with hesitation about breaking the silence which had become so precious and re-engaging in what could not help seeming like the needless commentary, mechanical enquiries and competing anxieties that made up ordinary conversation, as well as restoring the habitual echolocation of prejudice and impression from which he had only recently won a reprieve. When he was a child and his parents used to take him to the seaside, his mother had always insisted that he change out of his wet bathing suit before they went to have a pizza for lunch. Sometimes when he ran back to the beach, eager to return to his sandcastles and his books, his bathing suit was still damp, and he remembered the intense aversion with which he climbed back into it. Leaving the hermitage that morning, and stepping back into various roles – the abbot, the friend, or for that matter the person called 'Guido' by various people in various contexts – had somehow reminded him of those damp trunks.

Manfredi was encouraged by a guard at the airport to drive his Fiat Panda onto the tarmac right up to the steps of the plane. Guido was off to see his dear friends Hunter and Lucy, which, of course, would be a great pleasure, but he couldn't help wishing he was facing a less abrupt challenge to the lightness and simplicity of the last few days: the startlingly steep lift-off of the little jet, the platinum-blonde air hostess with her implacable hospitality, the sprawling cities glittering through the thick oval windows, the prospect of so many luxurious meals it would be rude to refuse and demoralising to accept. And yet he wanted to thank Hunter personally for paying to mend the monastery roof. Nobody knew about the gift except Guido and of course the fiscal authorities, who worked tirelessly to ensure that the amount of criminal money in circulation in Italy did not exceed the current level of one in three euros, and that organised crime remained a minority stakeholder in the business of government. Hunter was not even Catholic, and yet he had come to seek sanctuary at the monastery when he was suffering from 'compassion burnout', and now he was repaying the favour with his munificent gift. He had thanked Guido for helping him to establish 'appropriate boundaries' to his relationship with Lucy. Although Guido knew that modern speech would scarcely exist without 'appropriate' and 'boundaries' scrutinising every sentence, he felt in his own shy and undogmatic way that compassion was only limited when it took the form of a personal emotion competing with other personal emotions – as it so often did. The striking thing about the love that Guido experienced in the last few days of his retreat was that it had so little emotional content. It was more like breathing than feeling. Far from requiring an effort, it stopped everything from being such an effort. The only thing that could make him burn out would be to stop loving, not to love too much. He realised of course that he had gone through the looking glass and that love now seemed to him a boundless thought rather than a particular emotion, a source of energy rather than a threat to it, and that the old system would return, seeming to make excessive demands on a limited resource, but he hoped that Hunter would one day experience what he had just been through, and instead of looking for appropriate boundaries would find the idea of boundaries to compassion inherently inappropriate.

He must leave now. Hunter had told him they were going to the gallery opening of a 'light artist' – a category Guido was not familiar with. He had seen the sun rise yesterday morning, after so many days of rain, sending spokes of pink and yellow light through the vaporous trees. He had watched the shadows of the trees stretch out at dawn and then get partially reabsorbed and tilted as the low winter sun crossed the sky. He had felt the light soak his skin and warm his damp clothes and his old bones, and he couldn't help wondering what the 'light artist' would do to capture his interest, when in the hermitage all he had to do was sit in his half-broken chair and watch the day unfold. Still, now that he was only a few hours away from the exhibition, and was surrounded by various forms of artistic endeavour, including a waxwork of St Philip in a glass case under the altar, Guido was less inclined to measure all creativity against Creation. He was hoping for the best from this evening's exhibition, he was hoping that it would be a revelation for everyone who participated, including himself, and so he set off through the church towards the darkening streets and hailed a taxi whose white headlights would soon be crawling along Piccadilly towards Hunter's apartment building overlooking the park.

In all his years, Sebastian had only ever seen a couple of copper pots, and he wasn't even sure if they were in films or in real life, so walking into the Hare and Tortoise properly blew his mind. It must be the world's biggest collection of copper pots – assuming there was another one; this might be *the* collection, the biggest copper pot cluster-fuck on the planet – stuck to the ceiling, nailed to the walls, scattered among the tables, hundreds of gleaming orange eyes watching you from every angle. The pots on the tables and windowsills had red flowers in them, and the ones nearest to the fireplace reflected the orange flames waving warmly from the mock logs, tightening the noose of amber cosiness around the neck of the room. The burnished copper was intensified by the dark wood of the rafters, panelled walls and bar counter. It was all he could do not to run away. The ceiling reminded him of the Sky Mirror he had heroically shattered in his first episode. Most people thought of episodes as things you saw on TV, but some episodes took place on the inner telly, otherwise known as the human mind. For donkey's years, he had felt that his life was a series of episodes written by a committee of strangers, with a strong taste for false leads and hyper violence, and that he hadn't even been allowed to watch a lot of them, but thanks to Dr Carr he could now watch all the episodes and was even allowed into the committee room to make suggestions about slowing things down a bit, having less exploding heads and more human humane humanity.

In this evening's episode, he was going to walk across the floor to the bar and order himself a syphoned Coke with ice and lemon. As usual, he had arrived early because of his fear of being late, but he wasn't going to run away, even though Helio was nowhere to be seen and even though, when he did arrive, he would be seen everywhere: from the sides, from above and all around, burning in miniature bonfires like a religious martyr or a rebel scientist – countless copper Helios warped and stretched and scorched by the watchful pots. Sebastian had agency now, which meant he could make his own decisions. It was the opposite of having 'an' agency, which meant you had an organisation to make a lot of decisions for you. What a big difference a little word could make. That's what Helio wanted from the gallery tonight; he wanted it to become an agency that made decisions about his career. You needed agency to get a career and a career to get an agency, and then an agency so you could lay down the burden of all that agency that got you a career in the first place. One little step at a time.

'Excuse me, mate,' said a voice.

Sebastian realised he was blocking the entrance, staring at what looked to him like a looney bin on acid but was in fact a good old British pub.

'Good old British pub, Good old British pub,' Sebastian whispered to himself as he walked to the bar. As usual, he didn't have much money, but he was determined to buy Helio a proper drink as a thank you, so he was going to nurse his syphoned Coke with ice and lemon until his friend arrived. He settled into a little snug in the corner but had to turn away from the room to get some relief from the visual inferno. Instead of any respite, he found there was a small painting by the side of his bench depicting a kitchen in which a red-faced cook stood by a blazing fire beneath rows and rows of copper pots and pans dangling from the dark beams. It was relentless; there was no escape. It was death by a thousand cuts. He breathed out deeply and tried to focus on the carpet. It turned out to be a kaleidoscope of broken colours capable of absorbing any stain; a spilt glass of red wine, a can of Fanta held upside down by a confused customer, a sprinkling of crème de menthe, a dirty shoe, a nosebleed, a missing tooth; nothing could stand out from the chaos woven into it at birth. It looked as if the factory had got hundreds of volunteers to throw up on the carpet so that any subsequent accident would blend in obligingly with the original design. The whole place had that special smell of a good old British pub, of beer-sodden carpet; baked beans; half-burnt, half-raw sausages; and the damp, pungent aura of people who have just come in from smoking in the rain.

Sebastian realised that along with all the other assaults on his senses, the noise in the room was gradually increasing, the banging of doors, the thud and clink of glasses, and the ever-louder opinions about the trouble with men, the trouble with women, the local weather and whether the weather was the-end-of-the-world weather, and politics and the incorrectness of political correctness, and bicycle lanes and the character traits of mutual friends, and celebrities and the trouble with celebrities. It was as if someone had a recording of Pub Conversation, starring

Bloody Ridiculous, The Trouble Is and You Won't Believe This, and she was slowly turning the volume from six to seven to eight without ever changing the angry views and the cheeky remarks and the sports results and the conspiracy theories bouncing around the lustrous room.

'Who cares what happens after you die? You won't be there anyway,' said a thick-necked man. 'Logically, the battery runs out and that's it.'

'But, darling,' said the elderly lady opposite him, 'why won't you let me believe what I believe? If I thought I would never see Daddy again, it would simply be unbearable.'

'The Jews believe that death is the end,' said her son, 'but we go on through our genes.'

'Do they?' said his sceptical mother. 'I didn't know that; I thought genes had only recently been discovered and the Jews have been around for ages. Anyway, isn't the whole point that they're not *our* genes? We share most of them with chimpanzees.'

On the next table there was an angry man, putting down his glass of beer after taking a swig.

'Not a soul in sight,' he said, 'streets completely deserted, and it's still an Ultra-Low Sadiq Fuckwit Zone. I've been caught, not once, but *twice* for going at *twenty-two* miles an hour in a twenty-mile-an-hour zone. It's bloody ridiculous.'

There were two men on the third table surrounding the snug.

'Her pearls may have been cultured,' said the man with a huge head of white hair and big bags under his icy blue eyes, 'but she most definitely was *not*.'

He pounced on the last word, like a beast on its prey. His friend, who looked as if he had just arrived from the circus and only had time to remove his red nose but not his heavily checked mustard suit, scratched the air, and made a sound like an angry cat.

Sebastian had cut down on his meds to be at his sharpest for the party, but right now he wouldn't mind a whack over the head from the good old chemical cosh. He leant forward on his elbows and pressed his palms gently to his ears.

'Hey, Seb, my man!' said a muffled voice.

'Helio! Hi,' said Sebastian, surging to his feet. 'Wow, ya, this place, far out. It's properly *themed*, right? Copper pots: like 'em or leave 'em.'

Helio burst out laughing. 'That's right, my friend, it's a copper pot theme park.'

'More like a prison,' said Seb. 'Makes me long for a tin of white paint and some stainless-steel saucepans.'

'That's the artist in you,' said Helio, chuckling. 'You're going to see plenty of white walls in the gallery.'

'That'll be a relief,' said Sebastian. 'This place could drive you round the bend if you didn't have your feet on the ground and your head screwed on.'

'Yeah, but you've got your feet on the ground,' said Helio, stomping his Chelsea boots on the complicated carpet.

Sebastian immediately felt less strange and jumpy. Helio was great; there was something about him that always cheered Sebastian up. He had never had a friend like him before, someone who believed in him and wanted him to get well – and happened to have a girlfriend who was as close to being an angel as you could get, without telling a virgin she was pregnant, down on one knee, resting your rainbow-coloured wings respectfully on a chequered floor.

'They are,' said Sebastian, 'my feet are firmly on the ground.' He stomped his good trainers on the crazy carpet, just like Helio had. 'And my head is screwed on,' he added, making a series of little turns, as if tightening his head onto his neck. 'Let me buy you a drink as a thank you.'

'That's very kind of you, Seb,' said Helio. 'I would love a glass of red wine. A Malbec if they have it; rich and strong.'

'Rich and strong,' said Sebastian, 'that would be nice. What's it called again?'

'Malbec.'

'Sounds like the baddy in *Harry Potter*,' said Sebastian. 'That's how I'll remember it.'

'The baddy in *Harry Potter*,' said Helio, shaking his head in disbelief at the wizardry of Sebastian's mind. 'It should be called Goodbec, or Bonbec; it's so delicious.'

Sebastian walked over to the bar, hoping that his debit card was rich and strong enough to handle a glass of Malfoy or Goodboy or Bonfire or, eek, whatever the star-star-star-star it was called.

'I would care for a glass of red wine,' he said to the barmaid, dead sophisticated.

'Anything in particular, dear,' she said. 'We've got Pinot Noir, Rioja, Malbec—'

'That's the one!' said Sebastian. 'The last one.'

'The Malbec?'

'Rich and strong,' said Sebastian knowledgeably.

'Yes, a lot of the customers seem to like it,' said the barmaid. 'I'm not a wine person myself.'

'Neither am I,' said Sebastian, 'it's counter-indicated with my meds.'

She made no comment but measured out the wine and tipped it into a glass.

'There you go,' she said. After tapping some numbers on the screen of a white machine she put it on the counter in front of Sebastian, who held his card in mid-air, not daring to look at the price.

'It's contactless,' she said.

'Well, not completely,' said Sebastian, 'otherwise it would be free.'

'We're not running a charity, dear,' she said. She seemed to be irritated as people often were when he was only trying to make a little joke. Sebastian lowered his card, as if he had made a stupid bluff in a poker game and could only hope that the machine had made an even stupider one. To his amazement a huge tick appeared on the screen with the word APPROVED underneath it.

'Thank you,' said the barmaid somewhat curtly, trying to make it clear to the copper pot watchdog that the slow pace of the transaction was not her responsibility.

'Here you are,' said Sebastian, handing Helio the wine.

'Thank you, my friend.'

Helio clinked his glass of wine against Sebastian's sweating glass of Coke.

'*Saudé!*' he said. 'In Brazil we drink to good health.'

'I should have spent more time there,' said Sebastian.

Helio smiled, and then suddenly looked serious.

'Listen, Seb, when we go to the exhibition, I have to spend some time with Bill Maraschino, the owner of the gallery, face to face, just the two of us, and—'

'And you don't want to have to explain why you brought Looney Tunes to a job interview,' Sebastian cut in with a nervous laugh.

'Hey, seriously, man,' said Helio, 'we've talked about this: don't put yourself down. I think you are a very intelligent, interesting guy and it's beautiful the way you are opening up to the world, but I've got to network with Maraschino – it's a business thing. He's going to be super busy, so we're just talking about a few minutes, yeah? If I got the same dealer as Turrell, that would be my biggest dream come true.'

'I'm sure it will happen,' said Sebastian. 'Your jaguar thing was mind-boggling.'

'Thank you, my friend,' said Helio. 'Listen, a lot of people go to an art show, and they forget to look at the art. A gallery opening is half party and half museum, and they often forget the second half.'

Not if they've been abandoned by their only friend, thought Sebastian. Going to a party and being left all on his lonesome; if it was in a book it would be about the tragedy of the human condition, or something like that, but in real life Mr Morris might be doing the catering, and Gabriella might be there and offer him a tiny mushroom risotto, or some mozzarella, tomato and basil on a toothpick, and she would see that he had gone up in the world and that he was on the other side of the tray now. And they might run away together, back to Heron House, or the flat she shared with her boyfriend, or perhaps Dr Carr would let them crash on his couch.

'No problemo,' he said. 'I'll scout out the art and then you can tell me what it all means when you've finished with Masachismo.'

'Maraschino!' said Helio. 'My God, please don't call him Masachismo.'

Even Helio's ebullience seemed to be crushed by this prospect. He drained the last of his wine.

'Okay, you ready?' he asked.

'Ready as I'll ever be!' said Sebastian, doing his Homer Simpson voice.

'Everyone is so preoccupied with the poison of egoism,' said Hunter, who had politely taken the passenger seat next to Brian, his driver, leaving Lucy and Guido lounging in the well-padded back seats where he usually sat, 'they forget that altruism can be a poison as well.'

'Not with you to remind them,' said Lucy.

'That's what I'm here for,' said Hunter.

'So it seems.'

'There is a paradox the other way around,' said Guido

diplomatically, 'egoism can also be a virtue. If a person is not obsessed with themselves, they can never realise what a waste of time it is.'

'I'm still working on that,' said Hunter.

'While being poisoned by altruism at the same time,' said Lucy. 'You really have your hands full.'

'Busy, busy, busy,' said Hunter. 'Don't forget I used to run a hedge fund.'

'How could I ever forget that?' asked Lucy.

'Did your scan results come in yet?' said Hunter.

'They were perfect,' said Lucy altruistically. 'Even if they hadn't been, I wouldn't have told you tonight when you're having one of your Medici moments.' She stretched forward, with some difficulty, and managed to reach over the back of the passenger seat and squeeze Hunter's shoulder. He put his hand on hers.

'My whole life is a series of Medici moments,' he said; 'you can't help interrupting one of them.'

'This is another paradox, or maybe it is just ironic—' said Guido.

'A paradox is an irony that's been turned into an equation,' said Hunter, 'to hold contradictions in balance. Sorry, I interrupted . . .'

'No, not at all,' said Guido. 'I was just thinking that so much Christian art is built on patronage, but the patronage is often born of repentance, and behind the repentance is sin. So, we look at the beauty of a great painting or building, and we can imagine the anxiety and guilt that paid for it, and then we can imagine the crimes that created the guilt.'

'Well, now we've got vanity rushing in to fill the repentance vacuum,' said Lucy, 'often operating under the name of "Legacy".'

'And whimsy,' said Hunter. 'Don't forget whimsy: I'm

mending Guido's monastery roof because I like him, not because I'm cleansing a murder in the cathedral.'

'No,' said Guido, 'it is because you have a beautiful soul.'

'I think we can put that explanation at the bottom of the list,' said Hunter. 'It's because I've got a lot of money, and there's a basic guilt to being rich. It's not just criminal money that needs to be laundered: it's all filthy lucre. So, this violence–beauty thing, Guido, is it a paradox or just an irony?'

'I think maybe a paradox,' said Guido.

'What would we do without paradox?' said Hunter.

'Be even more confused than we are!' said Guido, with a little laugh. 'It's like when you are climbing a mountain and there are no trees.'

'The treeline,' said Lucy.

'Yes, thank you. After the treeline but before you need extra oxygen to reach the summit, this is the paradox zone.'

'Nice,' said Lucy.

There was a pause in the conversation. Guido felt he was being bombarded with concepts and moods, impressions and expressions, like insects splattering against a windscreen on a summer drive. He mustn't cling to the fragile clarity of his retreat. Silence still seemed to him the natural state, but he knew that it would eventually strike one of his friends as a social failure. For his part he mustn't make the opposite mistake. Conversation didn't pollute silence any more than stars polluted darkness.

'Mind you, the Medici didn't get everything right,' said Hunter. 'They got a bargain on their mausoleum in Florence by placing a big order for tombs, but then the dynasty died out before they could fill them.'

'Tomb futures,' said Lucy, 'just when you thought you'd made a trade that couldn't fail.'

'All they had to do was rebrand,' said Hunter, 'Medici and Friends – problem solved.'

'You're such a problem solver,' said Lucy, 'but there wouldn't have been a "they" to do the rebranding.'

'Somebody must have owned the building,' said Hunter, 'and decided that it was more valuable without the Friends. So, the trade worked out in the end.'

'In the limited sense that they always do,' said Lucy. 'You're right, though, there is something unbeatably pure about an empty tomb; not just the absence of life, but the absence of death.'

'Purity is a lousy ideal,' said Hunter, 'more likely to produce a bulimic or a Nazi than a saint.'

'Yes, yes,' said Guido, 'I was thinking about something like this only a moment ago!'

'Great minds,' said Hunter. 'Purity is a false summit; in fact, by trying to deny your "paradox zone" it's blocking the way to the summit. How long?' he asked, turning to Brian.

'About three minutes,' said Brian.

'Among his continuum of Medici moments,' Lucy explained to Guido, 'Hunter has contributed an installation to this evening. It's the same type that first persuaded him Turrell was a great artist. He saw it in Norfolk where the enlightened owner has one in an old water tower next to his house.'

'Ah, *magnifico*,' said Guido.

'It's a meditation on light,' said Lucy. 'Anyway, I won't say more, you'll see for yourself . . .'

'It's right up your street,' said Hunter.

'We have arrived?' said Guido.

'No, no,' said Hunter, turning back to smile at Guido, 'it's an expression we use over here meaning that it's your kind of thing; something you've already got a taste for.'

'Ah, I understand,' said Guido. 'Yes, *certo*, a meditation on light is, eh, "right up my street".'

Brian parked in front of the gallery.

'I'll be waiting here; it's a single yellow.'

'A single yellow,' said Hunter, 'sounds like a rival art show.'

'It isn't,' said Brian drily.

'Darling, if you want to admire the single yellow,' said Lucy, 'we could go in with Brian to have a look at the Turrells. There are double yellow lines as well.'

'And chevrons,' said Brian. 'You could have a good look at them and lose your licence at the same time.'

'Okay, you've persuaded me,' said Hunter, 'I'm going in. I'm through my road art phase.'

'Speedy Gonzales,' said Lucy.

Hunter got out and opened the door for Lucy. Brian did the same for Guido, who was so deeply reclined that his feet barely reached the floor.

Brian watched the party go into the gallery. The women in black dresses with guest lists on clipboards acknowledged Hunter without bothering to check his name. Mr and Mrs Medici and the family priest. Hunter and Lucy were nice enough, but they didn't half talk rubbish sometimes. What the fuck was the poison of altruism supposed to mean? When he went to see his mum in her old people's home, which was not exactly a barrel of fun, he wasn't going there to poison her (tempting as it sometimes was) but to cheer her up. When he gave money to charity, which he still did, despite the cost-of-living crisis, it wasn't to put cyanide in the water supply, although he could think of some people whose water supply could do with a dose. Rich people were so out of touch with reality, they had nothing better to do than come up with ideas that defied common sense. Christ, his back was killing him. He opened the boot and took out a Red Bull and a strip of painkillers from the little rucksack he had tucked away next to the first-aid kit. You never knew with Hunter. He might go straight home, or he might go to Hertford Street and on to Annabel's or to White's or Black's or Green's or Blue's while Brian was parked outside on a single yellow, the world bloody expert on road art.

Martin pulled the heavy cab door closed behind him and sank down into the seat next to Olivia.

'Poor Noah,' said Olivia, 'he so wanted to come with us, he wouldn't give up all day. Were Charlie and I that difficult to shake off when we were young?'

'It was easier to get a lifeboat on the *Titanic* than get out of the house,' said Martin, 'until we found Helene.'

'The face that launched a thousand lifeboats,' said Francis.

'Exactly,' said Martin. 'After she arrived you couldn't wait for us to go to dinner, or go and sit on a park bench, as long as you got to play with Helene.'

'She had a genius for playing,' said Olivia.

'Yes,' said Martin, 'that's what we liked about her. There's so much talk about spectrums and screens but it's the loss of play that really takes a toll.'

'I wonder where Helene is now,' said Olivia.

'Glasgow,' said Martin.

'How do you know?' said Olivia.

'Because we send her a Christmas card,' said Martin. 'You lost interest in her when you were teenagers, but we kept in touch in a tenuous but friendly way – we owe her so many evenings out.'

'Why did I never know that?'

'You never asked, or perhaps we couldn't handle the competition,' he said, smiling.

'You guys are so secretive,' said Olivia, 'or perhaps it's a professional thing, and I should use softer words like discreet or confidential.'

'Yes, it's not always easy to keep secrets,' said Martin, 'but I suppose it becomes a habit.'

'Everything is habit,' said Francis, 'even being surprised is a habit for some people.'

'OMG! You don't say!' said Olivia.

'There are so many ways to be surprised,' said Martin. 'You can be surprised that a hundred million sharks are being killed every year for their fins – ignorance; you can be surprised in bed with another man's wife – exposure; you can be surprised by something entirely inevitable like death – timing; you can be trapped in the OMG permafrost of perpetual amazement, more of a defence against surprise than surprise itself—'

'Is there any room for surprise in this ruthless model?' Olivia interrupted him.

'A tiny corner,' said Martin, 'is reserved for surprise-in-itself, the real deal. If it weren't genuinely rare it wouldn't pass the entrance exam.'

'Maybe we'll be surprised tonight,' said Francis.

'Well, it's highly unlikely, according to Dad,' said Olivia.

'I don't know his work,' said Martin.

'I did a bit of a background check,' said Francis. 'It seems it's about perception rather than any particular objects of perception. There's a lot of psychology, and physics and meditative practices, and astronomy, and aviation behind his art. Interdisciplinarity is king . . .'

'In exile,' said Martin.

'Well, maybe he's one of the people who wants it back.'

'Sounds interesting,' said Martin. 'There's such an absurdly early forking in the road: science or humanities, being forced to choose at fifteen or sixteen, as if the grown-up thing is to decide they will have nothing to do with each other again . . .'

'OMG,' said Olivia, who was glancing maternally at her phone in case Noah had set the house on fire or Lizzie had lost him in a game of hide-and-seek. 'Lucy has just asked us to dinner after the show. Typical Hunter, either he books you a year in advance or it's completely last minute.'

'The "spontaneity" of a control freak,' said Francis.

'Yes, he will have booked a private dining room a month ago and still has some places to fill,' said Olivia.

'Well, it's very friendly of him,' said Martin, 'before we rip his personality apart altogether.'

'Of course,' said Olivia. 'I don't know where I get this awful habit of analysing people from. Shall I say yes? It seems a bit unfair on Mum.'

'Not at all,' said Martin. 'She's being a grandmother tonight; it would be much more unfair for the three of us to pitch up hungry and full of gossip about things she didn't participate in. Far better to debrief at breakfast about our respective evenings.'

'So, yes,' she said, looking across at Francis enquiringly.

'Sure,' he said, 'could be fun.'

'Okay,' said Olivia. 'We . . . would . . . love . . . to . . . come . . . to . . . dinner . . . what . . . a . . . nice . . . surprise!' She spoke the text out loud as she wrote it. 'I've gone for "nice", rather than predictable, exposing, shockingly timed, artificially spontaneous, and so forth.'

'Good decision,' said Martin.

'Sent,' said Olivia.

Sebastian had tactfully separated from Helio as soon as they got past the clipboard guards. A willowy woman with dark red lipstick and artistic hands had found his name with no trouble at all and welcomed him to the gallery, hoping he would enjoy the show, which was very friendly of her. He and Helio had beaten the crowd and arrived right at the beginning of the show at about the same time as a small man who didn't seem to have got the memo about it not being a fancy-dress party and had come as an Italian priest in *The Godfather*, although that lot often turned out to be assassins dressed as priests and this man didn't look as if he could hurt a fly. Sebastian set off on his lonesome leaving Helio to network with Bill, The Man, Maraschino, and make his greatest dream come true, but he saw that Helio was held in a queue, as if he was ringing a bank (which in a way he was), behind a man who looked familiar to Sebastian for some reason he couldn't put his finger on. Big Bill was making a right old fuss about the bloke in front of Helio, who had a beautiful woman standing next to him on one side and the man in the priest costume on the other, so Seb didn't rate his friend's chances of getting his job interview any time soon. Bill was wearing a black suit and a white shirt with no collar – so his business couldn't have been doing *that* well. He had huge, black proud-to-be-wearing-glasses glasses. Yes, I'm wearing glasses, and I'm proud of it. Have you got a problem with that? No, Bill, I love them, I really do. They're ever so stylish with their thick black frames.

It was a huge bright white room, although there was a wall at the far end with a little doorway into what seemed to be a much darker space. Now that he was all on his owny own, he surveyed the gallery to see which exhibit he was going to check out first so he could have an art chat with Helio once he had finally finished his networking. Scanning the room, Seb felt that the decision was a no-brainer: about two thirds of the way down, slightly off-centre, was a ramp leading up to a large white spherical chamber. A white-coated attendant stood at the foot of the ramp and another by the entrance to the chamber. It looked like a nuclear generator – perhaps it was, reducing the carbon footprint of all the light art, which would be very ecologically sensitive in this day and age.

Dead curious to know what was going on, Sebastian walked up to the first attendant and asked him what this artwork was all about.

'It's part of the Cellular Cell series,' said the attendant.

‘This particular one is called *Bindu Shards*. It’s a highly immersive pre-programmed light cycle that plays for about fifteen minutes and eventually enables you to experience behind-the eyes seeing.’

‘What’s that called when it’s at home?’ said Sebastian.

‘We don’t want to overmanage your expectations, but the physiology of the eye itself will become visible to you. The eye is the outermost layer of the brain and, as I’m sure you know, is made up of structures like rods and cones and blood vessels which you will be able to see within the sphere. It’s really far out,’ said the attendant, briefly ditching his technician’s persona, ‘and there’s usually a big queue, so you’re lucky to get here first.’

‘Great,’ said Sebastian. ‘I’m up for it. I didn’t know art could be like this. It sounds more like a rave or something.’

‘We have to warn you that it is a very intense experience,’ said the attendant, re-establishing his flat but solicitous tone, ‘and so we ask you to sign a disclaimer, confirming that you don’t suffer from epilepsy and have not taken any drugs today.’

‘I never take drugs,’ said Seb, ‘I don’t even drink; it’s counter-indicated; and I don’t have epilepsy.’

‘Good. Please print your name and sign here and choose between the soft and hard options.’

Sebastian did as he was told and walked up the ramp to the entrance of the sphere. The second attendant helped him mount a sliding table and slotted him into the cell headfirst. He couldn’t help being reminded of a film he had seen about the French Revolution and how they used to slide people under the guillotine. Inside, he lay beneath a blue light that was so rich and strong (it should probably be called Malbec Blue) that it seemed to be solid, as if all the blue photons had been crushed together to squeeze out the space that might normally be separating them. Instead of looking at a blue-coloured dome, he was under a blue hemisphere. Then the lights started pulsing so fast that he hardly had time to read the images of flowers and crystals that flashed among the saturated, changing colours. Gradually the images of things that were clearly not inside the pod, like skyscrapers, were replaced by images of things that were not only inside the pod but within his own eyeballs. The rods and cones that enabled him to see were seeing the rods and cones that enabled him to see. He was seeing seeing, inside out and outside in, and he felt his mind shimmering and floating in this new space, which he seemed to have been waiting for all his life. He'd had ever so much trouble over the years working out what was real and what was not, what he was imagining and what was really going on, but now he was imagining what was really going on. It was such a relief. And then he wondered if he already had an inner image of the crystals and flowers and skyscrapers he had seen before because if he didn't, how did he know what they were when they flashed before his eyes? In a way he was just recognising stuff, and you could say that a baby wouldn't know what the images represented, but in this space, it seemed to be much deeper than that, it seemed like he had been misled all these years, thinking his eyes and ears and the rest of them were antennae for picking up a broadcast that he was being forced to watch on the old inner telly, otherwise known as the human mind, but now he felt that there was an inner and outer version of the world and that they were rushing to meet each other like lovers, like lovers who catch sight of each other in a crowd, and that their meeting was in this richly coloured solid light. Reality was (in reality) a love affair. He had never had a love affair, as such, and because it was so incredibly beautiful, it made him want to cry but it also made him want to cry because he had missed out on this all his life, and so it was incredibly sad as well. He felt joyful and terrified and terrified that the joy would be taken away. And then it stopped, and the attendant slid the table back out and helped him to get to his feet.

Sebastian walked dazed down the ramp, trying to keep his grip on what had happened, feeling that it was immensely important but difficult to hold on to now that he was no longer in that extraordinary space. The priest impersonator was standing at the bottom, next in line.

'That was properly mind-blowing,' said Sebastian.

'This is a good thing?' said the man, who had gone the extra mile and put on an Italian accent.

'Yeah, inside out, outside in, super intenso. I couldn't tell whether I was imagining it or if it was really the inside of my eyes. I totally got it for a while but now I feel I'm losing it.'

'Maybe they work together,' said the man with a smile and a charming simplicity.

'Yeah, right, yeah, that's what I was feeling,' said Sebastian. 'You really should be a priest. My head was spinning a bit there, but you've set me back on the right path.'

'But I am a priest! My name is Father Guido,' said Guido, handing back the signed disclaimer to the first attendant.

'Really!' said Sebastian. 'Well, I suppose somebody must be a priest, or there wouldn't be any – like skyscrapers,' he added obliquely. 'I'm Sebastian. I don't know why I'm surprised that you're a real priest; I met a cardinal at a party once, waxy-faced bloke in a scarlet dress.'

'Here in London,' said Guido, 'at the Happy Helmets launch?'

'Yeah, that's the one!' said Sebastian. 'Happy Helmets, how did you know that?'

'I was there! So, we have met before at one of Hunter's parties.'

'I'm sorry, sir,' said the first attendant, 'I'm going to have to ask you to move up the ramp.'

'*Scusa, scusa*,' said Guido. 'I did not expect to meet a friend. *Arrivederci*, Sebastian, we will talk later.'

'Defo,' said Sebastian. 'I really enjoyed talking to you, I really did.'

Guido waved to him from the top of the ramp, like an unwisely dressed astronaut about to get into a rocket.

What a nice man, thought Sebastian. He wished he had a father like Father Guido, rather than a father who thought that babies were human ashtrays for stubbing out your cigarettes in. Father Guido had called him his friend, which meant he didn't just have one friend here any more. He looked for Helio and saw that he had made it to the front of the queue and was now having his moment with Big Bill. He would have to wait a bit longer before he could reconnect with him. In the meantime, the party had transformed during his rave in the *Bindu Shards*. The gallery now looked like the Intergalactic Bar in *Star Wars*, an indistinct hubbub full of jabbering aliens, a bubble and squeak of languages and cries, of wobbling jowls, and ribbed foreheads bulging with brains and Botox.

He had to get away and have a moment to think about what had happened in the nuclear generator, he had to find somewhere quiet to sit down and take the weight off. He knew the inner telly had been blown up but what was he going to put there instead?

'I think I'll go and take a look at some of these artworks,' said Martin, rather suddenly.

He gave Olivia's forearm a little squeeze and started to work his way through the crowd until he felt he was no longer visible from the position where he had seen Carmen come into the gallery. He was sure she would respect the confidentiality of their relationship, but he would rather avoid running into her if possible. It would have been an innocuous enough encounter, except that he knew Carmen had considered Francis a competitor for Hope's affections at some point during her brief tenure.

'At least Hope didn't leave me for another woman,' Carmen

had told him stoically. 'I can forgive myself for not having a penis.'

'We used to be taught that not all women can,' said Martin, 'although I think the rumours of envy may have been exaggerated.'

'You guys must envy our wombs and vaginas,' said Carmen.

'Absolutely,' said Martin. 'Karen Horney introduced the idea of "womb envy" long ago. A lot of male boastfulness is based on envy of women's primary role in creating life.'

Carmen had seemed to be pleased by the acknowledgement of this fundamental deficiency in a phallocentric world.

Luckily the gallery was by now quite full, and Martin felt it was safe to pause in the middle of the chattering throng, whose strongest common purpose was to ignore the art menacing its wagon formation of comments and complaints.

'The only way,' said a man with a mane of white hair and icy blue eyes, 'to get into the House of Lords these days is to have inflicted enormous harm on this country, or to have well-known ties to the Russian Secret Services – it's no use being the Duke of Devonshire.'

The man next to him scratched the air and made the sound of an angry cat.

'*Lord* Cameron, if you please, the noble life peer, or death peer, as he should be called, since his grotesque title will, thank goodness, die with him, must have *begged* to be made Foreign Secretary so that he could spend more days abroad than the rest of us after the catastrophe of his second unconstitutional *pleb*-iscite,' he said, leaping on the first syllable of the last word, like a beast on its prey.

Martin decided that perhaps he should find an even more remote place to wait until Carmen had moved away from his family and friends.

'There's room for one more,' said a friendly woman by the entrance to a dark space at the far end of the gallery.

'Is this an installation like the one at Houghton Hall?' asked Martin.

'Yes, that's right,' said the usher. 'Have you ever been there?'

'No, but I have a friend who was first impressed by the artist after seeing that installation.'

'Well, it's quite dark inside so you'll have to feel your way down the corridor and there should be a seat at this end of the bench. When you've settled down, I can close the door, and we can begin. It takes about fifteen minutes.'

'Marvellous,' said Martin.

'Olivia,' said Lucy, 'do you know Carmen?'

'Oh, you're Carmen,' said Olivia. 'Pleased to meet you. Francis, my husband, told me that he met you a while back at Yab-Yum. He didn't mention that you had moved to London.'

'Oh my God, so you're Olivia!' said Carmen. 'I never got in touch with Francis because I met him so briefly in California, I thought it would be presumptuous.'

'I'm sure he would always be happy to hear from someone close to Hope.'

'Oh, we haven't been together for a while,' said Carmen, 'that's part of the reason I moved to London. Hope leads to disappointment and disappointment to fresh victims for Hope.'

'Sounds like a well-oiled machine,' said Olivia.

'She could have "well-oiled machine" on her tombstone,' said Carmen, with a loud but unfriendly laugh. 'What's that white pod over there, the thing that looks like an observatory?'

'I suppose it is a sort of observatory,' said Lucy. 'You should check it out. They slide you in on a morgue table until your head is in the middle of the dome and then . . . I won't say too much.'

'I think I will check it out,' said Carmen. 'I'm intrigued. It's been a pleasure to meet you, Olivia. See you later, girl,' she said to Lucy.

'The pleasure of meeting Carmen was minuscule,' said Olivia, watching her walk away, 'compared to the relief she gave me when Francis went to visit Hope and Carmen turned out to be her girlfriend.'

'Really?' said Lucy. 'She's always struck me as energetically superficial, while hinting at hidden depths, like a skater dashing across the ice in a wetsuit and mask. She's gone up in my estimation now I know that she helped stabilise your marriage.'

'That's her hidden depth,' said Olivia, smiling. 'So, what is it like in "the observatory"?'

'It couldn't help having a medical feel for me,' said Lucy. 'You get to see inside your eye, which also felt rather medical. Sometimes opticians can see tumours when they shine a light deep into someone's eyes, and so now they're going to be allowed to refer people directly to a specialist, rather than hint that the person who came in for a new pair of reading glasses should make an appointment with their GP as soon as possible, without being able to tell them why. Anyway, that's the sort of thing I thought about, but of course it's also an extraordinary work of art.'

'So, how are your scan results?' asked Olivia.

'It turns out that the tumour has grown a tiny bit, by a millimetre here and there. It's asymptomatic, as it's not pressing on the motor strip, and anyway the brain can find ways round a certain amount of obstruction.'

'What are you going to do?'

'I don't know. Paul says we can just leave it, if I want, or we can do a new kind of heat treatment that stimulates an immune response. They normally give that with Temozolomide, but I'm not sure I can face the whole chemo thing again . . .'

'Can you have the heat without—' Olivia began, but interrupted herself, seeing Francis move towards them.

'Hi there,' said Francis.

'So, how's Ecuador?' said Lucy rather abruptly. 'Are there any trees left, or is it all oil refineries and birth defects and illegal gold mines and murdered ecologists and shackled attorneys and rivers flowing with mercury and money?'

'Well, I know you've got me down as a purveyor of eco gloom,' said Francis, 'but . . .'

'But what?' said Lucy. 'Has General Power taken responsibility for all the illness and contamination?'

'No, of course not,' said Francis. 'Natural resources are limited but General Power's capacity for judicial dishonesty is infinite. What's encouraging, though, is that everyone else has recognised where the illness and the contamination come from. General Power will end up like a Mafia boss with dementia, muttering in his prison cell about making offers they can't refuse to opponents he murdered forty years ago. There's been a breakthrough case, led by a wonderful woman called Nemonte Nenquimo, which has resulted in a court ruling protecting half a million acres of Waorani land. She is now teaching other indigenous people how to win similar cases for their own territories. General Power will never admit to the harm it's done, but perhaps they can be prevented from doing it again. If no one wants them on their land and the only place they can drill for oil is under their own headquarters in Houston, then that would be a good enough compromise.'

'He's so hardcore,' said Olivia.

'*Que hombre*,' said Lucy, with a smile.

'I'm excited, though,' said Olivia, 'because I'm thinking of doing a new series called *Solutions*, also with six programmes, but with a rather different flavour. I might start with Nemonte Nenquimo's story.'

'Sounds great,' said Lucy. 'But your *Apocalypse* series hasn't been broadcast yet, has it?'

'No, the first one goes out in early January. On the sixth.'

'Twelfth Night.'

'Exactly,' said Olivia. 'We've decided to start with nuclear weapons.'

'The logical choice for a launch,' said Lucy. 'I'll listen from under a school desk.'

'Obviously, we'll be recommending that at the beginning of the programme,' said Olivia.

Martin had groped his way into the installation as instructed and heard the thud of the closing door. He was now sitting on the end of the bench in total darkness, waiting for what he hoped would be more than a symbolic non-appearance, the visual equivalent of Godot – *Waiting for Photot*. The usher had said 'it' would take about fifteen minutes, but for all he knew, 'it' would be their liberation from this room, and the light art would turn out to be light itself, or something like that. Mind you, it was quite relaxing, not having to make conversation, leaning against a reasonably comfortable wall, in darkness and silence. It was certainly unlike any other art he had experienced, defying the fetishistic craving for something to look at, a crucifixion, an Arcadian landscape or a haystack, a portrait of a grandee, or of the artist's wife having yet another bath, an abstract work with a very definite name which smuggled a figurative fantasy back among the spattered paint or fields of colour, or one with no name at all, refusing to provide any respite from its austerity, and so on and so forth. Perhaps there wasn't even a Godot, and it was more like John Cage's famously 'silent' *4.33*, only three times longer. Perhaps someone would cough soon or walk out, to generate some ambient noise; or maybe everyone else on the bench knew something he didn't. At least he was safe from Carmen. That's why he had come in here, and he really couldn't have asked for a better place to hide, given that he was at an exhibition. Martin could only assume that part of his strange discombobulation was caused by his anxiety about the inevitable revelation of his relationship with the patient he cared about most, rather than the one he cared about least, the rich, discontented nomad who treated psychoanalysis as an extension of her skincare regime. All patients were equal, but some were more equal than others, and he had to admit that he would have thrown Carmen to the wolves of professional ethics if it could have saved Sebastian from their snarling fangs. It would of course be a useless sacrifice, but the unconscious had its own strange logic and accountancy, which it was his job to understand, and in his own case to see through at inception.

Hold on a moment, the room was not entirely dark after all. There seemed to be some kind of nascent glow rising from the base of the wall opposite the bench. Slowly, what had seemed to be a black wall was becoming suffused with a faint pink light. As the room grew brighter Martin realised that his eyes had been adjusting to the dark, that he had been blind but now he could see, and that what he was seeing was a light that had been there all along. For some reason, it was immensely moving. He was filled with gratitude that he had not been in the dark after all. He wanted to reach out and touch the light as he had reached out and touched Olivia's arm before he disappeared into the crowd, to communicate something simple and whole that words would have disintegrated.

'Beautiful,' he murmured.

Hunter had not told him why this was the installation that first excited him about Turrell's work but now he felt he understood. As the light grew more visible, people started to get up and file out. They had got the point, or not, and were moving on. Martin wanted to stay a little, to shelter himself from the storm of voices and photons outside the refuge of this room. It had been a long day and he wanted to linger for a second round, although of course there could be no second round unless he went outside and allowed the strong light to decompose the rhodopsin in the rods of his eyes.

'Is that you, Dr Carr?'

Martin looked up, thinking he must be in some twilight zone created by the low light conditions and be hallucinating what he had been thinking of only a moment ago.

'Sebastian?'

'Fancy meeting you here?' said Sebastian. 'What are the chances, hey?'

'Gosh,' said Martin. 'I suppose they're one hundred per cent now that we have met.'

'Quick as a whistle,' said Sebastian. 'I like that: once something has happened the chances of it happening are one hundred per cent. No flies on you, Dr Carr.'

'I have to keep on my toes around you, Sebastian,' said Martin.

'What I'm not so sure about,' said Sebastian, 'was that thing we just saw. Call that art? Someone behind a screen turning the dimmer up! It's probably done by a computer anyway. I liked the other one, though: behind-the-eyes seeing, they call it.'

'I don't think there was someone turning a dimmer switch,' said Martin. 'I think it was about our eyes adjusting to the dark in low light conditions. That pink light was there all along.'

'Ohhh,' said Sebastian, tapping his temple with his index finger. 'Well, I never. That's dead clever, isn't it? How did you know that?'

'I don't really,' said Martin, 'I'm just guessing. Partly because of what you said. There wouldn't be any point to someone turning a dimmer switch – however slowly.'

'Exactly,' said Sebastian. 'Not so much a case of "Don't try this at home" as "Try not doing this at home". You must be right. And the other installation was also about the eyes, and seeing and how it works. I think that's Desert Dad's main gig: looking into seeing. Makes complete sense. Another insight for the old insight album, hey, Dr Carr? We'll have a hundred volumes before we're finished working together. It's ever so nice to run into you like this. I know three people here now. Makes it more of a party if you have other people to talk to.'

Martin moved up the corridor slowly, trying to work out how he could escape from Sebastian without making him feel rejected or abandoned, but before being spotted with him by Olivia, and without running into Carmen.

'Are you enjoying the party?' said Sebastian.

'It's one of the most extraordinary evenings I've had for a long time,' said Martin.

'Me too,' said Sebastian, as they emerged into the main room. 'It's good practice for me. I can say things like, "Do you come here often?" That's the sort of thing people say, isn't it?'

'Yes,' said Martin. 'They're certainly reputed to.'

'So, Dr Carr, do you come here often?' said Sebastian playfully.

'No,' said Martin, 'I've never been here before and I doubt I'll ever come again.'

'Don't say that!' said Sebastian. 'It's lovely here.'

'Sebastian,' said Martin, allowing himself to rest a hand on his shoulder, 'I didn't mean to sound negative. It's wonderful that you're enjoying yourself and it's wonderful that you can be playful.'

'Well, a lot of that is down to you, Dr Carr,' said Sebastian. 'I've been practising and I'm sure I'll get better at it over the years.'

'I've no doubt about that,' said Martin.

'Sebastian?'

Sebastian turned around.

'Olivia! What are the chances? Oh,' said Sebastian, smiling at Martin, 'a hundred per cent, right? Meeting/not meeting.' He held one palm above the other and then slapped them together. 'Meeting. There's nothing faster than reality, right? From nought to a hundred in a single collapse.'

'It's a lot to take in,' said Martin, frowning significantly at Olivia.

'It is, it is,' said Sebastian. 'There's Helio, and Olivia, and the priest fellow (we go way back), Father Guido, and Dr Carr. Oh, I should introduce you. Olivia, this is Dr Carr, he's my psycho-nannylist, I mean analyst. Whoops. We'll be talking about that slip in the next session, hey, Dr Carr! One for the old insight album. I'm a bit overexcited, to be honest. This is my Bio Sis, Olivia, Dr Carr, my psycho-an-a-lyst. Phew, got there in the end. Better late than never.'

'Is he?' said Olivia. 'Really? Well, what are the chances, as you would say?'

'One hundred per cent,' muttered Sebastian. 'What's the sound of two hands clapping? Collapse. There could be two things and then there's actually one thing – that's what Professor Al-Khalili said on the telly. I should probably find Helio, he brought me here, and it's not fair to be abandoned by him, I mean, to abandon him. Same difference. I'm not used to meeting so many people all at once, to be honest.'

Sebastian clapped his hands together repeatedly.

'Total Claps,' he said quietly, 'that's reality for you.'

'Well, let's go and find Helio together,' said Olivia, giving Martin an amazed and somewhat reproachful look.

'I think we were going to go to the same dinner,' said Martin to Olivia, with a polite but neutral tone. 'I wonder if you would be kind enough to tell Lucy and Hunter that I am not feeling on top form and think it might be better if I head home. I have a very busy day tomorrow.'

'That's me!' said Sebastian. 'Dr Carr sees me tomorrow: I'm an extremely busy day. I'm only joking, I know there are others.

He helps ever so many people. I can honestly say that my shrink has made me a bigger man – ba-boom! I've been practising my jokes. Everyone likes a joke, don't they? How do you two know each other anyway?'

'Oh, we go way back,' said Olivia.

'Like me and Father Guido,' said Sebastian.

'At least that far,' said Olivia.

'But not as far as you and me,' said Sebastian to Olivia.

'Oh, no,' said Olivia, 'nobody goes back that far.'

'Aren't you coming with us to look for Helio?' said Sebastian.

'No, no, I'll see you tomorrow,' said Martin.

'All right then,' said Sebastian sadly. 'I'll tell you what happens.'

'I look forward to it,' said Martin warmly.

'I last saw him over there,' said Sebastian to Olivia, 'he was talking to Big Bill, The Man, Maraschino.'

Martin watched Olivia and Sebastian work their way back towards the front of the gallery. So, it had finally happened, the collision he had been anticipating for so long, but instead of being on top of the hill watching it, Martin felt that he was in the front compartment of both trains.

Olivia and Sebastian arrived at the front of the gallery, looking for Helio, but before they could find him, they ran across Hunter and Lucy.

'This is my brother Sebastian,' said Olivia, sounding more surprised than she had intended.

'The long-lost twins,' said Lucy. 'It's so great that the two of you have found each other.'

'I'm sorry to say that Martin is feeling a little under the weather and won't be able to come to dinner,' said Olivia.

'Too bad,' said Hunter. 'Maybe Sebastian would like to come instead.'

‘That’s very friendly of you, I’m sure,’ said Sebastian.

‘If we lose track of each other, it’s the private dining room in Wilton’s, eight fifteen.’

‘What? You mean we’re each going to eat on our own?’ said Sebastian.

Hunter burst out laughing. ‘Solitary confinement, the ultimate dinner invitation. Eat your heart out, Buñuel.’

‘Eating your heart out, all on your lonesome. You couldn’t get more Buñuel than that,’ said Sebastian, like a child who has just read a word without knowing what it means but wants to test it out as soon as possible.

‘Where have you been hiding this guy?’ said Hunter, smiling at Olivia. ‘We’ve got a few places left. This is an improv dinner. We just took the room and then thought we’d assemble a party along the way. Bill is coming! Bill, come and meet my friends, Olivia and Sebastian. Bill, whose gallery we’re in.’

‘Pleased to meet you,’ said Maraschino. ‘Are you enjoying the show?’

‘I love it,’ said Sebastian. ‘I hope it’s a big success and that you can afford to get some collars for your shirts.’

Maraschino looked grave for a moment, but hearing Hunter laughing merrily, he smiled and said, ‘Here’s hoping!’ holding up the crossed fingers of both hands.

‘He’s been saving up for years,’ said Hunter confidentially to Sebastian, ‘and I think this is going to be the breakthrough show.’

‘Defo, it really gets you thinking,’ said Sebastian. ‘I mean, the “the visible spectrum” and its opposite number: the invisible spectrum. The conscious mind and the unconscious mind. I mean, reality is what we can see and what we can’t see as well; what we know and what we don’t know. The bit we don’t know is like the long-lost twin Lucy was talking about earlier.’

‘Well, that’s a remarkable observation,’ said Maraschino. ‘Are you an art critic?’

‘Well, not as such,’ said Sebastian, ‘but I have been thinking a lot about art recently, very recently.’

‘Maybe we could persuade you to write a catalogue essay, while the thoughts are still fresh in your mind,’ said Maraschino.

‘Don’t know about that,’ said Sebastian, ‘it’s been donkey’s years since I have written an essay.’

‘Well, we must get you back into the fold,’ said Maraschino.

‘Seb, my friend! I’ve been looking for you.’

‘Helio, I’ve been looking for you everywhere – or not everywhere, as I would have found you if I had done that. This is my Bio Sis, Olivia, and this is Hunter and Lucy who’ve been very friendly and asked me to a private dining room, although my vote is for all of us to sit around the same table, as it’s ever such fun having conversation.’

‘The critic’s mind,’ said Maraschino, beaming a smile at Hunter, “private dining room”. So, you know Helio as well?’ he asked Sebastian.

‘Of course I do,’ said Sebastian. ‘I was checking out the gallery to see if it was the right home for his work.’

‘We’re very impressed by his work,’ said Maraschino.

‘I should hope so too,’ said Sebastian. ‘Have you seen *The Jaguar Brings Down Fire from Heaven*? It’s genius.’

‘We have just agreed a date,’ said Maraschino, finally committing to a studio visit.

‘This man,’ said Sebastian, putting an arm around Helio’s shoulder, ‘is the best person you could have on your team – along with Dr Carr.’

Maraschino looked momentarily lost, making a note to get his assistant to find out who this rapper-styled young artist was. He seemed to have lost track of the cutting-edge of London’s art scene. Dr Carr must have sprung up while he was in New York for six months. He couldn’t afford to let these long periods go by without checking out the new talent.

'Of course,' he said. 'I love his work too. If we take on Helio, would you do us the honour of writing a catalogue essay?'

Sebastian puffed out his cheeks, remembering the sarcastic reception Mr Bracket had given his last essay, a few weeks before his disastrous GCSEs. 'Sebastian Tanner, your essay is history in this sense only,' Mr Bracket had said, tearing the pages in half and dropping them in the wastepaper basket. 'Causes of the First World War, without the benefits of a Martian perspective, thank you, Sebastian, on my desk by tomorrow morning, or you'll be facing another detention.'

That was the last essay he had written, but this one wasn't for Mr Bracket.

'All right, then, I'll do it,' said Sebastian defiantly. 'What are friends for, eh?'

Noah had persuaded Granny to give him almost all the crunchy top layer of the fish pie and then put some tomato ketchup on it. After she had dug into the soft potato and fish goo under the topping, he saw some pieces of salmon which he carefully picked out. His plate then had slightly burnt brown potato, bright red tomato, and pink salmon on it, whereas poor Granny had a pile of white mud on her plate with a yellow puddle of buttery water spreading around it.

'Would you like some of mine?' he asked, finally broken by pity.

'No thanks, darling, I've got just what I want. Peas?'

'No, thanks.'

Then there were stewed pears, but they had cloves stuck in them, which looked like rusty old nails, so he decided to have some of the vanilla ice cream that was supposed to go with them and asked Granny if he could have two squares of chocolate because if you stuck them in the corners of the scoop, they looked like ears. Granny was great, she agreed to more or less anything, unlike his parents who made him eat sticks of cucumber and carrots dipped in squished-up avocado. He liked some healthy things, but it was fun getting Granny to give him delicious things without asking for anything back. Usually it was, 'If you learn your times table', or 'After you've washed your hair'. Nobody said to grown-ups that they couldn't have a gin and tonic unless they were doing the school run or could only watch a film if they were driving a combine harvester at the same time. It was so unfair. He had complained to his father about it, and Dad had said, 'Yes, it's called "double standards", darling.' And Noah had said, 'Well, that's not good, is it?' And Dad had said, 'Well, it's good for some people and not good for others – that's rather the point – but it's certainly not fair.'

While Granny was clearing up, Noah went next door and put his secret plan into operation. He took all the cushions off the sofas and armchairs and made a cushion fortress in the middle of the room and put all the lamps on the ground behind chairs and under tables so that they cast giant shadows. He looked for a children's book in the shelves and found one called *The Drama of the Gifted Child*. It sounded like it was a Christmas story, which was perfect as Christmas was coming up soon, and he put it in the middle of the cushion fortress, next to his Little Sun. The Little Sun had been invented so that a child who lived off the grid could still be read a bedtime story. And then he climbed into the cushion fortress and sat there next to the book. It turned out that *he* was the child who lived off the grid, so he shouted 'Granny!' because he couldn't be expected to wait for ever after arranging everything so perfectly.

'Coming,' said Granny from the kitchen.

When she came into the drawing room Granny was truly wonderstruck, especially when he turned on his solar lamp and it glowed among the cushions.

'Goodness, Noah,' she said, 'you've made a light show of your own!'

'That's right,' said Noah.

'And you've built a sort of Stonehenge with the cushions.'

'It's a fortress,' said Noah. 'Is Stonehenge a fortress?'

'It's more to do with celebrating things like the winter solstice – the shortest day of the year – which is coming up next week. It looks very like what you've done with the cushions, but done with stones instead, and the sun comes up in between them at special times of the year.'

'Like this!' said Noah, his sun lamp rising slowly behind his standing cushions.

'Exactly. Shall I take a photo for Mum and Dad? This is so wonderful; I think I should make a record of it.'

When Granny came back into the room, she was reading something on her phone and seemed less cheerful than before.

'What's wrong?' said Noah.

'Nothing . . . nothing,' said Granny.

Now Noah was sure there was something wrong, or she wouldn't have said 'nothing' twice.

'Is it about Uncle Charlie?' he asked.

'Why did you ask that?' said Granny, looking at him sharply. She sat down in one of the armchairs, but she seemed much smaller because the cushions had gone.

'I don't know,' said Noah. 'I often think about him when I'm staying in his room.'

'Synchronicity,' said Granny, who was talking to grown-ups who weren't in the room, which she didn't usually do. 'A Jungian would go bananas.'

'What's a Jungian?' said Noah.

'They're like me and Grandad, they try to help people understand what they're really feeling.'

'Well, maybe I'm a Jungian,' said Noah, 'because I'm trying to understand what you're really feeling.'

Granny laughed and put her phone down after taking a photo and typing a short message.

'Come and give me a hug,' she said, holding out her arms.

Her cardigan was very soft against his cheek.

'Shall we watch *Incredibles 2*?' she asked.

'No,' said Noah. 'I liked the first one, but now they have a new baby who has too many superpowers. There's no point in someone who has too many superpowers. That's why Achilles has his heel in the book of Greek myths I have at home, and Superman can't be in the same room as Kryptonite.'

'That's so true,' said Granny, and she hugged him a bit too hard, as if someone might be trying to take him away.

'Grandpa!' said Noah.

'Oh,' said Lizzie, 'back already? Are the others with you?'

'No,' said Martin, 'I came ahead, there was a dinner plan I found intimidating.'

'It's not like you to find a dinner plan intimidating,' said Lizzie.

'It's not like a dinner plan to be intimidating,' said Martin. 'I think I'll go to bed. Imagine that, Noah, Grandpa going to bed before you!'

'But you haven't seen my light show,' said Noah.

'I'm looking at it right now,' said Martin, 'and I think it's magnificent. I wish I had stayed for your exhibition instead of going to the one at the Maraschino Gallery.'

'Don't worry, Grandpa,' said Noah, who felt that there was something sad in his grandfather's demeanour, 'you're home now, so it's all alright.'

17

Last night turned out to be, beyond the shadow of a doubt, the best evening of Sebastian's entire life. It had started with him being brushed off because he might be an embarrassment to his friend's business dealings with Big Bill Maraschino, but in the end, it had been Sebastian who nailed the studio visit that Helio was afraid he would undermine. Not only that, but when Hunter heard that Helio might be represented by Maraschino and was a friend of Sebastian's, he had included him in his private dinner party. Wilton's was the poshest restaurant Sebastian had ever set foot in. The logo above the entrance was a dead-sophisticated prawn with a top hat, leaning on his cane, looking as if he was in the mood for a cocktail or a cocktail sauce, and about to say something that Oscar Wilde would have killed for. The carpet was so rich and thick, he wanted to kneel down and stroke it like a sleeping puppy; the light was gentle and reassuring, like the light in the dark space of the gallery which Dr Carr had explained to him had been there all along, blushing like a woman who has been paid a compliment by someone she is secretly in love with. The waitress was so polite that Sebastian almost asked her to stop because he didn't feel he deserved it. When his smoked salmon arrived, the slices were as thin and bright as window-panes at sunset, and the lemon was wrapped in a white net, tied with a green silk ribbon, and the pepper instead of being the grey powder he was used to was like broken black pearls scattered across his plate. It was so perfect he hardly dared touch it.

When he arrived for his session, Dr Carr was standing by the open door as usual, in his dark grey suit and maroon woolly tie, smiling and welcoming. Sebastian lay down and started talking before his head had settled on the back of the couch.

'You should have come last night, Dr Carr. It was a winner; in fact, it was the all-time best. I kept thinking: Why would Dr Carr turn down a dinner like this? I hope he's not feeling too poorly. Maybe you go to dinners like that all the time, but it's hard to believe, because even Lucy and Hunter, who gave the dinner, said it was a very special occasion and that they were delighted to have met me. I don't think anyone has ever said they were "delighted" to have met me. I was ever so touched. I was sitting between Lucy and Olivia, and they looked after me, and showed me the ropes, as they knew that I'd never been to a place like that before. I was going to take the little mesh off my lemon, but Lucy explained that it was for stopping the pips falling onto my smoked salmon, and that there was probably someone who had spent the whole afternoon wrapping half lemons in little muslin nets, and I said I wouldn't want to hurt her feelings (for some reason I imagined she was a nice old lady with a smiley face who had been doing it for donkey's years and could tie the ribbons in a jiffy) and Lucy said that was very considerate of me. And Olivia advised me to have these sole nuggets with a French name and a delicious creamy sauce that was the same thing twice, like chin chin, or Mau Mau . . .'

'Tartar,' Dr Carr suggested.

'That's the one!' said Sebastian. 'Have you been to Wilton's?'

'I haven't,' said Dr Carr, 'but I have had tartar sauce in my time. It's interesting that you should say "the same thing twice" when you were sitting next to your twin sister for the first time at a meal. From what we know of your history, you were never together at the same meal, even when you would naturally have expected to be: at a time when your mother would have been breastfeeding both of you. Perhaps you wish that your mother could at least have been like the nice old lady who you imagined in the kitchen: someone who knows exactly what she's doing and has been doing it for decades; perhaps for all your life, quietly in the background, knowing just how to hold things together and secure them with a beautiful ribbon.'

'You're on fire today, Dr Carr. That's one for the old insight album,' said Sebastian cheerfully, but with no intention of being distracted from his narrative. 'I didn't even know there were places like that. I felt ashamed that I had thought a private dining room was one where you ate all on your own, but Olivia said that it was a very natural thing to think and that my interpretation – that's the word she used, which reminded me of you – was much closer to the real meaning of the actual words, and that Hunter and Big Bill Maraschino had thought it was a brilliant joke, so I had turned it to great advantage. She gave me so much confidence. Instead of feeling like I was a stupid fool, I felt like I was a big success. I'm ever so fortunate to have her as a sister. She must have lucked out in the old adoption lottery, unlike yours truly.'

'Well,' said Dr Carr, 'we know that you were adopted by people who were too rigid and conventional for someone with your powerful imagination and your fragile ego, but the way in which you were truly unlucky in "the old adoption lottery" was that you didn't get adopted *immediately*.'

'Yeah, yeah,' said Sebastian, 'Bio Mum did her best, but my Bio Dad was The Creature from the Black Lagoon. Anyway, Lucy advised me to have the Bread-and-Butter Pudding, and I said that I'd been having bread and butter all my life, and it was practically the only thing I recognised on the menu, so perhaps I should have the Gateau Opera, or Pavlova whatnot, and she said, "Trust me." And I did trust her, and it was the best dessert I ever had in my whole life, covered in double cream. And when I'd finished, I felt so happy it made me sad, if you know what I mean, and I said to Lucy, "I don't suppose I'll ever eat something that delicious again," and she said, "Don't be silly, we can come here again. I know it sounds ridiculous, but this is my local. Hunter's flat is just down the road." Can you imagine anyone being that kind?'

Sebastian leant forward and pulled a couple of paper handkerchiefs from the box on a ledge by the couch.

'That was very kind of her,' said Dr Carr. 'It seems that it was trust that transformed the most ordinary thing in your life, bread and butter, into the most extraordinary thing, the Bread-and-Butter Pudding you had last night.'

'You never stop, do you?' said Sebastian, laughing a little and blowing his nose at the same time.

'I have been your "psycho-nanny-lyst", as you pointed out last night.'

'Yeah, that was a classic!' said Sebastian. 'Freudian slip of the century.'

'I think that when we started working together five years ago,' said Dr Carr, 'you did need something like a psycho-nanny-lyst, someone who would look after your most basic needs, but that now you have come to enjoy having a psychoanalyst with whom you are collaborating on making interpretations, on building up "the old insight album". You have grown to trust the process that lies behind the relationship.'

'Yeah, I suppose,' said Sebastian, 'I've learnt a trick or two. That's why I was reminded of you when Olivia used the word "interpretation" about what I thought a private dining room was.'

'Yes,' said Dr Carr. 'It's wonderful that you are developing a relationship with Olivia.'

'We're going for a walk next Saturday,' said Sebastian.

'Oh, good,' said Dr Carr. 'I'm sure that will be very enjoyable for both of you, but there is a complication that I should bring up at this point. When the three of us met last night, you asked how Olivia and I know each other.'

'She's not a patient of yours, is she?' said Sebastian. 'What are the chances, eh? Of all the psychoanalysts in all the world for two long-lost twins to have chosen the same one. It's not against the rules, is it?'

'It's not against the rules for two patients to have the same analyst,' said Dr Carr. 'Unless the analyst is very unpopular, he is bound to have more than one patient. They might know each other. They might discover that they share a therapist. All of that is outside my control. What is against the rules is for the therapist to be directly involved in their lives outside the consulting room, or to comment on each other's lives within it, using confidential information. Unfortunately, the relationship between you and me and Olivia is much harder to reconcile. There is something that I hoped would not arise and which, obviously, I was unaware of at the beginning of our work, but which we must now address. Olivia, who is clearly delighted to have found you after all these years, is my adopted daughter.'

'Blow me down,' said Sebastian. 'I didn't see that coming.'

'How could you have?' said Dr Carr.

'So, we don't only have the same Bio Mum, we have the same Psycho Dad,' said Sebastian.

Dr Carr couldn't help smiling at that one, almost as if he knew Sebastian so well, he'd seen it coming.

'Yes, that's a typically pithy way of putting it,' he said.

'So, what are you saying?' said Sebastian, who was sitting up by now and staring at Dr Carr with a mixture of bewilderment and ferocity. 'Is that against the rules?'

'I am not aware of a situation of this exact kind ever having arisen,' said Dr Carr. 'We are in uncharted territory, but the breach of confidentiality and the conflict of interest and the heightened dangers of transference and countertransference are off the charts, so I think we—'

'Why didn't you adopt me?' Sebastian interrupted him. 'Then I wouldn't have needed psychoanalysis because I would be like

Olivia, and we could have been together all this time, like peas in a pod, sane as all get out. I'd probably be a professor by now, being interviewed on the telly when people couldn't make head or tail of what's going on. "What's your interpretation, Professor Sebastian Carr?" "My interpretation, Kirsty, is that we should move the Middle East to the Far East, so it's not so close to home."'

'You were not available for adoption,' said Dr Carr. 'We were aware that Olivia had a twin, and would normally have been inclined to keep twins together, as they have had the exceptional experience of being together *in utero*, but your parents were determined to keep you. We were unaware that you were later available for adoption, and it was only when you exercised your right to get in touch with your natural mother that it became an established fact that you and Olivia were siblings.'

'So, what are you saying?' said Sebastian. 'Are you just going to abandon me?'

'I am not going to abandon you, Sebastian, of course not. We have tomorrow's session and Friday's session. The Christmas break then begins, but what I suggest is that, exceptionally, we carry on working the week before Christmas and that we fit in three more sessions next week, at your usual times. In the meantime, I will ask around among my colleagues to find one who is suited to carry on the process with you; the process that you have grown to trust.'

'It's you that I have grown to trust,' said Sebastian.

'Thank you,' said Martin, 'but let's not forget that you also trusted Lucy last night and followed her recommendation for Bread-and-Butter Pudding. I think that trust is now something that is in you and not exclusive to our relationship, although it's there that you may have learnt to develop it, which is a tremendous achievement.'

Sebastian rested his elbows on his thighs, refusing to look at Dr Carr, but holding his downcast head in his hands. He stared at the carpet, wondering whether to jump.

18

'No,' said Lizzie, 'he doesn't get to be part of this family because you have discovered each other after forty-two years. It's taken forty-five years to build the family, and we can't just tack on a new wing overnight for someone who we did *not* adopt.'

'He's not "someone" you didn't adopt, he's *the* child you didn't adopt,' said Olivia. 'You knew that I had a twin when you adopted me. He's been a shadow member of this family since inception, or at least since my arrival.'

'Well, he can live in a shadow wing of a shadow house,' said Lizzie. 'Shadows can't be incorporated, they can only be cast.'

'Oh, really? I thought the whole point was to incorporate our shadows,' said Olivia. 'Whatever happened to "This thing of darkness I acknowledge mine"? Anyway, shadows are cast by light. They aren't the opposite of light; they're one of its consequences.'

'Oh, for goodness' sake,' said Lizzie, 'I'm sorry I was looking after Noah last night and was unable to go to what was clearly a very instructive exhibition, but we're not here to discuss the physics or metaphysics of shadows, or the incorporation of the unconscious into an individual psyche, we're here to talk about family. And,' she added, casting an inquisitive glance at her husband, 'if Martin is going to participate, about professional ethics. Even the most senior analyst needs a supervisor at times of high pressure, and you haven't had anyone to go to since Margaret died last year. Why didn't you come to me?'

'Precisely because I thought it would violate professional ethics, given the nature of the problem,' said Martin. 'In a conflict between my obligations to a patient and my obligations to my family, you are *not* a neutral observer, as I think this conversation demonstrates. Besides, if we are going to talk about professional ethics, I think it would be unprofessional and unethical to do it in front of our daughter.'

'Fair point,' said Lizzie, breathing out slowly. 'So, let's discuss Sebastian without dragging professional ethics into it. Are we going to allow an ambulatory schizophrenic, an especially resistant and relapse-prone category of patient, free access to the building *in which* he was analysed? Oh dear, it's beginning to sound as if we can't keep professional ethics out of it. Is he going to drop in for Sunday lunch with the man who has re-parented him and be allowed to witness what that man is like as an actual parent?' Lizzie was already speaking more rapidly than she had been immediately after her studied exhalation and was now accelerating further. 'Might such scenes fill him with a sense of volatility or banality or envy that would throw into question the heroically even flame with which I have no doubt you have been burning over the last five years – in the new framework, let's not forget, of his no longer being the sole topic of a carefully structured style of conversation?'

'Dad didn't know Sebastian was my brother when he took him on,' said Olivia.

'Well, he didn't find out last night,' said Lizzie. 'We don't know how long it's been because it would be "unethical" to tell the truth. Just to pick an example at random,' Lizzie said to Martin with a curt smile, 'would you like Sebastian to be here *now*?'

She shot out the last question with a vehemence that surprised her, even though her strong feelings on this subject were making her heart pound.

'No, obviously not,' said Martin quietly. 'Although I would say in passing that banality, as you call it, or ordinariness, if we don't want to denigrate it, would be a great victory for someone whose mind has been assaulting him with harrowingly bizarre thoughts and fantasies and images for so long.'

'Point taken,' said Lizzie, who was cultivating calm again. 'I am just questioning whether we can be the ones to provide that ordinariness which, as you say, would be the holiday of a lifetime for a person with his mental health history, or whether we might undo the work that has got him to wherever he is now.'

'I was with him last night,' said Olivia, 'and he's certainly unusual, but he's also incredibly touching, for some reason, and naturally intelligent, with a strong sense that the more he is released from his psychological constraints the more intelligent he will become.'

'Well, that's true of anybody,' said Lizzie.

'Yes, but not everybody has been treated for most of their life as if they're in a state of complete confusion . . .'

'And not everyone has been in a state of complete confusion for large parts of their life,' said Lizzie. 'Let's not overlook that detail.'

'Nobody is trying to win an argument, Mum,' said Olivia.

'I am,' said Lizzie.

'Well, what I want is to find a consensus,' said Olivia. 'Maybe coming to this house is a boundary Sebastian shouldn't cross after he's stopped working with Dad. Perhaps coming through the main door would undermine the benefits of having come through the basement door for so long. This is yours and Dad's house; it's obviously your decision, but if Francis and I decide that Sebastian can come to Willow Cottage, and you refuse to visit because he is there, that would create a schism in the family that would make me feel very uneasy.'

'Well, you could ask us separately,' said Lizzie, 'so as not to cause yourself needless torment. There are fifty-two weekends in the year.'

'Asking you separately would be the schism,' said Olivia, 'not the solution to it.'

'Are you happy,' said Lizzie, ignoring her daughter's grating logic, 'with the prospect of Noah spending time with his new pop-up uncle who manages to be nothing worse than "unusual" on a high dose of antipsychotics but might stop taking them one day and become *unusually* unusual? Is Noah ready for a second grandmother, one who abandons her children, and a second grandfather so shockingly unlike the saintly figure he has grown to love, a shadow grandfather, an alleged but untraceable monster, a Grendel that can never be killed, however courageously Noah sets off with his wooden sword and his plastic helmet? You would also have to accelerate the revelation of the adoption story. Are you ready to do that? And where does all this leave his Uncle Charlie, who Noah also loves and misses and feels connected with, as he told me last night. Why should Noah be thrown into confusion about who his real uncle is?'

'There's no confusion,' said Olivia, 'he has two uncles, both real. As to the double grandparents, I'm sure he'll be even more grateful for the ones he has ended up with, when he learns about the grim alternatives. Besides, aren't we in favour of the truth?'

'For a five-year-old? Absolutely not,' said Lizzie. 'And my whole point is that Sebastian is one of the "grim alternatives". Noah doesn't have to meet him now; he can be told about him in due course and then contact him of his own volition, as you did Karen.'

'Sebastian is not grim,' said Olivia. 'Whatever else Dad has done, he has stripped away a lot of paranoia, if there was a lot of paranoia in the first place, which obviously is an assumption on my part. Sebastian does not come over as someone who feels threatened in a delusional way; he seems authentically fragile, and since he doesn't feel threatened, he doesn't behave in a threatening way. I want to protect him, rather than feeling I need to be protected from him.'

'Indeed,' said Martin. 'He is not a dangerous person. That is not the issue.'

'He didn't need analysis to learn how to free associate, like the rest of us,' said Olivia, 'he needed it to find out how to *stop* – by doing it lucidly and systematically, something like that, you're the experts. Some people need to read books about lateral thinking, he needs to put a brake on it because it sometimes takes him so far off course.'

'Hmm,' said Martin, resisting any further commentary on his daughter's analysis of her father's analysis of her brother. 'For now, I don't know what the answer is, other than finding him someone else to work with.'

'The main thing is that he is so grateful for kindness,' said Olivia. 'If he were too unwell to respond to kindness, there would be no point, but he has passed that crucial threshold.'

'I think I have come to the absolute limit of what I can say as someone who is trying to help resolve a family conflict while still being Sebastian's therapist,' said Martin. 'I would not have allowed myself to say anything at all if Sebastian had not breached confidentiality in such an innocent but explosive way. However, until I have found him someone else,' he said, standing up, 'I will let you discuss the matter among yourselves. It's my email hour, as you know.'

'To be completely honest,' said Olivia, 'some of this professional ethics stuff is beginning to get on my nerves. The analytic term ends tomorrow and I'm going for a walk with Sebastian on Saturday. What can I say to reassure him?'

'You can continue your conversation as siblings, and you can tell your mother about it,' said Martin, 'and I will continue my conversation with him as my patient, which I cannot tell you about, even if I wished to – which I don't. I will re-enter *this* conversation when I have found him someone to carry on the work with.'

Martin kissed Olivia on both cheeks.

'I know you have your Soil Association dinner tonight, so I'll say goodbye now. I'll see you later,' he said to Lizzie, opening the door to the basement.

Olivia waited to hear his footsteps descending the staircase.

'I suppose my point is that underneath professional ethics,' said Olivia to Lizzie, 'there must be basic ethics: compassion, kindness, inclusion.'

'Oh, give me a break!' said Lizzie. 'What do you think your father and I have been doing all our working lives? I will not be characterised as someone who wants to send your brother to Tierra del Fuego because it rhymes with inferno and is therefore his natural habitat, or because Rwanda is not far enough away. Our professional ethics are not a pedantic little rule book effortlessly overruled by your "basic ethics"; they are an application of basic ethics to a profession especially concerned with the protection of vulnerable people.'

'Great,' said Olivia, 'in that case we should be in perfect agreement. I just want to know what this family really stands for, that's all.'

'You know perfectly well what it stands for,' said Lizzie. 'The question is not what we stand for, or stand up for, or stand against, but what we can *stand*.'

19

Walking uphill towards the Hollow Tree, Olivia rediscovered the shape it had always suggested to her from this angle: a crouching mythological beast, with its forelegs planted in the ground and its chest bulging forward. Isolated by its celebrity it was cordoned off to discourage people from compacting the soil around its roots. Climbing inside, as she and Charlie had done on most of their childhood visits to Hampstead Heath, was now a transgression against a 'veteran' tree. The familiarity of the old beech had only deepened their childhood delight at taking refuge in the polished interior, gouged out by bacteria and fungi over the last hundred years but continuing to flourish with only the perforated tube of its trunk left to generate an overarching mass of fresh green leaves each May from the bare branches that now stood out against the brief winter sky. Olivia paused where the two elliptical windows in the trunk aligned and imagined an arrow flying through them perfectly and landing in the trunk of the oak on the other side. She felt ambivalent about the security detail surrounding the old tree which she had known when you could just walk up to it and say hello. Of course, she wanted it to be protected and understood that the footfall of ten million visitors a year was threatening the root systems of the outnumbered trees on the Heath, but she could still remember lifting Noah into the hollow before the cordon was put in place. She remembered crouching down with him and looking out of the windows and shaking hands with Francis on the other side, but of course she could not pass on in one visit the accumulated meaning the tree had for her and Charlie, and if she brought Sebastian here after lunch in the café at Kenwood House, they would have to either perform this sibling rite of passage by committing some kind of ecological misdemeanour or stand by the cordon and reinforce the sense of exclusion which it was the point of this meeting to start dismantling, if that was possible and desirable. Her confidence was shaken by the position that Lizzie had taken on Wednesday evening, and she was of course barred from any further discussions with her father. Francis had barely managed to speak to Sebastian at the dinner after the show, but she and Francis had talked about the encounter deep into the night. Francis was not opposed to exploring ways to include Sebastian in their family life regardless of the position taken by her parents. His neutrality was perhaps the best she could hope for, but she would have preferred his encouragement in her current frame of mind.

Perhaps the whole thing was a stupid idea, a niche subset of survivor's guilt: Preferential Twin Adoption Syndrome.

'There's no way to sugar-coat this, Olivia, so I'm going to tell it to you straight,' she imagined a white-coated psychiatrist informing her in a rerun of a television hospital drama, 'you've been diagnosed with PTAS.'

'Oh my God, doctor, PTAS, is there a cure?'

'I'm afraid not. All you can do is shoot your twin brother and blow up the adoption agency. I'm also going to prescribe these pills, which will almost certainly make no difference unless you luck out and they have a placebo effect. They used to be prescribed for asthma and urinary tract infections, but we've found that in very low doses people sometimes report a reduction in Undeserved Good Fortune Anxiety (UGFA) and Pathological Fear of Success, or PFS.'

'You mean, I've got UGFA and PFS as well?'

'There's no way to sugar-coat this, Olivia, so I'm going to give it to you straight: the answer is "Yes, our randomised multiple choice test results show that you have PTAS, UGFA and PFS. It's a tough diagnosis but you're a tough kid, and if anyone can survive this, it's you, but just in case you feel overwhelmed and get sick of people telling you how brave you are, I'm also going to prescribe a barbiturate, so you can take your own life.'

'That really means a lot, doctor, thank you.'

'Don't worry, kid, I've got your back. We're going to introduce as much needless violence, fake science and preposterous plot twists as we need to drive this show through what the ratings gurus call the Four O'clock Flops, that danger point in the afternoon when even a hardcore TV junky toys with the idea of having a break before the evening news kicks off another eight-hour binge.'

'I am so grateful to you,' said Olivia, putting her hand on her heart.

She passed through a gate into Kenwood and turned left down one of the woodland paths that led to the house. As she ditched her little fantasy dialogue, Olivia realised that in a way, she had been continuing a tradition that she and Charlie had formed of improvising stories for each other as they huddled together inside the Hollow Tree, but she also recognised that she was being silly about the roots of her relationship with Sebastian because they were so fragile and under threat from the footfall of so many opinions and the cordon of so many constraints. Lucy had been sweet to Sebastian and totally collaborated in making him feel welcome at her grand dinner the other night. Hunter had hoped to see him again. She had seen him talking to Father Guido in a friendly and easy-going way. Even Bill Maraschino seemed to be under the mistaken impression that he was some sort of art critic, but Martin had been forced to bow out of dinner and Lizzie had unleashed her scepticism the following evening. What Olivia had to do today was begin to find out whether their common origin felt to them more like a fundamental fact or a contingent one.

Despite her obvious claims to precedence, Karen had turned out to be a maternal anticlimax, but Olivia felt that Sebastian would somehow turn out to be different as a second brother.

Instead of being driven onto the banks of the path as she usually was by the frequent stretches of waterlogged ground, the frozen mud meant that she could walk straight down its centre, only pausing once because she couldn't resist breaking a sheet of clear ice with the tip of her boot. Here was another thing she would often have done as a child but never bothered to do these days. Perhaps she was thinking of Noah, who enjoyed cracking ice sheets whenever he got the chance. That was probably the part of Lizzie's tirade that had affected her most: the thought of Noah suddenly acquiring an eccentric 'Uncle Sebastian', who needn't be in his life at all. Would it do more to enrich or disturb his world? Was he ready to know that Granny and Grandad were not her only parents? More and more of the children in his school turned out to have two fathers or two mothers, a stepfather or a stepmother, half-brothers and half-sisters, a dead parent or a dead sibling; he might be relieved at having his seemingly ordinary background disrupted, and as Francis had said in his conscientiously relaxed way, 'If it doesn't work out, we needn't pursue it.'

She crossed the bridge at the end of the woodland path and looked up the vast sloping lawn at the white stucco building on the ridge of the hill. The survival of Kenwood House and much of its estate had depended on Lord Iveagh's philanthropy in the 1920s, just as the Heath below it had been saved by an Act of Parliament at the end of the nineteenth century. The fact that they formed this astonishing island in the torrent of metropolitan life was due to sacrifice and generosity and public campaigns and political acts; it was not that London had absent-mindedly forgotten to devour hundreds of acres of woodland and meadows, and to demolish an important piece of architecture, but that certain values had been fought for and prevailed, and consequently she would be meeting Sebastian in the old brewery of a country house, rather than in a café on yet another busy road. She hoped that the tenacity of her desire to help Sebastian rested on a set of values worth fighting for, but the deeper she dug all she seemed to find was more varieties of guilt. Apart from the PTAS so artfully diagnosed by the psychiatrist in *Four o'clock Flops*, there was the guilt of undermining Sebastian's arduous journey towards mental health by being the adopted daughter of his psychotherapist. Even the most ambitiously comprehensive diagnostic manual might baulk at creating a new disease out of such an outlandish set of circumstances, but behind that highly specific misfortune, Olivia felt a fog bank of guilt connected with her vague memory of reading R. D. Laing in her undergraduate years. She seemed to recall that there needed to be a family where 'double binds' – damned if you do and damned if you don't instructions – were used to displace the unacknowledged secrets and contradictions in the lives of the parents. The schizophrenic was the member of the family targeted as a scapegoat for the contradictions and the one most relentlessly persecuted for failing to find a way out of double binds which were designed to make escape impossible. What do you do if sex is disgusting and celibacy forbidden? What do you do if these riddles are reiterated a thousand times? Split and shatter on behalf of those who want to give their conflicts the shallowness of hypocrisy rather than the depth of insanity. She was haunted by having been told that in some South American countries when cattle must cross a river in which piranhas are known to live, the weakest animal is cut and forced into the water downstream, so that the rest of the herd could cross serenely while the chosen animal is devoured in a frenzy of blood and bellows. Was Sebastian the sacrificial twin who had enabled her to cross the river to understanding parents and Oxford University and worthwhile employment and the opportunity to live and bring up her child in the middle of a rewilding project, while he frothed and twisted behind a bend in the river? The fact that she had been rejected at birth made him the sacrificial animal in the sense that the piranhas were the family into which they had both been born but to which only he had been fed. There was also an amalgamated imaginary family to which they belonged, the Birth-Carrs, and from which he was now about to be exiled, if she didn't prevent it. Although she had never meant to do him harm, she had somehow benefited from the harm that had been done to him as a child and was at least unintentionally associated with the harm now being done to him as a patient. Was she going to let him be slashed and thrown downstream a second time? To hell with that. She was going to help get him to the other bank of the lethal river because he had suffered enough, and he was her brother.

She was early, as planned, but Sebastian was already in the far corner of the café, rocking on his chair, clapping his hands together silently, like a person absorbed in the favourite song on his playlist, but without the headphones or the music. The phrase 'It's all in the mind' came to her with the smugness of a traffic warden securing a penalty notice behind a windscreen wiper.

'Hi, Sebastian.'

'Oh, hi. They've got "goujons" here, like in Wilton's, but chicken instead of sole,' said Sebastian.

'Wasn't that a fun evening?'

'Yes, it was the best evening – followed by the worst morning,' said Sebastian.

'Well, let's redress the balance by getting some goujons,' said Olivia.

'Goujons time machines,' said Sebastian.

'This whole place is a sort of time machine,' said Olivia.

'Yeah, when I got here,' said Sebastian, 'I thought, The spaceship has landed; but of course it's London that's the spaceship, because it was all like this before London arrived – all countryside. Must be a flying saucer with a hollow centre, and this is the place that didn't get squashed.'

'Yes, I'd never thought of it like that,' said Olivia, determined to be unfazed.

They went to the back of the queue and started sliding two pale grey trays towards the till, gradually acquiring plates of crunchy chicken and metal pots of strong tea, and a slice of carrot cake for Olivia and a chocolate brownie for Sebastian. They returned to Sebastian's favoured table.

'Dr Carr would probably say that I'm feeling cornered,' said Sebastian.

'You're absolutely right,' said Olivia, laughing, 'that's just the sort of thing he would say, or think. Has he found you someone new to work with?'

'Yeah, I'm going to see her next Tuesday, and then I have three last sessions with him.'

'I'm so sorry your work with him has been interrupted. I feel responsible, although of course I never wanted anything of the sort.'

'That's a funny thing about guilt, isn't it?' said Sebastian. 'You don't have to do anything wrong to feel it, and sometimes you do something wrong and don't feel it.'

'That's so true,' said Olivia, 'although there's still room for what Silicon Valley would probably call "legacy guilt": the type you feel when you've done something wrong.'

'Yeah, but it's not the whole package, is it?' said Sebastian. 'To think something is "wrong" in the first place, you have to have a sort of pre-guilt, if you know what I mean. The worst kind is just feeling guilt and not knowing why, as if you'd done something horrible during a blackout. I don't get that so much now.'

'Oh, good,' said Olivia, feeling that she didn't want to become a surrogate therapist, but did want to get to know Sebastian. 'Listen, because I've lived near here most of my life, there are a few things I like to do when I'm on the Heath. Shall we do them together, it would mean a lot to me.'

'Yeah,' said Sebastian. 'What things?'

'You'll see.'

After they finished their lunch, Olivia led the way out of the garden door of the café and to the porticoed front door of Kenwood House around the corner.

'Do you know the people who live here?' said Sebastian.

'No, it's a museum now,' said Olivia.

'Does your family look at art every day?' said Sebastian.

'No,' said Olivia, laughing. 'That Turrell show was probably the first one I went to this year. It's just that there's a painting here that I particularly love, and so I wanted to show it to you.'

Olivia weaved her way rapidly through the ground floor of the house and into a large dim room, protected from the ravages of natural light, but filled with canvases that were individually lit. She moved to the far-right corner and stood in front of a painting of an ageing man with grey curls hanging from under his white linen hat. He wore a fur-lined black robe over a red garment with a white collar. He looked straight out at the viewer from a fleshy face with a bulbous nose, brightly lit on one side and shaded on the other.

'It's called *Self-portrait with Two Circles* by Rembrandt,' said Olivia. 'I don't know why I like it so much. His gaze is so penetrating, but seeing deeply into things hasn't made him proud or harsh, it's made him sad and understanding.'

'Yes, his eyes remind me of your dad's,' said Sebastian.

'Yes,' said Olivia, realising that wherever she took him she was inevitably going to be the confidante of Sebastian's anxiety about separating from Martin. 'I suppose he seems to be confronting the world, but he's really looking at a mirror, so it's introspection on display, the more intensely he looks outwards the more uncompromisingly he is really looking inwards – it's a portrait of the gaze the artist brings to the world. I just find it touching because he is vulnerable but so strong at the same time. I suppose we're all vulnerable and I would like to respond like him, if I am ever wise enough.'

'Yeah, vulnerable but strong,' said Sebastian, 'I like that. If he hadn't broken through the mirror, we wouldn't see him because he'd still be the other side.'

'Yes, I see what you mean,' said Olivia, trying to feel her way around Sebastian's mind.

'What are the "Two Circles" about?' said Sebastian. 'I mean, they're the outer edges of two circles going in opposite directions. They aren't even circles.'

'I know,' said Olivia. 'There's a big debate about it and nobody is quite sure. Shall we go outside? There isn't that much time before it gets dark.'

'Yeah,' said Sebastian.

'Apparently, Giotto,' said Olivia as she led them back to the hall, 'who was painting in thirteen hundred and something or other, not quite sure, once drew a perfect circle freehand to show what a master of his art he was. It was a famous story among painters, so some people think that Rembrandt was asserting his powers as an artist and was referring to that Giotto story. And then there are other interpretations. I don't really know – I just like his face.'

'Hang on,' said Sebastian. 'When what's-his-name painted the circle . . .'

'Giotto.'

'Right. They thought the world was flat, so he drew it on a flat surface, but by the time the other bloke . . .'

'Rembrandt.'

'Right. By the time Rembrandt drew his two circles, they knew the world was round. So,' said Sebastian, holding his head with both palms, trying to clarify the picture forming in his mind, 'those two curves are the outer edges of one circle, because it's on a globe and not a flat surface. The lines meet directly behind where he is standing on the other side of the world. Do you see what I mean?'

'I do,' said Olivia, taking Sebastian through a gate that led into a huge meadow beyond the Kenwood railings on the Highgate side of the Heath. 'I've been looking at that picture for years and I never thought of that. Bill Maraschino is right, you ought to be writing catalogue essays . . .'

'Now you're making fun of me,' said Sebastian.

'No, I wasn't! You have a way of thinking about things that's very original.'

'I just think that maybe it's not two circles but one,' said Sebastian, 'and he's standing on the edge of the globe with his palette and brushes – and that unflinching gaze. And . . . and,' Sebastian seemed to be excited but trying not to get confused, 'if it *is* one circle then the two lines meet where he's standing, but he can only show that by sending them off in opposite directions, just like we would meet eventually if we walked for long enough in exactly opposite directions.'

'In fact, we have,' said Olivia. 'We did set off in opposite directions and walked around the world until we met, and I'm very pleased we have.'

She stepped up to a stone fountain decorated with wreaths and a squirrel and a series of carved faces. From the centre of one man's face a spout poured water into a carving of a scallop shell. Wherever it splashed, into the shell, onto the grille of the drain next to it, over the plinth and on to the mud and grass beyond, the water left a bright orange stain.

'People used to come here to "take" the waters,' said Olivia, cupping her hand under the flow and lifting the icy liquid to her mouth. 'This is the last well head left on the Heath. Do you want to try some? It's full of iron and supposed to be very good for you.'

'So that we can be vulnerable but strong,' said Sebastian, copying what Olivia had done and scooping handfuls of water into his mouth hungrily.

'That's right,' said Olivia.

'I can feel it,' said Sebastian, 'I can feel the iron.'

'It's extraordinary, isn't it?'

'I wish I had known about this when I was younger; when I was at my most vulnerable.'

'Well, you know about it now, so you can come here when you feel you could do with a boost.'

'I might as well stay here!' said Sebastian.

'You can bring a bottle or thermos next time and always have some with you,' said Olivia.

'Like Asterix,' said Sebastian.

'That's right,' said Olivia. 'Are you ready? We can go on to the third place I always visit if you like.'

'Defo,' said Sebastian. 'I feel much stronger now.'

'Good,' said Olivia. 'The last place I want to take you is the Hollow Tree. The centre is missing but it's still alive and flourishing.'

'Same old, same old,' said Sebastian rapidly. 'Vulnerable but strong.'

Olivia burst out laughing. 'You are amazing,' she said. 'I hadn't spotted that and I'm the one organising this little tour. Maybe it's what I think is most important in life.'

'Personally, I could do without the vulnerable bit,' said Sebastian.

'I see what you mean,' said Olivia, 'but then we wouldn't have the strength either; there wouldn't be any need for it.'

'Yeah, but it would be better if there was a lot more strength, with just a dash of the old motivational vulnerability.'

'I think we can certainly send back the cocktail and try to get it just right,' said Olivia, walking slowly away from the fountain.

'Anyway,' she went on, a little hesitantly but seeing no alternative, 'my dad and Lizzie, my mum, had a child before they adopted me, a son called Charlie . . .'

'Hang on. So, you have a brother who isn't really your brother who you've known all your life and a real brother who you're just getting to know. So, this Charlie has lived with your dad and mum all his life,' said Sebastian, beginning to sound angry.

'Well, he is their child,' said Olivia.

'Right,' said Sebastian. 'Yeah, exactly, he is their child. I suppose I'm not used to it, because you didn't stay with your parents and it was a great idea, and I did and it was a terrible idea, and then I didn't, and it was a different kind of terrible idea. And Charlie did stay . . .'

'And it was a good idea,' Olivia completed the sentence.

'Right,' said Sebastian. 'Obelix fell into the Druid's cauldron when he was a child, so he didn't need a flask of magic potion or iron water.'

'Yes, but don't forget the books are named after Asterix; he's the real hero,' said Olivia. 'In any case, Charlie and I always used to visit the Hollow Tree. I want to take you there as a thing I do with my brothers.'

By the time they got to the Hollow Tree, Olivia still hadn't made up her mind what she was going to do about the cordon. They walked around the back so that Sebastian could get a closer look at the inside.

'How does it survive without a centre?' said Sebastian.

'I know, it seems impossible,' said Olivia, 'but there are human equivalents: a forty-four-year-old Frenchman went to hospital because he was experiencing weakness in his leg and when they scanned him, ninety per cent of his brain was missing, it was just filled with liquid – it's called hydrocephalus. He had a family and a job and was leading a normal life on ten per cent of the usual brain matter.'

'The Hollow Brain,' said Sebastian, 'blow me down.'

Olivia glanced up and down the path.

'Fuck it,' she said, 'let's go in.'

She took Sebastian gently by the wrist, stepped over the cordon and into the interior of the tree. Sebastian followed and the two of them crouched down together, their knees touching.

'Like peas in a pod,' said Sebastian, smiling for the first time, 'just like the old days.'

20

Francis and Olivia had invited Sebastian to Willow Cottage for a compressed weekend, beginning on Saturday afternoon and ending after lunch on Sunday. Martin and Lizzie were also invited to Sunday lunch, but Martin had decided that he could not see Sebastian until he was in a well-established relationship with his new therapist, and Lizzie also felt it would be premature to meet him. After Mrs Pellegrini agreed to take on Sebastian, it seemed that Martin was able to speak to his wife as a fellow professional and she had tempered some of her views about Sebastian's integration into the wider family; nevertheless, they both felt that they should only get involved once Olivia and Francis had decided what role he was going to play in their own immediate family. Charlie had written to Olivia from America saying that he and Minnesota would be happy to meet Sebastian as soon as they came over to England. 'Being your brother, he's bound to be wonderful,' Charlie's message concluded, 'as I know from personal experience.'

Sebastian's train arrived in time for him to meet Noah, but late enough for Noah to be launched into his tea and bedtime routine if the meeting didn't go well. As it turned out, Noah was unhesitatingly friendly.

'You are Mummy's old friend, Sebastian,' he said. 'I'm Noah.'

'Are you?' said Sebastian. 'Where's your ark then?'

'I'll show you.'

'You mean you've really got one?' said Sebastian, flabbergasted.

'Of course I do,' said Noah. 'If you're a king you have to have a crown, and if you're a Noah you have to have an ark.'

Francis was impressed by Sebastian's playfulness, as he had told him about the ark on the way back from the station, as well as explaining that he and Olivia would prefer not to go straight to Uncle Sebastian, as it was 'a big story for a little boy to take in'.

'I know the feeling,' Sebastian had said. 'It's going to take me a while to get *my* head round to being "Uncle Sebastian".'

As the ark was visible from the kitchen window, Francis let Noah take Sebastian out to inspect the increasingly seaworthy heap of logs and branches piled up on the edge of the wood. Although he couldn't hear what they were saying, he soon felt that an atmosphere of friendliness and shared excitement had sprung up between them and that he could get on with preparing the main dinner.

'Sorry, I was having a bath,' said Olivia, coming into the kitchen. 'I should go out and say hello.'

'Sure,' said Francis, 'although Noah is the only one of us he hasn't met, and they seem to be getting on pretty well.'

'Okay, good, I'll give it five or ten minutes then,' said Olivia, glancing out of the window. 'I wouldn't want to interrupt Noah explaining that our ark is so compact because we'll just be taking DNA samples rather than pairs of mating animals.'

'And Sebastian might have some top tips on why a crooked bifurcating mast is better than the conventional type.'

'There are certainly opportunities for bold design innovations,' said Olivia, getting the spaghetti from the cupboard. 'How was he on the way from the station?'

'A bit agitated at first,' said Francis. 'He told me he'd never been asked to the country before, but he's so appreciative, he soon calmed down. His originality may be rooted in pathology, but I find him rather good company. I think it might not just be the “right thing” to do to include him in our lives, it might be rather fun. Let’s see, maybe tomorrow afternoon we’ll never want to see him again.’

They looked back out of the window and saw that Noah was standing inside the ark, with Sebastian giving him a naval salute, as if asking permission to come aboard. Captain Noah must have granted permission, as Sebastian stepped among the wooden debris and mimed the hoisting of a sail by running his hands over a piece of rope dangling from the tormented mast. Noah relocated himself at the helm, a defunct bicycle wheel attached to a vertical branch at the back of the craft.

‘I doubt it,’ said Olivia.

It was already growing dark, and so Noah and Sebastian came in without Olivia needing to collect them. Sebastian sat with Olivia by the fire, while Noah went to have his spaghetti in the kitchen.

‘Sebastian is brilliant at playing,’ said Noah, ‘even better than Rory and Jamal.’

‘That’s great,’ said Francis.

‘We went sailing over England, not *around* England, which anybody can do, but over England, after the flood, and we went up to London and we saw Big Ben deep under water, and it was still tolling but in a muffled way more like a submarine than a bell, and then we sailed up to Belsize Park, where the water was less deep because it’s on a hill, and we saw Grandad helping one of his patients but they were both wearing scuba-diving outfits, and Sebastian said they were probably having a very good session because that’s what Grandad does: he takes people under the surface of things.’

‘Did he? I’m sure Grandad would be pleased to hear that,’ said Francis.

‘I’m going to tell him next time we meet,’ said Noah.

‘Good idea,’ said Francis.

Francis and Olivia had decided that, on balance, it would be better not to huddle around the radio together for the first programme of her *Apocalypse* series, like a family listening to a speech by Churchill or an episode of *The Archers*. They felt that Noah was not ready for the crushing logic of Mutual Assured Destruction; the dangers of nuclear proliferation and terrorism; the testimony of Hiroshima survivors; the lingering health problems of those lucky enough to witness the first hydrogen bomb test; the sinking of the *Rainbow Warrior* by the French secret services; the introduction of Uranium 235 and Plutonium 239 into the food chain, the first with a half-life of seven hundred million years and the second with a relatively fleeting half-life of twenty-four thousand years; the debauchery of a military policy that had seven hundred nuclear missiles aimed at Moscow in the late eighties, when one fifty-megaton Tsar bomb would have been enough; the avoidance of World War III having depended on a few isolated acts: JFK's decision, against the advice of his cabinet, to make a secret deal with Khrushchev agreeing to remove American missiles from Turkey in exchange for Russian missiles leaving Cuba; the Russian captain Arkhipov, who refused to release a nuclear weapon from his submarine during the Cuban Missile Crisis; the cool-headed Colonel Petrov who decided in 1983, on his own initiative and against a protocol which obliged him to report to his superiors, that the five incoming missiles showing up on the Soviet early warning system were evidence of a mechanical error rather than proof of American insanity. Nor should Noah hear that experts considered that the dangers of nuclear aggression were greater now than they had been at any time since the height of the Cold War. And so, they missed the broadcast and listened to a recording after dinner.

'It's amazing,' said Sebastian.

'Oh, thank you,' said Olivia.

'I mean you being on both sides of the radio, interviewing people on one side and sitting here with us on the other.'

'Oh, that,' said Olivia, 'yes. Is this the first time you've been with someone who's talking on the radio?'

'Yeah,' said Sebastian, 'I suppose that's it. I've always thought the people on the radio were "over there" – in another dimension. My Fake Dad used to enjoy what my Fake Mum called "a flutter on the gee-gees" so there was often racing on the telly. When I was four I remember asking him how they managed to make the horses so small and my dad told me not to be so bloody daft, and it really hurt my feelings, because he was always telling me to keep my eyes "peeled" and to pay attention to what was "staring me in the face" and to "use my common sense", because I was a dreamer, "lost in my own thoughts"; but I *was* looking at what was staring me in the face, and the horses on the telly really *were* small.'

'I remember thinking exactly the same thing about horses on TV,' said Olivia.

'Well, I thought it was an excellent programme,' said Francis. 'Congratulations.'

'Thank you,' said Olivia.

'Oh, yeah, excellent,' said Sebastian. 'It made me feel ever so grateful to live in London because you'd be vaporised in a jiffy rather than stumbling around for weeks with bits falling off. Even in the breathtaking scenery of New Zealand a nuclear winter wouldn't be a bag of laughs, would it?'

'Plummeting temperatures, sooty skies, failing crops,' said Olivia, 'starvation.'

'The Goldilocks nuclear winter,' said Francis, 'would reverse the global warming since industrialisation. It's so easy to overshoot, though.'

'Big cities are the answer,' said Sebastian, 'and military bases. The other good thing is that there are no sirens, no warning, except for top politicians, who'd probably be having a party anyway, so they'd die happy. The rest of us will be going about our business and then, Flash, Bang, shadows on the pavement. That's modern life for you, the rapid transfer of information.'

'I've never met anyone with such a positive attitude to nuclear war,' said Olivia. 'It's so refreshing.'

'Well, that's what families are for, aren't they?' said Sebastian. 'Encouraging each other. Doesn't it make you nervous living in the country, though?'

'I think we're close enough,' said Francis, 'to be wiped out quickly in the event of World War III, but far enough away if a dirty bomb was detonated in Parliament Square.'

'The ideal spot,' said Sebastian, impressed. 'When you think of what people went through in old-fashioned wars: shrapnel, bayonets, raping and pillaging, amputations without anaesthetic, no antibiotics; I mean, nuclear war is a big step forward. The great thing about extinctions is not to be around to experience them. I suppose that's why you put it first. A perfect field of mushroom clouds from shore to shore and nothing left to suffer. Some of the other extinctions are so slow-mo and complicated, people might get depressed and stop listening, so you kicked off with good old nukes. "Now I am become death, the destroyer of worlds." Great stuff. Hard to beat, really. It's just the people in remote locations I worry about. Not here, of course, this is the ideal spot.'

'Yes,' said Francis, 'no fun being a survivalist, sitting in a bunker for twenty-four thousand years, with a rifle and a top-of-the-range Swiss Army knife.'

'It would be a good opportunity to do some reading,' said Sebastian.

'Gosh, I'm glad we listened with you,' said Olivia. 'I must admit I sometimes got a little cast down making these programmes, but you've really cheered me up.'

*

After lunch the next day, Francis offered to take Sebastian on a walk, before driving him back to the station. They set off, up the short drive and turned right into a vast open field.

'Noah is such a nice boy,' said Sebastian.

'He likes you a lot,' said Francis. 'He said you were "brilliant at playing".'

'It's all I've ever done, really,' said Sebastian. 'Well, come to think of it, until recently it's been more a case of my thoughts and feelings playing with me – not the way Noah plays, more like boys who pull wings off insects, or drop their sister's doll head-first out of a high window. So, in a way, you could say I'm quite new to playing, as opposed to being toyed with. Whichever way around it is, some people would say that it's high time I got a job. Hang on, hang on, what are those tiny horses? Perhaps they're the ones that used to be on the telly when I was a child.'

'They're Exmoor ponies,' said Francis. 'They're part of the rewilding project I was telling you about in the car.'

'The grazing animals that stop the whole place from turning into a forest when you let the land do its own thing.'

'Exactly,' said Francis, 'the savannah effect.'

'Yeah,' said Sebastian. 'It's so strong, I can feel it. It's like the countryside has been taken off its meds – in a good way, like when I cut down on the old Clozapine because things were going well with Dr Carr. I was advised to go back up again but I haven't. They thought I might relapse because of what Mrs Pellegrini called "the unfortunate schemozzle" – not that I blame Olivia.'

'Well, she feels very concerned but optimistic, as your new therapist is an old and trusted colleague of Martin's.'

'Martin,' said Sebastian dreamily, 'Dr Martin Carr. Yeah, anyway, the countryside . . . I lost my train of thought.'

'What you were saying was spot on. We're trying to get the land off its meds: pesticides, herbicides, fertilisers, so that it can get back to its true nature. It's a complex process and these ponies are part of it . . .'

'Look, they're pricking up their ears,' said Sebastian.

The ponies gathered into a tighter group and started to trot along the hedge at the far side of the field. Suddenly riders in black velvet hats, standing up slightly in their saddles, came galloping in the opposite direction on the other side of the hedge. It was difficult to tell whether the wild ponies were running towards or running away from their huge, glossy descendants.

'Do the telly horses like the racing horses?' said Sebastian.

'The stronger the herd, the more inward-looking and secure it is,' said Francis, 'but of course it recognises and responds to other horses. The Exmoors could tell the other horses were coming long before we could.'

'On the old horse net,' said Sebastian, tapping his forehead.

'That's right,' said Francis, smiling and turning down a woodland path.

'Yeah, not that I've spent much time in the country – although I spent a couple of months there last summer – but it's more alive here – not that I got outside much last time I was in the country – it was hard enough to get out of my room, to be honest – but even in winter, it feels more alive here.'

'There's a simple explanation for that: it *is* more alive,' said Francis. 'I'm glad you feel it, though. I know the branches look starker in winter, but that makes them seem more like a mirror image of the root system spreading underground. It's always the case, but it just hits my imagination more at this time of year.'

'I'd never thought of it like that: the ground being a mirror,' said Sebastian. He struggled for a moment to redirect his thoughts. 'Really this whole place is a Noah's ark,' he said, more cheerfully, 'and your Noah's ark is like one of those little boats they have hanging from big boats.'

'The tender,' said Francis.

'Is that what they call it? That's how I'll think of it, then,' said Sebastian. 'It's a very nice name, but I won't tell Noah because he's the captain of the ark and he might be disappointed.'

'That's very considerate of you,' said Francis. 'We're going to need a fleet of arks, so maybe one day he could be admiral of the fleet.'

'I think he'd like that,' said Sebastian. '"Admiral of the Fleet", sounds just the ticket.'

'Here we are at the stables,' said Francis, leading Sebastian into the cobbled courtyard surrounded by redbrick buildings.

'The stables,' said Sebastian, 'so, this must be on the old horse net as well.'

'Horse net, owl net, stork net, internet, you name it: it's connected,' said Francis, unlocking a blue door and taking Sebastian upstairs.

'It's a hub,' said Sebastian.

'That's right, and this is my office,' said Francis.

'I like the round window,' said Sebastian. 'I've never been in a room with a round window before. They're like the sun on a Japanese flag, a James portal. And they're more like eyes, aren't they? Which makes perfect sense when you think about it.'

'Yes, it does,' said Francis. 'Good point. The funny thing is that the round windows were used in stables more than anywhere else, so I suppose horses would think they were the natural shape for a window, whereas we're stuck with rectangles.'

'Lucky horses, eh? Matchy-matchy, seeing eye to eye,' said Sebastian. 'Not that I want rectangular eyes. Nobody ever seems to have those, even on *Star Trek* when they meet aliens.'

'Hmm,' said Francis, sorting through a pile of deliveries on his desk. 'That's true: green, squelchy, tentacular . . .'

'Spiders from Mars,' said Sebastian.

'Exactly, but we're never prepared to go that extra mile and give our aliens rectangular eyes. Ah, here's the book I forgot to take home for Olivia on Friday.'

'What's that about, then?' asked Sebastian.

'It's called *We Will Not Be Saved*.'

'Oh dear, is she making more programmes about the end of the world? It can't really happen more than once, can it? Unless we're in a time-loop,' said Sebastian, sounding as if his enthusiasm was under strain. 'Although, I suppose there are lots of different ways it could come to an end,' he went on, struggling to get back to his feet as a supportive brother. 'It's a bit like pasta, plenty of variety: shells, strings, ribbons, but it's all pasta in the end. In the end, the end is the end. As a kid, I used to love alphabet soup, trying to see if there was a poem hidden in it, but even then, you're down to twenty-six basic choices, aren't you?'

'Actually,' said Francis, 'it's rather the opposite. She wants to make a new series called *Solutions*, to balance out the *Apocalypse* series. It is a sequel, but . . .'

'A same-opposite,' said Sebastian, puffing out his cheeks with relief.

'An antithetical sequel.'

'A what?'

'A same-opposite,' said Francis, smiling, 'you'd got there already. I see what you mean about *We Will Not be Saved*, though. It sounds like doom and gloom, but it's really defiance. It's written by an indigenous Ecuadorian eco-warrior, and what she is saying is that her people do not want to be saved by missionaries, or by Western "Syphilisation", as Beckett called it; they want to prevent their own culture from being erased by guns and Bibles. And that's what she's set about doing with extraordinary success. She's stopped loads of rainforest from being destroyed by logging and mining and oil drilling.'

'Oh, great,' said Sebastian, 'more power to her.'

'Yes,' said Francis. 'Shall we go back? I think the timing will be about right for your train.'

'Okay,' said Sebastian, taking one last look through the round window. 'Let's see what's through the round window, shall we?' he murmured.

'Strangely enough,' said Francis, after cantering down the steep wooden staircase and waiting for Sebastian, 'this book has another title in America: it's called, *We Will Be Jaguars*.'

'Hang on,' said Sebastian, 'hang on, *We Will Be Jaguars*. I got a text from my mate Helio this morning, the one who came to the posh dinner . . .'

'I remember, the Brazilian artist.'

'Yeah, so Big Bill Maraschino, is going to his studio *right now*, at three o'clock – on a Sunday, because he is going to New York tomorrow – and you won't believe this, but the piece Helio is showing him is called *The Jaguar Brings Down Fire from Heaven*.'

Sebastian stood in the courtyard beside an old metal trough, his hands undulating towards each other and his fingers interlocking.

'The jaguar brings down fire, we will be jaguars, the book, the visit, Helio, Olivia, the same-opposite sequel, solutions,' he spoke very rapidly, 'the new series, Brazil, Ecuador, you working there, and this place coming off its meds, and seeing eye to eye with the round window: it's all coming together, wow, all the strands, it's like, it's like a bride having her hair braided before a wedding, Helio and Isabella, everything all at once. It's blowing my mind. That used to be one of my bad phrases. Maybe when your mind is all over the place, it's like being turned into a sand-storm, but when your mind is in one place, it's like being a ship under sail, so now I sometimes love having my mind blown. To be honest, I'm so happy here, I didn't take my meds this morning. I'm rewilding myself, I suppose, but consequently I'm going a bit fast now, a bit ducks and drakes.'

'I'm sure you'll be fine,' said Francis, resting his hand gently on Sebastian's shoulder. 'You've certainly tuned into the jaguar net. Congratulations: not a lot of people manage to do that in Sussex. I think you should carry the book – not that I'm trying to fob you off with a chore – I just think you'll sail home even more smoothly with Nemonte's book in your hands.'

Sebastian unlocked his fingers, which were by now white-knuckled.

'Do you know her, then?' he asked, taking the book, and seeming to be released from the cascade he'd been caught in.

'Yes, she's a very impressive person, as is her co-author and boyfriend Mitch,' said Francis, setting off slowly.

'We will be jaguars and bring down fire from heaven,' said Sebastian, relaxing a little as he fitted two pieces of the puzzle together.

When they got back to Willow Cottage, Sebastian gave the book to Olivia.

'Perfect timing,' she said. 'Sam just called me to say that Silverline want to greenlight *Solutions*.'

'That's wonderful,' said Francis.

'Yeah, great . . . yeah,' said Sebastian.

Francis watched him sinking down into an armchair to absorb this further coincidence. He looked nervous, as if he were placing a final stone on top of a pile of stones and was bound to bring the precarious tower clattering down. Francis's own relationship with synchronicity was one of affectionate scepticism in the sense that he didn't interpret these sudden mesas of coincidence, springing up from the desert floor of one thing after another, as the secret code of a Californian 'Universe' especially devised to guide each of the eight billion individuals on the planet out of some maze of vacillation by showing that supernatural forces were all aligned in favour of their trip to Disneyland, or against proposing to a partner who has starred in both their nightmares and their dreams. Whatever the origin of these surges of coincidence, they could lift a person's preoccupations from the kind of reasoning that's indistinguishable from indecision, in which 'one hand' always precedes 'the other hand', and 'either' is always followed by 'or', into a metaphoric realm in which a jaguar, with the rippling gait of an apex predator, might come ambling down a road which seemed to have two forks, towards a dilemma which inevitably had two horns, and scatter the alternatives, leaving only one thing left to do. It was stalking through the light forest of Helio's studio, through the pages of Nemonte's book, and through her Waorani's traditional lands which she had helped to protect. The trouble for Sebastian, who was easily triggered into a chain reaction of associations, even when they were hard to find, was that these surges accelerated him in a direction in which he was already inclined to move too fast. Whereas a depressive had to deal with a world devoid of meaning, Sebastian had to deal with an excess of meaning. He had taken the most literal pause by slumping into the armchair and staring into an apparently blank space, crowded with associations only visible to someone with his combinational genius.

Francis decided to join him there rather than drag him back in chains to the mundane, if entirely unreliable, claims of the Southern Rail timetable.

'So,' he said, 'the jaguar net has secured a sequel for Olivia; any news of how it's worked for Helio?'

'Oh, yeah,' said Sebastian, getting out his phone, 'good point. Maraschino wanted me to introduce him to Dr Carr. He thought he was an artist, which in a way he is, as well as being a scientist, but I don't think he would do a session in the gallery. It would be a bit of a "breach of confidentiality".'

'No kidding,' said Olivia.

'Blow me down, you're right,' said Sebastian, 'there *is* a message: "Hello, my friend, Maraschino says he *loves* the work, and the gallery is going to get in touch tomorrow. Love and thanks, H&I".'

'That's striking,' said Francis. 'You were the one who persuaded Maraschino to make the studio visit. Maybe we should go to Ecuador one day to see some real jaguars – you obviously have a strong link.'

'Ecuador,' said Sebastian, incredulously.

'Jaguars are so cool,' said Noah, leaping onto the sofa with a roar. He padded and froze, padded again and paused, but instead of devouring his father, he climbed over his legs and up onto the arm of the sofa, poised for his great leap.

'Catch me!' he shouted to Sebastian and threw himself forward without the slightest hesitation.

'Wow!' said Sebastian, turning just in time to catch Noah under the arms and lift him into the air.

Noah laughed delightedly.

'One moment you're the captain and the next you're the jaguar,' said Sebastian.

'No problemo,' said Noah, who had heard Sebastian use that phrase at breakfast.

'I think we really need to set off for your train,' said Francis, seeing that Noah had lifted Sebastian out of his trance.

'Off we go then,' said Sebastian.

'Sebastian can't leave,' said Noah, 'I want to go on playing.'

'He'll be coming back,' said Olivia, 'assuming he would like to.'

'I'd love to,' said Sebastian. 'I didn't know families could be like this.'

'Well, it wasn't like *this*,' said Noah, 'until you came along. It was very nice but now it's even better.'

'Oh, well . . .' Sebastian didn't seem to know what to say.

'To be continued,' said Olivia.

'Yes,' said Francis, 'let's make sure that happens.'